WINNING
LOVE

WINNING
LOVE

ABBY NILES

Entangled Publishing, LLC
2614 South Timberline Road
Suite 109
Fort Collins, CO 80525

Visit our website at www.entangledpublishing.com.

Edited by Nina Bruhns
Cover design by Fiona Jayde

Paperback ISBN 978-1-62266-273-9
Ebook ISBN 978-1-62266-274-6

Manufactured in the United States of America

First Edition August 2014

10 9 8 7 6 5 4 3 2 1

Life begins at the end of your comfort zone—Neale Donald Walsch

Chapter One

Demolished homes. Mangled cars. Strewn bodies. All around him lay death and destruction.

Panic locked in a chokehold around Mac "The Snake" Hannon's neck, rendering him incapable of drawing in air. He squeezed his eyes shut and concentrated on mentally fighting his way out of the tormenting memory's submission hold. Forcing in a deep inhale, he held it for a few seconds, then slowly released, repeating the action until the death grip around his throat slackened, and only then did he reopen his eyes.

The destruction was gone. The only thing speeding by the passenger window of his childhood friend's truck was miles upon miles of flat open land.

The flat open land of Kansas, to be exact.

No place like home? *What a load of shit.*

What the hell had he been thinking in coming back? To actually step foot back on the cursed soil known as Tornado Alley?

Damn Lance and his whole "I could really use your help,

buddy." How the fuck was Mac supposed to say no? He shot a glare at his childhood friend, who was too busy driving to notice his edginess. Or maybe he did notice and was refusing to acknowledge it. Most likely the latter. Lance knew Mac hadn't wanted to return to Kansas any more than a fighter wanted to lose a goddamn fight—but that hadn't stopped him from asking Mac to help him train for an upcoming fight.

After trying to come up with every reason known to man to have Lance come out to Atlanta instead, and the asshole always having a damn good excuse why he couldn't, Mac had reluctantly agreed. Because he sure as hell couldn't say no. Not when this was the first favor Lance had asked for since he'd saved Mac's life four years ago.

"Mac."

Lance's deep voice cut into the thick silence, causing him to jolt. Fuck, he was whacked out.

"I know we haven't really stayed in touch since you moved to Atlanta," his friend continued. "So I appreciate you doing this for me."

Other than a few phone calls—made by Lance—over the years, Mac had cut all ties with the past the moment the plane's wheels had lifted off the runway and carried him away to Georgia.

"Yeah, well." Scowling at the roughness in his voice, he cleared his throat. "It's the least I could do, considering. Besides, your kid's here. I didn't want to take you away from your kid."

Especially after he'd learned Lance had moved over two hundred miles to stay near the child. It also meant Mac wouldn't have to return to Emerald Springs. Thank God.

"Skylar can't wait to see you," Lance said.

Mac glanced out the window. No clouds. Just endless blue skies. How quickly that could change, though, especially at the end of April. Mac clenched his teeth. Goddammit, he was going to drive himself fucking mad before he left.

"How old is she now?" he gritted out, determined to focus on their conversation.

"Eight. She remembers you. When I told her you were coming out for a few weeks to help me train, she was excited about seeing Uncle Mac again."

Uncle Mac. He remembered that man, too. He'd died, along with his wife, over four years ago.

He scrubbed a hand over his jaw and shifted on his seat. *Don't go there.*

He inhaled another steadying breath and sat back against the leather seat, studying Lance. Anything to keep from being crushed by the influx of fucked-up emotions this damn trip was already causing.

Except for a couple more tats added to the sleeve his friend had been working on for years, and a beefier build since he'd decided to fight light-heavyweight instead of middleweight, Lance hadn't changed. Same unruly dirty blond hair, same mischievous gleam to his gray eyes, same laid-back attitude. Mac used to be like that...before.

Fucking hell!

"When did you move out to Cheney?" The edgy feeling of wanting to crawl out of his skin had him scouring his palms on his jean-clad thighs until the skin burned. Trying to relieve the building tension, he worked his neck back and forth. He hadn't felt this tightly wound in years. It was what had pushed him into the cage—which had ended up being the best damn therapy a guy could've asked for. Pummeling the shit out of something released it all. And he sure as hell could use a pummeling session right now.

"You okay?" Lance asked.

Mac grunted. "Cheney?"

A sigh came from across the cab, which he ignored. If Lance thought Mac was the same guy he'd grown up with after all that had happened, he'd soon learn how wrong he was. That guy was long gone. Once his friend realized that, maybe he'd get the boot back to Atlanta early. He'd be okay with that.

"About two years ago Piper's husband got a job in Wichita, and I couldn't be three hours away from Skylar. Since I can technically work anywhere, I packed up and moved here, too. Cheney's nice. It's only thirty minutes from Wichita, but still has a small town feel."

"How are things between you and Piper?"

His friend shrugged. "Unlike popular belief, divorce doesn't have to be horrible. We have a great relationship, I like her husband, and he loves Skylar. He doesn't try to take my place or step on my toes, and he leaves the parenting to me and Piper. So I think I got a pretty good deal."

The more Lance talked, the more Mac's tension eased. If distraction helped, he'd make sure to keep him talking.

"That's great. If anyone could make a divorce work, it's you two."

"There's still love there, man. Just not *love*. I guess that's what happens when you marry right out of high school. We grew up together, then grew apart together. There're no hard feelings, the shit just happened. As a result, Skylar gets two parents who can be in the same room together and honestly like each other."

Lance veered right, off the main street running parallel to the town of Cheney, onto a dirt road. A few seconds later, he turned onto a long, gravel driveway leading to a large two-story farmhouse. He pointed to a wooden barn behind it. "I have a home gym setup in there. With my schedule, it's hard for me to get out to a training facility daily, but I have to train, even if the only time I can find is at two in the morning. It's a rough setup, but it gets the job done."

"You got to do what you got to do, man," Mac muttered. No one knew that better than he did. It was why he'd left in the first place.

"With your help, I hope to be ready for the fight in six weeks. There're supposed to be some big-name promoters from Cage Match Championship there. If I can get CMC to notice me, I'll be golden."

Mac hid a grimace. At thirty-six, Lance's chance of getting into the top dog of Mixed Martial Arts was slim to none. Though he'd give the guy credit— he never gave up on his dream, even if he'd had to postpone working toward it for a few years.

His friend parked the truck, and Mac climbed out, surveying the area. After being in the hustle and bustle of Atlanta, the endless expanse of land before him was almost overwhelming—made him feel like a walking target. He fucking hated it. "You really went for isolated, didn't you? There wasn't a part of you that wanted to live in, say…a neighborhood?"

Lance chuckled. "I did, actually. For Skylar. But I couldn't pass up this house. I got a killer deal. I would've never been able to afford a place like this if it hadn't been in foreclosure. The house needed a ton of work but, since I spent years working construction with Dad, I knew I could fix it up."

Looking at the house now, Mac would never have known it'd ever needed work. Soft sage siding made the white trim and shutters stand out. The gigantic wraparound porch was decorated with potted plants and hanging baskets, with a wicker seating area, and a porch swing. Lance had sown grass around the perimeter of the house so there was a large, lush lawn that stood out against the dried-out land surrounding them. The flower beds were filled with hostas, boxwood shrubs, and pansies. Cozy. A home. *Easily destroyed.*

He shook away the thought.

"You've been busy."

"You know me. I can't sit still. Always got to be doing something."

He did know that. Lance had the energy of ten men. His inability to just relax had been one of the problems he'd had with Piper.

"Surprisingly, I love it out here," Lance continued. "Skylar loves it out here. And if I had moved anywhere else, I wouldn't have meet Gayle."

"Gayle? She a new girlfriend?"

"Nah, man. It's not like that." Lance pointed to one of only two houses in the distance—another two-story farmhouse, but with white siding and black shutters. Though the house was beside Lance's, it sat farther back off the road and was at least a good five minute walk away. Talk about privacy. Sheesh. "She moved in about six months ago. She helps me with Skylar when I get a call. She's never bothered about the time, either."

"You still repo'ing, then?"

"And towing, jimmying locked doors. The life of a single dad, bro. Skylar comes first. I can't fight as much as I want. The little I bring in is a nice bonus but, with you here, I can get in a little quality training and hopefully knock those promoters' socks off." His friend slapped him on the shoulder as they started toward the house. "It'd be nice to get out of the smaller circuit. I'm only averaging about a grand a fight right now. Because of my schedule, I've only been able to do one every other month or so. Can't make a living like that."

"How's your record?"

"Won the last five consecutive fights, hence the grand payouts. Overall record is 12 to 2."

"Pretty good. Have they already slotted you against your opponent?"

"Yeah, some young kid. Man, it sucks to be old in a young sport." A strained smile came to Lance's face. "Do you think I'm chasing a pipedream? Should I just hang up the gloves and be happy with what I did get to do?"

No reason to sugarcoat it. "Ultimately your decision. It's not going to be easy. The chances are slim. But I got into CMC at thirty-two. Others have come in their mid-thirties—though few. We still have guys fighting into their forties. So it's not impossible."

His friend nodded. "As long as there's a chance, right?"

"Never give up."

As they neared the porch, a tiny body with a mass of blond curls came barreling around the house, squealing at the top of her lungs. The piercing shriek, however, wasn't from happiness at her dad being home. Mac tensed, preparing to take down whatever was chasing the child. The little girl suddenly dove to the left into a thicket of bushes.

"Ah-ha! I've got you now."

A figure jumped from around the corner of the house and a cold blast of water hit Mac in the middle of the chest, soaking his shirt to his skin. Stunned, he stared at the woman for a moment, his arms splayed wide at his sides, then he tugged the drenched material away from his body.

Lance burst into laughter.

The woman didn't miss beat. Turning slowly in a circle, she kept the water gun close to her face as if she was peering through a scope. "Did you see that, missy? I just took out a civilian. You will pay for that!"

She pumped the lever on the bottom of the gun and a peal of childish laughter erupted from the bushes. The woman spun around, pulled the trigger, and saturated the greenery in a spray of water.

Skylar crawled out, laughing so hard her sides heaved. "I-I surrender." She flopped on her side, giggling. "Did you...did you see his face?"

Heat crept up Mac's neck as his gaze bounced from the laughing child to the young girl who'd assaulted him with the water gun. He knew he should see the humor in the situation, but with all the suppressed emotions trying to explode forward since he'd stepped off the plane, being laughed at as soon as he got out of the truck irritated the piss out of him. "Who the hell is she?"

As Lance accepted the hug his daughter threw around him, he said, "Mac, I'd like to introduce you to Gayle."

"The neighbor you were just talking about?"

"One and the same."

Mac frowned at the girl. From the way his buddy had spoken about her, he'd expected someone more grandmotherly, hell, *motherly* at least. But this...this kid in front of him couldn't be more than twenty-one.

Her auburn hair was split into two low pigtails that made the gathered strands fall over her shoulders onto her upper chest. A tight blue tank that didn't reach her navel strained out of the lapels of the plaid overshirt she had knotted at her ribcage, making her bountiful breasts pop forward. The sleeves had been ripped off and were frayed at the seams, giving him the impression of a farmer's daughter.

Except for the indecently low ride of her nothing-there

jean shorts that displayed way too much flat stomach and tanned legs. Those things spelled trouble. His gaze lowered. Yep, the look was complete. Barefoot, with bright purple painted toenails.

"Hi, Mac. Sorry about the soaking. The little booger got away from me."

Uncomfortable with the appreciative way she was eyeing him so openly, he pressed his lips together in a disapproving scowl. "You should be a little more careful. Someone could get hurt."

Her lips twitched at the corners. "This coming from a cage fighter? How…ironic."

How in the hell did she know he fought? He glanced at Lance, who was watching the exchange with amusement.

"What I do has no bearing on the matter," Mac said, returning his attention to Gayle.

"Really? I'd say fists have a better chance of inflicting more damage than my poor little water gun."

Mouthy thing, wasn't she?

She sauntered closer to him, an alarming sway to her hips. The fact that he noticed horrified him.

"Let me rectify the damage. Dinner. My place. Eight o'clock."

At a loss for words, Mac blinked. Not that he hadn't been asked out before by a woman. He had. Just not so bluntly.

"I have better things to do than play tea party." He needed to get control of the situation. She might find it fun to hit on older men, but he wasn't going to be a part of it.

Those twitching lips split into a full grin, revealing a radiant smile brimming with mischief and mirth.

"Come on, handsome. I make a *mean* cup of tea."

He got the craziest idea she was laughing at him. He shot

a glance at Lance for help, who grinned and shrugged.

"That's Gayle," he said. "She holds nothing back."

A throaty chuckle that was all woman came from her, and an odd sensation crackled in Mac's chest. Frowning, he instinctively moved into his fighter stance, preparing to mentally knock that unwanted feeling into submission.

She either noticed his defensive movement or decided to change tactics, because she stopped in her advance and studied him in an extremely unnerving way that made him shift his feet. "Well, I'll let you get settled in."

She turned and started to walk away, Skylar right on her heels. Mac breathed a sigh of relief. She'd picked up on his disinterest and was taking the hint.

The relief was short-lived as she glanced over her shoulder at him. "See you at eight, handsome."

Her eyes eased up his body with such appreciation he felt it all the way to his groin. Another husky chuckle came from her as she turned her head back around. The seductive sway of her jeans-covered backside held him captivated. Mac shook himself, appalled he was gawking.

He spun on his friend. "She's trouble, Lance."

"Gayle? Ah, you'll love her."

"Really? What could I possibly have in common with someone that young? For that matter, what do *you* have in common with her? For God's sake, Lance, she's teetering on the edge of jailbait for guys like us."

Lance laughed. "Dude, she's thirty-two."

Mac whipped his head back toward her. She and Lance's little girl had made their way to the side of the house. She was only four years younger than him? "No way."

"Way. She has a damn doctorate in meteorology or something to that effect. But don't feel bad, okay? I made the same mistake when I met her. I even asked where her parents were after she moved in. I got the same amused reaction. She knew you thought she was young. She's a lot of fun. She doesn't have a filter, though. So be prepared."

Okay, so the age difference was a no-go as a reason to stay the fuck away from her. Damn it, he didn't like that. Didn't like his reaction to her. He needed something negative to focus on. She seemed to be a handful. Two handfuls, actually. And he didn't have time for a handful. Or any woman, for that matter. "I don't need to prepare, because I'm not going."

"Come on, Mac. She doesn't bite." He nudged him. "Unless you want her to."

Mac jerked back, scowling. "I don't want her to bite anything. I have absolutely zero interest in women."

Except for just now. And it completely freaked his shit.

His friend sobered. "Wait. Are you telling me you haven't dated at all since… It's been over four years, Mac."

"Yeah. That's exactly what I'm saying."

"I knew it." Lance scratched the back of his head and gave a derisive snort. "I *told* Piper she was wrong, but I let her convince me otherwise. Damn it."

At his friend's sudden change in attitude, Mac's defensive shield locked into place. "What the fuck are you talking about, man?"

"That cold motherfucker I've been watching on the TV for the last few years. The one who is short with reporters. Never smiles. That's not for show. That's who you are now." Lance glared at Mac. "I *told* you to stay here. That leaving your home wasn't going to fix anything, but you were adamant. Now look at you…you didn't *heal*. You're hollow. Lifeless. Ally would be horrified."

Rage erupted so quickly he charged forward, raising his

fist to slam it into Lance's disapproving face. At the last second, he made himself stop, and instead grabbed a handful of shirt and tugged him forward until their noses almost touched. He said between gritted teeth, "If you've got a problem with the way I've dealt with my wife's death, I'll be more than fucking happy to leave."

The man didn't even flinch, just gave another snort as he shook his head. "Man, you really have changed. In almost thirty years of friendship you have never raised a fist at me in anger."

Stunned, Mac jerked back. Jesus. He'd never snapped like that. "Lance, I—"

"So, that's it," he interrupted. "That's how you've coped. You beat the shit out of people—legally."

Anger started to fester again. "You know what? Fuck you, man. I didn't come here for a goddamn intervention. It's *my* fucking life, and I'm fine with the way it is." He took an aggressive step forward and pointed a finger at him. "People change, *buddy*. If you can't handle that, that's your deal, not mine. Just count yourself lucky your life has been so perfect you haven't been forced to change *to cope*."

"My life has been anything but perfect, and you would know that if you'd checked in *at all* over the last four years. But you haven't. The few times I called, you rushed me off the phone because you were too busy becoming"—Lance's chin notched up—"Mac *'The Snake'* Hannon." Distaste coated his voice as he used Mac's fighter name. "It's time for you to get reacquainted with just plain old Mac Hannon."

They squared off for a few moments, then Mac muttered a string of curses and stormed toward the house. He didn't need this shit. Had he known this was what he was in for, he would've said to hell with debts owed and found a reason to stay the fuck at home. Lance didn't know him anymore, and it was complete bullshit for him to believe Mac would be the same person. So he preferred solitude to hanging out. Who gave a fuck? He wasn't hurting anybody.

So he took his anger out on his opponent in the cage. Who the hell cared how he beat his opponent, as long as he did?

If Lance pushed this, Mac would find the first flight back to Atlanta.

Eight thirty.

He wasn't coming. Mac Broom-Shoved-Up-His-Ass Hannon.

Gayle twisted her lips in annoyance. Not that she was really surprised. The man had been uppity to the point of humor. But if he thought for one second she'd let him off the hook, he had another think coming. Gayle Matthews didn't back away from a challenge—and unknowingly, he'd issued a very exciting one she couldn't ignore.

After making the trek to Lance's place, she stomped up the porch steps and rapped on the door.

As Lance answered, an amused snort came from him and he shook his head. "I should've known it was you." He leaned against the doorjamb. "You know I admire your tenacity, right?"

"*Uh-oh*. Did the terrified fighter make you pinky swear that the next time you saw me you would convince me he wasn't interested?" He chuckled, but it quickly faded to a seriousness so unlike him it put her on alert. "What, Lance?"

"Listen, I know you. You're going to do what you're going to do. I can't stop you. Hell, you might be exactly what Mac needs. Just be careful, okay?"

The warning intrigued her. "What are you saying that you're not saying?"

"He's damaged, Gayle. I don't know this Mac, and I don't know what he is capable of if he's pushed into a corner. I'm not telling you to back off, because honestly, I think he could use a good dose of you, just…tread carefully."

So the grrr-worthy fighter was damaged goods. That worked to her advantage and made him safer for her. The last two men she'd enjoyed a few weeks of fun with had been too emotionally available—a mistake she didn't plan to make again. "Message received."

Over his shoulder, Lance yelled, "Mac!"

A few seconds later, the man himself trotted down the stairs. He'd exchanged the soaked shirt that had given her a panty-wetting glimpse of the hard muscles underneath for a black wife-beater that displayed his powerful arms very nicely. A Celtic half-sleeve decorated one bicep and the curve of his shoulder with different shades of black and gray.

For the second time that day, her breath caught tight. When she'd come around the side of the house, she'd been stunned at the towering hunk of male hotness before her. She'd known Lance was going to pick up a friend who was helping him train, knew this man would probably be as attractive as Lance, but the reality of Mac blew her imagination to smithereens.

Tall, possibly six-four, nothing but bulging muscles. Dark brown hair topped his head and was a little long, so a strand fell onto his forehead.

As he approached the door, she didn't miss the clench of his jaw or the slowing of his steps.

Undeterred, she crossed her arms over her chest. "You know, it's rude to stand a woman up."

He mimicked her stance. "I believe I told you I had better

things to do."

"And I believe I told *you* eight o'clock."

A moment of shock lit his brown eyes. He seemed to catch the slip and put his grumpy face back on.

"Now, come on. The sun is about to set. The food is past cold and I didn't slave away at a stove for nothing."

She bounced down the steps. No footsteps followed. She twisted and lifted a brow. He was still rooted to the spot. The mask had completely fallen off, revealing an interesting amount of reluctance. She turned all the way around and tilted her head to study him. How could a man who looked like him have a second of hesitation at being alone with a woman? Lance had said he was damaged. Just how bad was it?

Mac glanced at Lance, who had his eyes narrowed on him. Tension crackled between the two men. Oh. Something had happened here.

"Gayle is a fixture at my house," Lance said. "You might as well get used to her. She's going to be around."

She could almost hear his teeth grind. "Fine."

Gayle hid a smile of triumph and started walking. This time, footsteps followed her. She didn't slow her pace or look behind her. When she reached her yard, she went around the side of the house toward the back.

Those footsteps stopped. "Where are you going?"

She didn't slow, nor did she respond, just headed for the four-wheeler ATV parked outside her backdoor with a picnic basket strapped to the back. She hiked the hem of the sundress she'd changed into to mid-thigh and climbed on. Twisting, she patted the area behind her.

Mac stared at her as if she'd lost her mind.

She revved the engine and inched the four-wheeler forward until she was by his side.

"Lance is right, you know. I'm not going away, so you might as well give me what I want. I promise to be on my best behavior…at least for tonight."

As his gaze roamed over her face, his brows pulled together in a fierce frown. "You have laugh lines."

To keep a burst of laughter in, she pressed her lips together and then worked her face into a serious expression. "It's never nice to point out a woman's wrinkles. Though, if we're being honest with each other, you could use a few laugh lines." She circled her index finger in front of his face. "You've got that curmudgeon look down to a science."

Again those lips didn't even begin to initiate a smile. Wow. Curmudgeon might not be that far off. Not that he appeared old—not with a body like his—but his features carried a haggard edge to them, especially around the eyes. And in those eyes was a sadness that made her wonder what had put it there.

"Sorry," he said. "You just seemed so young before. But I can see now you're not as young as I first thought."

Another chuckle tried to erupt. She mock-scowled. "Are you calling me old?"

Being mistaken for a kid in her early twenties happened on a regular basis. That was, until they got a really good look at her. However, having her crow's-feet pointed out was a first.

"I'm just stating an observation."

"Fair enough." She pointedly nodded her head at the ATV. "Get on."

Mac muttered, "What the hell," and climbed on behind her. Muscular thighs surrounded her hips, causing tingles to erupt over her. She wanted to feel his chest pressed into her back, his hands wrapped around her waist, but he didn't move to hang on to her.

We'll see about that. She gunned the four-wheeler forward. As his body jerked back, his thighs instinctively clenched around her and his arms flew around her waist. She smiled.

Better.

"Hang on, handsome. It's going to be a bumpy ride."

She took off toward the wheat field that billowed behind the farmhouse. The heat of Mac's touch seeped through her sundress and she inhaled a pleased breath. When she moved out here from Kansas City, she'd worried she'd have a hard time meeting someone, especially since the very hot Lance didn't do a thing for her. Not that she would've started anything with him even if he had. Having a fling with her neighbor carried the risk of upsetting her day-to-day life. The men she chose to play with were temporaries, and when she moved on, seeing him every day wasn't an option. Which made Mac perfect. Not only did he make everything inside her come to life, but he was out of here in a few weeks. Just long enough for her to scratch her itch.

She just had to get him on board—and she would.

Five minutes later, she stopped in the middle of the field. She loved this spot. It was far enough away from the houses so the artificial light didn't dim the night sky. With no moon and the sun having set, they were in complete darkness. Stars glittered above them, and the canopy seemed to go on forever.

She climbed off the ATV and waited for Mac to stand. When he did, she stretched around him, making sure her breasts caressed his arm as she unhooked the picnic basket behind him. Every muscle in the man's body tensed and he moved back into the same braced position he had when he met her. All he needed to do was bring his fists up next to his cheeks as she'd seen Lance do when he trained and he'd be in fighter mode.

Interesting.

Lifting the basket, she flipped on the ATV's headlight, then carried the picnic things to the lit spot. She pulled a blanket out of the basket and spread it out over the ground.

As she did so, Mac relaxed his stance.

So the fighter didn't like anyone getting near him. Even more interesting.

"Aren't you worried about being out here alone with me?" he asked.

She strolled toward him until she was inches from him. Smiling, she looked up at him through lowered eyelashes. His entire body froze. She walked her fingers up his chest. Instantly, he shifted back into the same stance.

At his reaction, Gayle chuckled. "Lance has put his stamp of approval on you, so I don't think I have anything to worry about." She reached into the pocket of her dress. "Besides, I have this."

She dangled the pepper spray from her fingers. Nodding, he grunted in approval. "At least you're not completely reckless."

Good. Lord. Even his praise was grumpy. Luckily for him, that made him all the more entertaining.

"Are you as hungry as I am?" To toy with him, she put a seductive undertone to the question.

A deep groove formed as his eyebrows dipped down, his suspicious gaze unwavering. "If you think we—"

"For food, handsome." She winked, then walked over to the blanket and sat down. "Since *someone* was playing hard to get, I'm about an hour late for dinner and starving."

A rushed exhale sounded behind her. "You really don't hold back, do you?"

"*Hmm.* Has Lance been talking about me?"

"Just said you don't have a filter and I needed to prepare."

"That's pretty accurate."

Mac finally strolled over to the blanket and sat down. Crickets chirped in the background as she tugged out the fried chicken, potato salad, and green beans. "Thank goodness this stuff is awesome cold. Next time, just show up when I tell you to, okay?"

"Next time?"

As she followed the muscular lines of his arms, she bit her lower lip. "If I get my way, there will be." She lifted her gaze to his. "And I *always* get my way."

A flash of heat warmed the coolness from his eyes, then he glanced off into the distance.

So, he felt it, too. Good.

She made Mac a plate and handed it to him. An awkward tension settled between them. He seemed to be filling it by munching on his chicken, but she refused to just sit there mute. If she had to steer the conversation, so be it. "How long have you known Lance?"

Mac froze, and she got the distinct impression he wasn't expecting her to speak. Too bad. She loved to talk.

He swallowed his food and wiped his mouth on a napkin. "Since we were kids."

"So you know Piper, too?"

"We all hung out. I take it you know her?"

"Yeah. Lance has me keep Skylar when he goes out on runs. Today, he could've taken Skylar with him to the airport, but he wasn't sure if there'd be a delay, and Piper was supposed to pick Skylar up."

"It's nice that you help him out."

"I believe in community, and there are no better ones than the ones you live beside."

Community had been there for her during her darkest

days, and she always made sure to reciprocate.

"Well, it's still nice of you."

"Lance mentioned you were going to help him train. I'm sad to say, I don't really follow MMA."

"Not a fan, huh?"

She had the man talking. Holy hell.

"I'm not *not* a fan. I've just never really watched it."

"Not even with Lance as your neighbor?"

"Nope." Again she let her eyes do the talking as she surveyed the very male body beside her. "However, I think I'm a little more interested now."

Red crept into his cheeks, and she thought it was the most adorable thing she'd ever seen. Such a strong, imposing man embarrassed by a little compliment.

She turned her gaze to the sky. "Beautiful, isn't it?"

"Doesn't look like this in Atlanta. I'd forgotten how endless the night sky is out here."

Will wonders never cease? Had there been a hint of awe in the curmudgeon's voice?

Since she was on a roll, she asked, "When did you move to Georgia?"

His body tensed, jaw clenched. Okay. Touchy subject.

"Almost four years ago."

"Ah. Won any major titles out there?"

She kept close tabs on his body language. His muscles relaxed as he turned his head toward her. "Nope. One day, maybe, but my usual opponents are extraordinary fighters who are all out to win a title fight."

"Humble. I like that."

"It's the truth of the business." He placed his empty plate beside him. "I'm friends with two title holders. Neither one of them came about their title bid easily. They busted ass for it. I got into fighting much later in life than they did. It was really only a hobby until a few years ago. Fought amateur, but never had any plans to make it a career."

"What changed?"

Again, his body tensed. So, the move to Atlanta and the fighting were connected in some way. In a way he really didn't want to talk about.

He finally looked over at her, his lips pressed into a hard line that tightened her chest. "Life just has a way of changing in a split second."

They stared at each other. The haunted look in his eyes was all too familiar. She'd seen it reflected in her own. Mac had obviously been through something traumatic, but had lived to face life anyway.

He toyed with a chicken bone, then tossed it onto the plate. "Dinner was great. Thanks."

She took the cue. She'd gotten him out here. Had made him relax a smidge in her company, but he was ready for the evening to end. She gathered up the plates, quickly folded the blanket, and attached everything to the ATV.

Instead of driving back to her place, she passed it by and dropped him off in front of Lance's porch, just wanting a few more seconds of feeling his powerful body behind hers, his muscular arms around her waist.

He slid off, and she immediately missed the warmth.

"Feels weird having a woman drop me off," he said.

She grinned. "I've never done things the way people expect."

He snorted. "I'm not surprised. But you're not as much trouble as I'd initially thought."

She climbed off the four-wheeler, walked up to him, and placed a kiss on his cheek. "You haven't experienced the full Gayle yet. I'm all kinds of trouble."

CHAPTER TWO

You haven't experienced the full Gayle yet.

Mac surveyed the contents of the refrigerator for something for breakfast, found nothing, and slammed the door closed.

She was wrong. He had. And *that* gale had destroyed everything he'd loved. He had no desire to experience another one. No matter how much he'd tossed in bed last night replaying the crazy woman's antics or how often he felt the lightness of amusement bubble in his chest from the memories—especially over her calling him a curmudgeon and the exaggerated, grossed-out expression she'd used while saying it.

The corners of his lips twitched. Groaning, he rolled his eyes at himself and stalked to the coffee maker. *What the fuck?*

There was no question about it, he had to stay away from that woman. Last night she'd been on her *best* behavior, and he'd actually relaxed, begun to think she wasn't so bad. Yeah. Then she'd sucker punched him with her "I'm all kinds of trouble" warning.

He didn't want trouble…didn't need trouble. Hell, judging by the way he'd assaulted Lance yesterday, he had more than he could handle as it was. How could he have almost hit his friend? No matter how far gone he'd been in his anger and grief, he'd never physically attacked another person unless it was within the confines of training or the cage.

The only explanation for his momentary snap was that no one in Atlanta really knew him, and everyone there respected the clear I-don't-want-you-to-know-me vibe he gave off. Lance already knew every dark demon of Mac's past and wouldn't hesitate to bring them up…and there was nothing Mac could do to stop him. Add in the horrifying kick of attraction he'd felt for Gayle, and he'd, well…snapped.

He rubbed his hand over his face, then shoved a filter in the coffee maker and added three scoops of grounds. Nothing had been within his power to control, either, which had made everything worse.

He took the pot to the sink, filled it with water, and poured it in the maker. If he was going to get through this with any of his sanity still in check, he needed to regain control. He could prepare for Lance. Though it was the first time Mac had wanted to hit him, it wasn't the first time they'd exchanged heated words. So he wasn't going into that blindly.

Gayle, however, was a live wire. He couldn't anticipate what she'd say or do next. She was anything *but* predictable. She was outrageous. Blunt. Crazy. And his structured life had no room for her disturbance, even temporarily.

Once the coffee maker finished its burbling, he poured a cup and glanced out the kitchen window. He bit back a curse. Speak of the devil and she will rise.

Striding across the field between the farmhouses, carrying that damned picnic basket, was Gayle in another pair of too-short khaki shorts and too-tight green tank top sans an overshirt this time, so her generous chest stood out proudly. Last night, the plunging neckline of the sundress she'd worn had tempted his eyes more than once. And that hadn't been all that had tempted him—which was all the more reason to put a lot of distance between him and her.

On top of everything else he was dealing with, he didn't need an unwanted attraction to an unpredictable woman, especially at this particular time and place. It was not exciting, nor was it welcome.

It was time to make it clear to her that he wasn't interested in pursuing even a friendship.

He waited for her to rap at the back door, then opened it, but kept the screen door closed between them. Crossing his arms, he stared down at her. "What do you want?"

"*Oooh.* Curmudgeon McMudgeonson this morning, huh, handsome? Had a few hours to think, did you?"

Stunned, Mac's arms slipped a fraction of an inch. He jerked them back up. She hadn't blinked. Hadn't even *hesitated.* How did he deal with a woman like this?

Bluntly. Just like she did.

"I have," he said. "I think it would be best if we keep our association to a minimum while I'm here."

Way-too-enticing plump, pink lips pursed as she cocked her head to the side. "Why? Scared you might have some fun?"

What. The. *Fuck?* "I'm not on vacation. I'm here to help Lance train."

"And if you'll notice, Lance is gone. You're going to realize he's gone a lot and you'll be sitting in this house alone with nothing to do."

"I'm quite capable of keeping myself busy."

"I have no doubt you can. But that doesn't mean you can't have a little fun with more than just yourself. Unless, of course…you like playing with yourself." A mischievous sparkle danced in her hazel eyes.

Words left him. Vanished from his mind as though he hadn't used them all his life. He opened his mouth, snapped it shut, then finally managed, "That was inappropriate."

"Did I say something racy?" Her nose scrunched, then she laughed lightly and wagged a finger at him. "Shame on *you*, handsome. I was merely playing with words, since we were talking about having fun. *You're* the one who put the dirty spin on it, not me."

He didn't believe a damn bit of that. "I don't have the patience for your antics today."

"Such a stick in the mud."

Through the entire exchange, he'd studied her movements as he would any opponent in the cage, waiting for the first signs of frustration or anger. There was none. Her body was just as relaxed as it had been when she knocked on the door. What did it take to ruffle this woman's feathers?

He jerked his chin to the area behind her. "You know the way home."

Intending for that to be a dismissal, he started to back away from the door to close it. She grabbed the handle to the screen door and swept past him into the kitchen. Stunned, all he could do was gape at her audacity as she placed the picnic basket on the kitchen counter.

"I didn't invite you in."

"I'm not a vampire. I don't need to be invited." She held up a hand and lightly shook it. Dangling from her middle finger was a silver key on a large key ring. "Besides, I have this. I get to use it. Any. Time. I. Want. I thought this morning was perfect. Thought maybe I could catch you in bed and slip underneath the covers…you know…wake you with a very pleasant 'good morning, handsome.'" Pursing her lips seductively, she winked.

Jesus. Christ. Mac swallowed, alarmed by the way his body responded to the image she'd painted. She was fucking with him, she had to be, and she was enjoying every damn second of it, while he was floundering. Never had he felt so outmatched by an opponent. Gayle just kept throwing one surprise punch after another, and all he could do was cover his face with his gloves and wait for the round to be over. Desperate to get the topic away from anything sexual, he cut his gaze to the picnic basket.

"What's in that?"

She ran her palm over the top in a slow back and forth motion as she pressed her body against the side of the counter. "Wouldn't you just love to know? It's a surprise. One I think you'll really enjoy."

The woman was going to be the death of him. He pinched the bridge of his nose. When she chuckled, he shot her a dirty look. She pressed her lips together and twisted her face into such an outrageously innocent expression, a bubble of laughter tickled his chest. From irritation to arousal to amusement. All within the span of mere minutes. She was driving him *mad*!

"Whatever," he said, exasperated. "Do what you want. I'm going to my room." As he stalked toward the door that led to the hallway, he threw "alone" over his shoulder as a precaution.

"*Aww*, you're no fun, handsome," she called after him. "I had so many naughty things planned for us to do."

The husky chuckle trailing her comment was like a kick in the ass and he hustled for escape, wanting nothing more than a locked door between him and Gayle and all the erotic innuendo she kept tossing at him.

Just as he was about to reach the staircase, a movement from outside the front door caught his attention. Pausing, it took him only a moment to realize it was Piper and Skylar climbing the steps to the porch. Everything clicked. He rolled his eyes at himself and groaned. *Mother. Fucker.*

Gayle must have been eating up every second of their encounter, thinking him a damn idiot. No wonder she had been so outrageous with her suggestions. She wasn't even here for him. She was here to watch Skylar. And he'd looked like an arrogant asshole while also proving himself to be the curmudgeon she accused him of being. Damn infuriating woman.

Cursing himself, he opened the door before Piper knocked. With a pink pig clutched in her arms, Skylar pushed past him and immediately clomped up the stairs as fast as her eight-year-old legs would take her.

Familiar blue eyes rounded. "Oh. My. God. Mac Hannon. Aren't you a sight for sore eyes?" Piper embraced him in a tight hug that he awkwardly returned, then extracted himself and offered her a stiff smile.

"Piper. Good to see you."

Unlike Lance, Piper *had* changed. Her once long, straight, blond hair had been cut off into a very short pixie, which she pulled off well. And it was no longer blond, but a deep raven color. Thick cat-rimmed glasses were perched on her nose. The woman who'd always dressed in chic clothing was now sporting loose jeans and a tight baseball style T-shirt.

"What's with the getup?" Mac asked. "Halloween was months ago."

The jest just slipped out and took him aback. Wow. Time

didn't change all things, it seemed. He used to kid around with Piper like this all the time. Anytime he saw her, he picked something and made some sort of snarky remark, which usually got him—

"Ha. Ha." She stuck out her tongue.

Yep. Exactly that reaction. He fought back a smile.

She grabbed one side of her glasses. "It's different, right?"

"Definitely, but it suits you."

She grinned. "I found *me*, Mac. It took a while after Lance and I separated, and he thought I was going through some kind of personality crisis, but I was getting to know myself." She waved her hand at him. "Hell, you know, we'd been together since we were fifteen. I had no identity outside of him. Now I'm the happiest I've ever been."

The emotion rolled off her in waves. Piper had always been a giving, loving person, but there was a new freeness about her that he envied.

"I'm happy for you, Pipes. You deserve it."

"You do, too." Her expression sobered. "Is Atlanta treating you well?"

"It's doing right by me." The raw edginess he always got when people started asking him personal questions had him shifting his feet and looking around the room.

"You're doing great in the CMC. I watched your last fight. You dominated the other guy."

"Yeah." He shrugged.

"Have you got yourself working in a kitchen anywhere?"

"I'm retired from the kitchen, remember? That means I'm not returning to it." A chilly bite he couldn't stop crept into his tone, warning her she needed to steer to a different topic.

"Well, that's a shame," she said, without reacting to his icy response. "Your food was always so delicious. At least tell me there's a special someone in your life."

Goddammit. He hated being back here. None of these people respected his boundaries. He openly scowled at her. "No. The last thing I have an interest in is dating, much less finding someone *special.*"

This time the pure hostility that saturated his words couldn't be ignored, making the air heavy and silent. Piper studied him for a very long, unnerving moment, then she sighed and slowly nodded. "Okay. I see how it is." She peered over his shoulder. "Is Gayle here yet?"

"Back in the kitchen."

"Skylar! Come on." Seconds later, the little girl came bounding down the stairs with the pig and now a doll.

As they moved around Mac, guilt kneed him hard in the stomach, which was crazy since he never felt that way when it came to getting people to back off their Q&A, but there it was, laying thick. He turned around. "Hey, Pipes?"

When she faced him, he grimaced. He'd kept his emotions bottled up for so long he was uncertain how to express what he needed to say.

"I'm sorry about that." He rubbed his hands together, then cracked his knuckles. "It— It's been an adjustment."

Compassion softened her gaze and he wanted to turn away from it. Those looks had been one of the reasons he'd left in the first place. Everyone had gazed at him with it. Everywhere he'd gone. All he'd wanted was privacy. Instead, he'd become a specimen under a microscope. Blinking, he quickly glanced away and cleared his throat.

"Mac."

He resented her intrusion. Wanted her to leave him be as he fought for control, but he bit his tongue and forced himself to meet her eyes.

"It's time to heal. You've been carrying this for far too long. You couldn't have saved her."

Why did everything come back to Ally? His wife was dead. He hadn't been there to save her. End of story.

"Couldn't I?" Bitterness darkened his tone. "If I'd been there like I should've been, the outcome would've been a hell of a lot different."

"Why torture yourself with that? You weren't there. You can't change that. Now you need to make peace with it."

Without another word, she and Skylar walked down the hall into the kitchen. Mac ground his teeth as resentment spiked hard and fast. Everyone was a damn armchair psychologist filled with helpful advice about what he needed to do.

To hell with them all. He was doing just fine on his own.

Shaking his head, he shoved all the festering emotions aside. He owed Gayle an apology for his behavior. He might as well get it over with before he went upstairs.

As he strode into the kitchen, Piper was heading out. She laid her hand on his forearm. "Remember what I said."

He managed a nod, but all he wanted to tell her was to mind her own damn business. As she proceeded down the hall and out the front door, he pushed out a breath and turned to Gayle, who was standing in front of Skylar by the kitchen counter.

She put her hand on the basket and said, "I brought the makings for homemade pizza for lunch. What do you say we roll out the dough while we wait for your daddy to get home?"

"Yeah!" Skylar jumped up and down.

Heat crept up Mac's cheeks. And now he was an even bigger asshole.

"Hey, Uncle Mac, would you like to help?"

Instinct pushed him to immediately say no, but the hopeful, excited gleam in the child's green eyes froze the word on his tongue as a slice of pain tore across his chest.

"Yeah, Uncle Mac, what do you say? Want to roll some dough?"

The challenge in Gayle's voice jerked his attention to her. Her gaze was steady. Knowing. *Mocking.* He clenched his jaw. Okay. He deserved that. He'd made himself look like an idiot, which gave her the advantage. For now.

"Sure," he grudgingly agreed.

Her lips twisted into a cocky smile. "Good."

With the agreement, an awkward silence fell in the kitchen—or maybe it was only awkward to him. He spent his social time in a gym with fighters. Men. The rest he spent in solitude. He didn't remember how to chat up women or interact with little girls.

Running his hands through his hair, he flicked his gaze toward the hall—toward escape—as pressure started to build in his chest. A ridiculous reaction. But Gayle scared the ever-loving hell out of him, and Skylar—well, that sweet little girl was just a little too hard to look at.

"We're not going to bite, handsome."

Damn it. His gaze shot to Gayle. The arched brow and amused lips sent anger blasting through him. *Okay, Hannon. Time to bring The Snake into action. Treat this like you would when meeting an opponent in the cage.*

Wiping his face of emotion, he squared his shoulders and started toward the counter.

That brow notched up another fraction. "Impressive. I take it the cage fighter is among us now, and not Mac."

He froze. Jesus Christ. The woman called him on every damn thing he did and left him fumbling for footing. He hated every second of it.

She shrugged and started pulling things out of the basket. "Whatever you've got to do, handsome." She shoved a bag of flour at him. "Take this and measure out four cups. You can handle that, right?"

It was his turn to lift a brow. So, she had no idea about his past career. Good. "I think I can handle it." He glanced down at the bag of all-purpose flour. "Bread flour would've been a better choice."

As she stared at the package in his hand, her nose scrunched in confusion. "That would make bread, right?"

At the outright bewilderment she didn't even try to hide, a laugh tickled his chest. Covering it up with a cough, he shook his head. "Never mind."

He grabbed a measuring cup and a bowl from under the counter and scanned the ingredients Gayle had pulled from the basket. He tried not to scowl at the assortment of canned items. He made a killer homemade marinara sauce, but it would go unappreciated by an eight-year-old. His eyes landed on the table salt. Nope. He twisted, grabbed the kosher sea salt from the counter behind him, and switched it out with the other, which Gayle didn't miss.

She slowly turned her head to stare at him. "You got a problem with regular salt?"

Deciding to keep his mouth shut, he just shrugged his shoulders.

"Whatever floats your boat, handsome," she muttered, lightly shaking her head.

A smile tugged at his lips, taking him aback. That seemed to happen a lot around this woman. Not only did she infuriate him and shock him, she amused the hell out of him. A worrisome combination. If he didn't watch it, he might actually find himself enjoying her company.

As she instructed Skylar to pour the pre-measured flour, yeast, and salt in the bowl of a stand mixer, he looked around for the missing ingredient.

"You forgot a teaspoon of sugar."

"The recipe didn't call for sugar."

"Well, I'm telling you it needs a teaspoon of sugar."

One hand popped on her hip. "What are you, some secret Martha Stewart ninja?"

There went that damn tug of the lips again. "No. I'm definitely not Martha Stewart." He couldn't decorate to save his life. "I just happen to know a thing or two about making homemade pizza."

She lifted Skylar to sit on the counter, then waved her hand toward the machine. "By all means, handsome, take the helm and show us ladies how it's done."

Just as a few minutes earlier, the challenge rang clear in her voice as she kept eye contact with him. She had no issue throwing out one, did she?

"Be prepared to be amazed."

He added the needed sugar and turned on the mixer. As the metal hook slowly turned and combined the ingredients, he poured in the water and oil. Keeping tabs on the consistency, he added more flour or water until the dough was a perfect ball. Then he spread flour on a wooden board, put the dough on it, and started kneading.

An appreciative "*Mmm*," came from his left.

He glanced over to find Gayle leaning her elbows on the counter with her chin perched on her palm. Their gazes collided, and she mouthed the words, "So hot."

A rush of heat suffused his entire body. He halted in mid-knead. *Fuck.* There wasn't a misinterpretation of her intentions she could play up with outrageous behavior right now. Jerking his gaze away, he refocused on the dough. The memory of those lips mouthing those words seared into his brain. Was this Gayle in full Gayle mode? He didn't know if he could handle this Gayle.

When he finally had the dough where it needed to be, he placed it in a bowl and put plastic wrap over the top to let it rise. "Done. It should be ready in about an—"

A sharp smack to his ass shocked the words right out of his mouth.

"Great job, handsome. Let's play a game while we wait."

He stood ramrod straight as Gayle swept by him, uncertain if he was more stunned by the sudden smack to his butt or the frightening jolt of lust he'd felt from her bold action.

Taking a steadying inhale, he focused on expelling the tension from his body.

Let's play a game, she'd said.

He didn't think he wanted to play games with Gayle Matthews. Something told him she was a master gamesman and he was going to end up on the losing side every time.

And he didn't like to lose.

For a third time, Gayle had to chomp down on her bottom lip to keep a laugh in as Mac's stunned expression filled her mind again—one of two stunned expressions he'd given her over the course of the last half hour. The one that had twisted his handsome face when she suggested this full-body contact game had almost topped the one when she'd smacked his ass. Almost.

She flicked the spinner. "Left foot on the green circle."

Mac sent her a furious scowl and she sucked in her cheeks to keep her mirth from spilling out into the open. God, the delicious man was too much fun not to mess with.

She *had* taken pity on him and let him be the caller the first round. But when she'd fallen on her ass trying to reach a blue circle, he'd had to take her place. Those were the rules—which she'd reminded him of when he'd resisted her attempt to take the spinner from his hand.

Mac somehow maneuvered his left foot around his right hand and got it on a green circle about a mile's stretch away. Nice. The view was nice, too. In camo shorts and white tank top, he was giving a magnificent muscle flexing show. The man was simply magnificent. Even his curmudgeon attitude couldn't detract from that.

Besides, he allowed enough amusement to show through his gruff exterior that she wasn't the least bit daunted by his attempts to push her away. He would have a better chance if those enticing lips would stop twitching at the corners, letting her know he wanted oh-so-badly to smile. The fact that he fought the impulse made him all the more intriguing to her.

"Okay, Skylar, your turn." Gayle spun the arrow. "Right foot, red."

The little girl groaned. "Really?"

With her little hands splayed on the red dots on one side of the plastic mat and her feet on the green dots on the opposite side, the move wasn't going to be easy. Skylar hated to lose.

Gayle grinned. "Sorry."

She brought her right foot forward, getting it as far as the line of blue before she simply tilted over onto her side. The fall was so fast and so dramatic, Gayle burst into laughter, and Skylar followed with her childish cackle, which made Gayle laugh even harder. She loved the pure, unapologetic joy of a child.

She glanced over at Mac to share the moment, and all her enjoyment faded. What would have brought an immediate grin to anyone else's face, failed to do so on Mac's. The stricken expression was filled with such sadness and longing as he stared down at the child, Gayle's heart clenched tight.

He jerked his gaze away and directed it across the room, shoving his hand through his hair, a swallow working his throat.

This man must have one hell of story.

Time to lighten the mood again. "Okay, Skylar. You know what that means?"

The little girl jumped up. "It's my turn to call and it's yours and Uncle Mac's turn to twist."

If his head had whipped around any faster it would have flown clean off his shoulders. At least he was distracted from whatever past demon had surfaced.

"That would be correct, Skylar." She cocked the challenging eyebrow she was quickly learning goaded the hell out of him. "How about it, handsome? A friendly competition between adults. Which one of us has the best balance?"

As expected, the angular jut of his jawline tightened. He really shouldn't make it so easy for her to read him. The man simply could not back down from a challenge—even from her. Which gave her all the power.

He walked toward her. "I'm the only one in the room who hasn't fallen yet."

"Because you've only played once."

"And I stayed on my feet. The one time you played, someone landed flat on her a—" He cleared his throat, his gaze shooting over to Skylar. "*Er*, backside. Seems to me I'm already the victor between the adults."

The man was just as bad as Skylar about winning. Gayle would have to change strategy. "It's pretty sad that a grown man would claim victory over an eight-year-old when the only reason she couldn't make the move was because she is an *eight-year-old*. I would've been able to make that move."

He pressed his lips together, but not before she saw the twitch at the corners. To seal the deal, she crossed her arms over her chest, cocked one hip out, and pursed her lips in a *what-are-you-going-to-say-to-that?* way.

He immediately dropped his head, but she'd seen it. Oh. My. God. She'd seen it. A flash of white teeth. Handsome had smiled. Unfortunately, she hadn't received the full effect or seen how it transformed his face, but still, he'd failed to keep it buttoned up.

She was getting to him.

It wouldn't be long and he'd smile just because he wouldn't remember not to. The thought almost brought a smile to her own lips.

When he looked up, he had control over his mouth muscles again and had them set in a stern line. "You're on."

"Bring. It." Waving her fingers in the motion that went with those words, she stepped onto the mat.

Again the stern expression cracked as he squared off with her. He was a good head taller than she was and she tilted her head back to gaze up at him. Narrowed brown eyes glared back down at her. Good gracious almighty, she liked this. A lot. Everything about the man was commanding. Compact. Tight.

A flutter swept low in her belly. Yeah, she wanted this man.

"Gayle, right foot, yellow circle."

With Skylar here, she would have to keep things G-rated, but that didn't mean she couldn't have a bit of fun. Without breaking eye contract with Mac, she slipped her foot between his spread legs to the lone yellow circle between his feet and brought her breasts closer to his chest. Other than a slight jerk back and some major tensing of his body, he gave no reaction.

"Uncle Mac, right foot, green circle."

An audible exhale came from him as he shifted backward until the required foot was on the correct color, putting the lines of yellow and red circles between their bodies. Okay, so he responded to verbal challenges, but was still gun-shy about physical ones. She could respect that—for now.

"Gayle, left foot, red." She moved her foot to the assigned color, inching closer to Mac again.

"Uncle Mac, left foot, green circle." Noticeable frustration crossed his face at having to remain in the same spot. The thrill of the chase shivered through her. This was a lot more fun than she'd expected.

"Gayle, left hand, red."

She glanced down at the rows before her, where she had one foot already positioned on yellow and one directly in front of Mac on red, then glanced up at him. Her naughty side roared forward with a vengeance. Hadn't she just thought she could respect his unspoken cues? She studied the circle again.

Nope. Forget respect. She had to do it. Opportunities like this didn't arise often enough, and she would not let one pass by. Plus, it was fun watching the yummy fighter who faced big, bad, aped-up gorillas in a cage get all awkward when she did something outrageous.

Thankfully, Skylar was way too young to read into this, but Mac would see the adult intention crystal clear. Keeping her expression innocent, Gayle slowly crouched until she was zipper level with his camo shorts, placed her hand on the circle, and tilted her head back to look up at him. His head tilted up toward the ceiling, and softly mumbled *Fuck*s rolled from his mouth.

Oh, yeah. He was reading into it exactly what she wanted him to.

She heard the spinner turn on the cardboard. "Uncle Mac, right hand, red."

An audible groan sounded as he bent to place his palm on the circle beside her, bringing his face in close. Tension carved deep grooves around his tightly pressed lips and anger burned as he glared at her. She flashed him a bright smile. His eyes narrowed dangerously. Man, if she could get all that built-in hostility to channel into passion, this man would rock her socks off.

"Gayle, right hand, blue."

Twisting her body away from Mac, she slapped her palm on the correct color.

"Uncle Mac, right foot, blue."

Muttering another curse, he stretched his foot from its spot on the green circle to the blue, bringing his torso forward, so they were once again facing each other.

"Hello, handsome. Good to see you again."

"Can't say the same."

She chuckled. "If you can't handle the heat, you know what to do to end it."

"No way in hell that is happening."

"Gayle, right foot, green."

She peered around the mat. Her right foot was currently on yellow. Left on red. Green was behind Mac. This could prove difficult. She faced forward, and came nose-to-nose with a smirk—*a smirk!*—twisting Mac's usually cantankerous lips.

Oh. It was *so* on.

With some careful maneuvering, she stretched her right leg between Mac's and barely tiptoed the green. And Mac wasn't smirking anymore. He was blanching as the outside of her thigh pressed to the inside of his. Yet he didn't waiver in his determination to win. Stubborn, stubborn man. He had no idea what a weakness that actually was.

And the game continued like that. No matter how provocative Gayle got with her move choice—at one time she straddled him—Mac refused to give in. But with each play, the tension slowly eased out of his muscles, a light air started to replace the dark, stormy aura he always seemed to carry, and before the new mood could be ruined, Gayle gave him what he wanted.

"Gayle, left hand, blue."

She slid her hand out from under Mac's back, then reached between her legs for the blue circle. Biting off a curse, she strained for the circle and then collapsed to the mat.

Mac shot to his feet with his arms raised above his head. "Yes!"

The grin that stretched his mouth wide, revealing his straight white teeth, made her breath catch hard in her chest as an excited jolt zapped her low in the belly. The curving of his lips took years off his face and erased the haunted gleam from his eyes. He radiated happiness.

He caught her staring at him and the smile faded. "What?"

"You should really smile more often, handsome. It suits you."

And she planned to make Mac Hannon smile a whole helluva lot more. Even if it was against his will.

CHAPTER THREE

Mac rolled over in bed and groaned, from both lack of sleep and the constant whirling of his thoughts. That damned *woman* wouldn't leave his mind.

Why?

Because after he'd perfected a stone-faced expression and only allowed the occasional small smile to those he called friends, Gayle had wrenched a fucking teeth-baring, shit-eating grin from him—*without* him being aware of it. He'd been so caught up in the moment, if she hadn't pointed it out, he might have never realized it. But she had, and he'd immediately wiped his face clean of emotion. She hadn't missed a beat, though. She just hopped up, clapped her hands, and announced it was time to roll the dough.

During the hour that followed, she'd acted as if nothing had happened, once again making him relax. He'd caught his lips stretching at her clever phrases so often he'd stopped fighting the impulse. By the time they were done with the pizza and Lance had shown up, Mac had grudgingly admitted to himself that Gayle radiated life in a way that drew him—at least, until she threw her sexual innuendo at him. The uncomfortable moments where he'd felt more like an amateur fighter facing his first big fight instead of a pro who'd won against countless opponents were usually few and far between. Not with her. And he hated how green she made him feel.

Not that he had any plans to act on a single one of her suggestions. The weird attraction troubled him, though. Right now it was easy to keep things under control because she was so outrageous, but if she changed tactics…

He shook his head. He couldn't think about Gayle anymore. She'd already stolen too much of his damn sleep. She wasn't going to steal his day, too.

Tossing back the covers, he jumped out of bed, pushing thoughts of the infuriatingly irresistible woman out of his head. What he needed to do was fix shit with Lance. After his buddy had returned home, he'd taken Skylar out on a daddy-daughter date. Gayle had gone home, and Mac was left at the house alone. Lance and his daughter hadn't returned until well after ten. He'd taken his sleeping child upstairs, tucked her in, and gone straight to his room. The message had been clear. Lance wasn't ready to talk.

Today, though, they needed to clear the air.

Mac threw on a pair a of black training shorts and red cotton tank, then hurried downstairs to the smell of frying bacon. As he stepped into the kitchen, he found Lance manning one pan with sizzling strips and another with scrambled eggs.

"Smells good," Mac said.

Lance glanced over his shoulder. "I always make Skylar breakfast before she goes back to her mom. She's getting dressed. Piper should be here in about twenty minutes." A click sounded as four pieces of toast popped up from the toaster. Lance motioned to it with the spatula. "You want any of this?"

"Nah. I'm good. Going to make a protein shake in a bit." Mac perched on one of the stools around the island, studying his friend's back as he grabbed two plates from the cabinet and loaded each with food. It seemed like Skylar did a lot of back-and-forth between her parents, which was an odd arrangement. "What kind of schedule do you and Piper have worked out for Skylar?"

A slight shrug moved Lance's shoulders. "What we can fit in. I wasn't supposed to have Skylar yesterday, but I had the afternoon off. Since those are so rare, I had Piper drop her off with Gayle before she went to work, so I could spend the rest of the day with her when I got home. Thankfully, I have an ex-wife who makes sure I get to spend more than a few minutes with my daughter."

"Why don't you cut back on a few of the jobs you take?"

The muscles in Lance's shoulder bunched. "Some of us don't have the luxury of being choosy, you know?"

This wasn't the conversation Mac wanted to have this morning. Seemed he was making things worse, not better. He just needed to get to the heart of things. "I'm sorry about the other day. No matter what you think, that wasn't me."

"I pushed your buttons." Lance faced him, leaning back against the counter. "I've had time to think on it, too. I shouldn't have come at you the way I did. You've spent the last four years dealing with your grief in your own way, and you're not with me for an hour and I'm all in your face about it. So, yeah, you exploded. I probably would've done the same in your shoes. In fact, I'm pretty certain. I felt anger rising just now at you asking why I didn't cut back my hours."

"Hey, man, I didn't mean to upset you with that."   •

"I know, but it did. The same way you got upset with my

remarks." Lance remained silent for a moment, then said, "About a year after you left Kansas, Skylar was diagnosed with leukemia." Mac shot to his feet in shock. Lance held up his hand, shaking his head. "You were going through your own shit. She's in remission now, but Piper's insurance sucked, and so did mine. The approved treatments weren't working, and the hematologist recommended something different. Of course, insurance denied coverage. But I wasn't going to let anything happen to my little girl, and it sure as hell wasn't going to happen because some suit in an office was denying her healthcare. So I found the money."

"How?" Mac sat back on the stool, stunned by what he'd just learned. How had he not known? How could he have not been here for Lance?

"Piper thinks I took out a loan. In a way, I did, just not a traditional one. The truth is, money like that isn't given to a guy like me by a suit in a bank."

Unease curled in Mac's gut. "Who did you borrow from?"

"There're a few guys I used to gamble with. Remember them?"

Mac closed his eyes. "You didn't."

"I'd die for her, Mac," Lance paused and swallowed. "Going to two rich-ass goons was an easy-peasy decision. I think you, of all people, would know something about that."

Yeah, he did. He would've done anything to save Ally if he'd had the chance. Unfortunately, that chance had never been given to him. "How much do you owe?"

"A lot." Lance shrugged. "It's not like the movies, though. They don't come banging on my door in the middle of the night and crack their knuckles, threatening to take out my kneecaps with a baseball bat if I don't get them paid back on time. We have a loan agreement, just like I would with a bank.

I pay a set amount each month, about the price of a really nice home. As long as I pay, we've got no problems. Except…" He sighed. "I've been doing this for two years…and I'm getting tired. But there's no end in sight."

Mac would never have believed he'd ever hear those words come out of Lance's mouth. Mac surveyed his friend's face, really studied it. The other day, he'd been too caught up in himself to notice anything except surface things. Upon closer appraisal, dark circles and bags aged his friend's eyes. Deep grooves bracketed his mouth. Lance did look tired… exhausted actually.

"I can write a check right now, Lance. Help you out."

"No." Lance shook his head sharply. "Absolutely not."

"This isn't the time for pride."

"I pay my own way, Mac. I always have. I always will."

"If it's that big of a deal, we'll set up an arrangement like you have with these guys. Just a lower interest and stretch out the life of the loan for a few more years."

"No. We both know how fast shit can happen. If you ended up needing the money you let me borrow, I'd never forgive myself. All I want you to do is help me train so I can win this fight and hopefully get a shot in the CMC. Things would be a lot easier if that dream came true."

"Why don't I just talk to Ethan Porter? I might be able to get you a fight without all of this."

Lance's jaw tightened. "No. I do this my way or no way. Got it? I don't want to be known as the fighter who got into CMC because of a favor. I want to get in because I earned it. If I'm not good enough, I'm not good enough. All right?"

Inhaling, Mac nodded. Although at this particular moment he didn't agree with his friend, he understood his need to prove himself and take care of his own. "Okay. We'll train our asses off, then. How about we start right after you feed Skylar?"

A grimace contorted the other man's face. "Got to go, bro. I have a repo out in Wichita. Big job."

"How are we going to train if you've always got to drop everything for a job?"

A look of helpless determination gleamed out of Lance's eyes. "Pipedream, right? It's what I want, but real life has to come first. We'll train. I was hoping to have my bills squared away before you got here, but it was slow at the beginning of the month, which put me behind. So I'm cramming in everything I can to make my bills. I've almost got it all. Once I do, we'll get busy. Just give me a few more days, okay?"

"All right. If there's anything—"

"Just be here when I've got everything squared away."

"I can do that."

Lance turned, lifted the two plates, and walked over to the kitchen table. "Skylar! Breakfast!" he yelled, then went to the refrigerator and grabbed out a carton of OJ "How did things go with Gayle yesterday? I was surprised she stayed over here. I thought she'd take Skylar back to her place."

Mac shook his head. "You were right. She doesn't have a filter. *And* she knows how to goad the hell out of me."

"What do you mean?" The caution in his friend's voice was unmistakable. Damn. Lance still wasn't certain how Mac would react to stress. A pang thumped him hard in his chest.

"She's able to throw challenges at me I can't resist." He watched Lance pour two glasses of orange juice. "She got me to play Twister, of all things."

Lance blinked as he slowly lowered the carton to the counter, then guffawed. "No shit! I would've paid good money to see that."

"I bet you would."

"She's good people. She has this way with life. She just goes with it. Doesn't sweat things. It's rare." Lance inhaled then yelled, "Skylar! *Break*. Fast!"

"I'm. *Coming*!" came the child's voice from upstairs.

"Gayle most likely never had any reason to sweat anything," Mac said, once Lance stopped chuckling at his daughter's irritated tone.

It was the only thing that made sense to him. People who'd gotten raw deals in life had the scars to prove it. And they showed. Every last one of them. His did. Lance's did. Gayle came across as a person who had never been touched by anything bad. If she hadn't, good for her. She was able to embrace life and all it had to offer—without knowing there was a dark side that could snatch the good away in seconds.

"Maybe," Lance agreed. "Funny, now that you mention it, I don't think Gayle and I have had a serious conversation about either of us since she moved in six months ago. Hell, she doesn't even know about Skylar's illness, unless Skylar has told her. Gayle is always clowning around, and you just have a fun time with her."

Not shocking. He didn't think this woman took anything seriously. "Does she really have a doctorate in meteorology?"

Not that she seemed dumb by any means, she just seemed the sort that didn't stick with something for very long—a little on the flighty side.

Lance snorted. "She does."

"And she actually works in her field, or is she like a career student?"

The career student would fit the way she came across.

"She actually works in her field." The feminine voice behind him had Mac twisting around.

Gayle stood on the top step outside the screen door. His

eyes locked on the black spandex shorts hugging the swell of her hips and barely covering the top of her thighs. *Holy shit*. He slowly lifted his gaze. A matching black tank top with bright purple trim encased her torso and breasts.

Typical workout attire he'd seen numerous times in the past on the women at the gym, but on Gayle...she wasn't a tiny wisp of a woman. She was lush, curvy, and filled out her clothes in a way that made his gut clench.

He cleared his throat, trying to shake off the reaction. Hadn't he just decided he didn't need another catastrophe in his life? And Gayle would most certainly bring catastrophe.

"Hey," he finally managed. The one word had a husky edge to it that dismayed him.

A grin curved her lips as she opened the door and stepped into the kitchen. "So...should I be honored or offended that I'm the topic of two sexy men's conversation this morning?"

"Honored, of course," Lance said. "Mac was just letting me know how you got him to play Twister."

Mac shot a scowl at his friend. Why would he tell her that?

"Was he, now? And what did handsome have to say about it?"

"That he can't resist your challenges."

What the hell was Lance *doing*? This would just feed her impulsiveness. Not that she needed any help with that, but this would definitely not curb her clever tongue. Thankfully, the pounding of little feet sounded on the stairs and, seconds later, Skylar roared in like a whirlwind. Mac breathed a sigh of relief at the distraction as the little girl kissed her dad on the cheek, then ran to hug Gayle.

"Hey, cutie pie," Gayle said, squeezing Skylar to her side but staring right at Mac. "You don't say? You like my challenges, handsome? Want some more from Gayle's bag of dares?" She winked at him and that dreaded jolt hit him low in the gut.

Fuck. How was the woman always so *on*? She never missed a beat. Never got flustered. And it flustered the hell out of *him*, especially since she caused this new need to spiral up in him. One that seemed to be growing stronger the more he was around her—if his reaction to her sudden presence at the door was any indication.

He needed to get control of this right now, before the woman got any ideas. "What are you doing here so early?"

"Go eat," she said to Skylar. She waited until the little girl was sitting at the table, scarfing down her breakfast, before she returned her attention to Mac. "I came for you, handsome."

At the unexpected answer, his mouth dropped open as his stomach clenched tight again. *Came for him.* Did she have any idea how damn erotic that sounded? Of course she did. She was Gayle. Was she fucking with him again? She'd enjoyed the hell out of that yesterday.

Either his expression asked that very question, or she read his mind, because a wicked gleam entered her eyes. "Not this time. I really came for you."

"For what?" He was pretty damn proud of himself for keeping his tone guarded.

"I'm getting ready to go to the rec for Zumba. Want to join me?"

"Zumba?" All evocative thoughts evaporated at the mention of the workout class. Was she for real?

Lifting her arms above her head, she swung her hips in an erotic circle that drew his gaze to them. He jerked it back up, determined to keep his wayward eyes on her face and not her luscious body.

"Yeah," she said. "You know, Latin aerobics class?"

"Are you asking me to go to Zumba?"

Lance guffawed in the background, seconding how outrageous the idea was.

"Uh. Doesn't 'want to join me' imply that?" Her brows drew together in confusion, then she laughed. "Don't tell me you're one of *those* guys."

"If you mean the type who doesn't participate in a chick's aerobics class then, yes, I'm exactly that type."

There was no way in hell he was going, and it wasn't because of the dancing. His gaze dropped back to her hips. Dangerous. She was fucking dangerous.

She pouted out her bottom lip, drawing his attention to the plump, inviting flesh. That tightening hit his gut yet again. Damn, he was going to have to stare at the ceiling to be able to have a conversation with this woman.

"Oh, is the poor manly-man scared he won't be able to keep up?"

And then he felt it…the tug at the corners of his mouth. He clenched his teeth together to keep his lips from curving into a smile. "Men do not dance to work out."

Not with her, anyway.

"Really? Tell that to the founder, who also happens to be one fine-as-hell Latino." She sashayed over to Mac. "Show me how you can move those hips, handsome. I. Dare. You."

So, this was what she had in her bag of dares today.

Refusing to let her bait him this time, he said, "Not going to work, Gayle. I'm privy to your game now. You're not going to goad me into this one."

She gave a long sigh and shrugged. "Oh, well. It was fun while it lasted. Besides, it's better not to be disappointed. A curmudgeon wouldn't have the moves to keep up, anyway."

Lance howled with laughter, irking the piss out of Mac.

"Curmudgeon. That's. Perfect," Lance said between gasps of air.

"What's a curmudgeon?" Skylar asked.

"A grumpy old man." Gayle's pleased expression mocked Mac, causing his rebellious side to storm forward.

"Uncle Mac isn't an old man," Skylar said.

"Thank you."

"But he is grumpy," she finished.

Lance doubled over, laughing even harder.

Fine. He'd show them. "I have the moves. Prepare to be awed."

And that's when he realized the woman had won.

Again.

M ac most certainly did not have the moves.

Gayle stifled a snort as he stumbled over his feet while trying to do a simple meringue. The man was the epitome of the saying "white men can't dance." He didn't have a lick of rhythm in his amazing body. Every dance step, from the salsa to belly dancing, was stiff and cumbersome.

She'd give him credit, though. For the last forty-five minutes, he hadn't backed down from any of the hip-swinging moves. Nor did he seem embarrassed. Not even after the twenty or so women in attendance had gathered in groups and started ogling as soon as he walked in the door.

Even in his awkwardness, Mac was eye candy delight for every woman in the room—including her. The sleeveless red workout shirt showed off his impressive tattoo and chiseled arms, hugged his broad chest and tight torso. Though he'd believed this was going to be a girly workout, sweat coated his skin—and increased his sex appeal. She would need a cold shower after all of this.

Thankfully, the class was almost over. All that was left was the hip-hop routine and the cooldown. Since the instructor was notorious for picking songs she was in the mood for, instead of following a pre-made track list, there was no telling which track she would use. Gayle was hoping for a really fun one. As the current song wound down, the instructor paused her iPod to allow everyone a second to grab a sip of water.

Mac ambled closer to Gayle. "Okay, I'll admit it. This isn't easy. My damn heart feels like it's going to jackhammer out of my chest." He patted his stomach. "And my abs are on fire. I will never speak ill of Zumba again. It's a thorough workout."

"For your first time, you're doing pretty well."

"Seriously?" Skepticism rang clear in his voice.

"No." She shook her head, laughing at his mock-hurt expression. "You look like a deranged animal."

A dimple dented his right cheek and her heart fluttered. How had she missed that yesterday? The dimple gave him a youthful appearance that showed a glimpse of the man he kept carefully hidden behind his tough exterior.

"That bad, huh?"

"Yeah." If possible his grin grew, making her knees weak. Good Lord, this man didn't need to be a professional Latin dancer to make her want to melt to the floor. He just had to look at her with all his barriers down. The Mac she saw right this second was spellbinding.

Their eyes connected, and the air between them thickened. Mac's throat worked on a swallow, but he didn't look away. A first. Gayle made sure she wasn't the one to break the connection.

The instructor did by starting the music. As the opening

beat and an, "Oh! Oh! Oh!" of the best hip-hop Zumba routine *ever* filled the fitness room, Gayle couldn't stop a little squeal of delight.

"What?" Mac asked, a suspicious frown marring his face.

"You're in for a treat, handsome. Have you heard of The Wobble?"

His eyes widened and his head jerked back. Well, yes, he had. She grabbed his hand, faced the front of the room, and started wobbling her hips. The abject horror on Mac's face had her sputtering out a laugh as she let go of his hand to clap to the beat and move from side to side, kicking out a leg with each shift. "It's not hard. Just shake your hips. No different than what we've been doing."

His gaze lowered to her gyrating booty, then jerked back up. "I completely disagree."

Oh, he liked what he saw and didn't want her to know it. Okay. She'd let him get an eyeful without worry. "Just watch me."

She jumped in front of him just as the, "wobble, baby, wobble, baby, wobble, baby," chorus started. She rotated her hips four times in a large circle, hopped back just inches from Mac's body, and repeated the hip-wobble for another four count. He didn't move a muscle. She shifted her body to the right, moving her shoulders just as vigorously as she moved her bottom, keeping the momentum as she shifted toward the left. She was pretty sure at this second Mac wouldn't be able to decide between watching her breasts or her ass. She cha-cha'ed on her right foot and did a quick three step, cha-cha'ed on her left, then turned to face the left wall and did a pelvis thrust while pumping her fist at chest level for a very quick eight count. She chanced a glance at Mac.

Eyes locked on her ass. So, handsome liked the booty.

Might as well have fun with it.

She repeated the series of steps facing the left wall. Anticipation shivered through her. What would he do when the class turned in unison to face the back of the room? How would he react when he realized she was standing directly in front of him? She was about to find out.

She finished the second cha-cha, pivoted to the back of the room, inches from Mac—who didn't seem to care he still hadn't moved—and immediately went into the eight count pelvis thrust. The hop forward brought her so close to his thigh she might as well have been grinding on it through the four count gyration. As she jumped back for the next step, the abnormal redness of his face made her heart catch. He hadn't taken his eyes off her body. So she squatted down just a little bit farther, gyrated her hips a little more provocatively. She pivoted to the left side of the room, and then he stunned the crap out of her.

One moment he was frozen. The next he was beside her, revolving his hips and pumping his arms as hard as she was. A shocked laugh burst past her lips. The women around them hooted and clapped. When it was time to hop forward he didn't hesitate, continuing the rotation of his hips. He hopped back in sync with everyone, shifting to the left, shifting to the right, making many of the other women in the class look novice in comparison. Had he been watching her…or watching the steps?

Maybe she should feel slightly offended at the idea that he hadn't actually been watching her, but she didn't. Mac Hannon was dancing. Unlike before, when everything had been stiff and awkward, his body went with the hip-hop. He got down into the movements as his shoulders circled along with his pelvis. He got low into the lunge forward during the cha-cha. And then the pelvis thrust. Ohmygod. Gayle froze and covered her mouth with her hand. Now *that* was just sinful.

And what did Mac do?

He winked. The man flipping winked. Gayle couldn't stop a grin, and as the class started the last rotation facing the front of the class again, she joined him. She glanced over at him and his dimple creased his cheek. He looked so in the moment. Just free and not a care in the world, and it was the most breathtaking thing she'd ever seen.

The song ended, and she couldn't fight the disappointment. She could've wobbled with Mac all day. As the song transitioned to a slower one, the class did the cooldown, and then it was over.

She wiped the sweat off her face and said, "I didn't know you knew how to wobble."

"I didn't."

So, he'd just been watching her to learn the steps. Bummer. "You picked that up pretty quickly."

He shrugged slightly, his lips curving downward. "Weren't a lot of moves to learn. I used to do a lot of those types of dances. I can do Cotton-eyed Joe, Tush Push, and the Cupid Shuffle."

"Seriously?"

"And that surprises you, why?"

A brow shot up. "And you have to ask that question, why?"

He smiled, but there was a trace of tightness to it. "It's been a few years."

Ah. So this was a before thing. Sadly, she had a couple of those herself. The before-Gayle would've never gotten so down and dirty with the song. The after-Gayle believed in living in the moment. Looked like Mac had taken the completely opposite approach, but maybe he was ready to start doing some living again.

"Well, you sure showed us women how it's done." She shoulder bumped him. "So…Zumba, it's pretty *freaking* cool, right?"

His smile stretched a bit more and he shook his head as he softly chuckled. "I'll admit it. I had fun. Other than the wobble, it's harder than it looks, that's for sure. You make it look simple."

She cast him a sly glance. Maybe there had been a little watching her in there as well. "Checking out my moves. were you, handsome?"

"Uh…"

"It's okay. I wanted you to."

He swallowed and cleared his throat. "Um." He ran a hand over his head. "So what other types of things do you do to work out?"

"Running and Zumba are really it."

"*Oh, really?*"

The way he drew out the two words in a slow, challenging drawl caught her attention. She stopped, faced him, and put both hands on her hips. "Yes, really, but I'm always up for something new. What do you want to dish out?"

He mimicked her stance as amusement softened his face. "Just wanting to return the favor. Lance's barn. Tomorrow. Eleven o'clock."

She bit back a smile at having the invitation issued in the same blunt manner she had given him her dinner invite. "You're on."

The gloves felt heavy on her hands as she hit the bag in front of her. What was her reward for taking Mac to do something fun yesterday?

Torture.

Seriously, the man was trying to torture her. What was supposed to be thirty easy seconds of hitting the bag felt like a damn eternity. The searing pain started in her knuckles, traveled up her arms, and settled in her shoulder blades until the entire length of her limbs and back were screaming in pure agony.

Since they'd returned to Lance's barn thirty minutes ago, Mac had been mean like this. First making her "warm up" by jumping rope. She hadn't jumped rope since she was a kid, but Mac had made it look so damn simple, like he and that stupid rope were one, she'd figured it would be like riding a bike. Yeah-freaking-right.

Seconds after she'd started, her calves had ignited into a fiery storm that had her wanting to beg for a time-out. Though breaks proved unnecessary, since she'd had plenty of those while untangling herself from the blasted rope every fifteen seconds. Mac hadn't hidden his enjoyment at her ineptitude, either, which had earned him a thorough sticking out of her tongue. His laughter had boomed through the room, making the torture worth it—then.

Not so much later, which had included way too many burpees—no one in the history of ever should have to do these evil things—drop squats—what was wrong with regular squats?—then he'd strapped some thingamajig around her waist that was attached to a flipping huge-ass weight, and made her run across the barn—these men were nuts—before shuffling her onto the bag.

"Done." He clicked a timer he held in his hand.

She groaned and dropped her arms. "You're a complete ass, you know that?"

Mac grinned. "What? The poor girly-girl can't keep up?"

At having her words from earlier tossed back at her, she chuckled softly. "This girly-girl can think of a few better ways to work up a sweat than killing my arms." She ripped off her gloves, tossed them on the ground, and walked the tips of her fingers across his forearm. "Come on, handsome, why don't you show me some body-to-body combat?"

Red crept into Mac's face. God, he was so easy. With a grin, she dropped her hands and went over to the black mat covering the middle of the floor. "I've watched Lance train a few times. How about putting me in one of those holds and letting me squirm around?"

"You've watched Lance train?"

That was what he took from her suggestion? Jeez. "Skylar likes to watch him. I've sat in a couple of times."

Mac's lips pressed together, then he shook his head. "Okay. Which move do you want to try?"

She blinked. Holy crap. He was game. Quickly flipping through her limited knowledge of MMA, she decided to focus on the one that would get her pressed closest to Mac.

"There's one Lance did that was really interesting to watch," she said, trying to keep an innocent expression in place as she delivered the rest of her description. "He wrapped his legs around the other guy's head."

Mac's eyes widened a fraction. "You want to try a triangle choke?" A croak cracked his voice and made her struggle to keep up the innocent charade.

"Is that what it's called? It looked...intense. Can you show me how it's done?"

The conflicted expression she'd seen a couple of times

crossed his face. As though he wanted to, but didn't, at the same time. She remained silent, letting him make the decision without pressure from her. If he said no, or tried to get her to do a different hold, she'd let him off the hook.

"Okay. Lie on your back on the mat."

She had to stop herself from doing a giddy dance. The man was slowly warming up to her. When he'd completely thawed, she wanted the attraction he was fighting to be filled to the brim with all the naughty images she'd deliberately put in his head.

She had every intention of reaping the benefit of all her hard work.

W as he really going to do this?

Mac shot a glance at the woman now lying on her back with her knees bent. Not once had he ever thought about the intimacy that came with this hold. He was an MMA fighter. He grappled. And grappling meant very close contact with his opponent. All he thought about in those moments was what his opponent was going to do to break out of his hold.

Now? All he could think about was Gayle's legs wrapped around his head.

He wasn't fool enough to believe she just *happened* to choose this submission hold out of thin air. She'd picked it on purpose, and again he found himself flamed by the silent challenge she'd tossed at him.

Now that he'd agreed.

What the fuck was he *thinking*?

As he inhaled a small breath and released it, he paced back and forth at the edge of the mat.

You can do this. Think of it as just a training exercise.

"All right, first thing you need to know is the triangle choke comes in handy when you're caught on your back and have your opponent punching you."

He swallowed but made himself drop to his knees in front of her.

"Oh, that's right," she said. "Lance was on his back and his training partner was between his legs. Like this." She parted her thighs and scooted forward.

Fuuuuck.

He wasn't completely inserted between her legs yet, more bordered by them, but for him to show her the move correctly, he'd have to get intimately close to a certain very appealing area. His breath locked in his lungs. He'd give his left nut right now to have on a cup. *Anything* other than her womanly center to rub against.

She's a dude. Just another guy you're grappling with.

As he moved his body deeper between her knees, the back of her thighs brushed against the top of his. His chest tightened more.

Focus.

"When your opponent throws a punch at you, his body will come forward," he explained. "That's when you grab the arm while wrapping one leg around his neck. Then you grab the shin of your other leg and pull it close to the opposite knee, locking the hold into place."

"Okay. Come at me."

He threw a fake jab toward the side of her head. She grabbed on with both arms, lowering him farther. One feminine leg latched around the back of his neck, pressing his cheek to the soft skin of her inner thigh while sliding his forearm straight up the warmth of her mound. Two tempting thighs clamped tightly around his face. She had him locked in.

He expected her to immediately release him. Instead, she tugged the back of his head down a little farther, bringing him closer still to a forbidden area. And he realized she knew more about this hold than she'd let on. He hadn't told her about holding his head down, which helped keep the opponent immobile. Though he was nowhere close to being in danger of losing consciousness—she didn't have the strength to do that—he was in all kinds of danger of losing coherent thought.

His face was just inches from her mound. The skin of her thighs burned into his cheeks. And he had the insane urge to break the weak hold and bury his face where she was damn near begging him to go. Then she suddenly released him, and a stuttered exhale shot from his mouth as he leaned back and closed his eyes.

Fuck. He wasn't going to be able to handle much more of this. He didn't *want* this attraction to Gayle. He just wanted the fucking friendship. Why couldn't he just have the friendship?

"How was that?"

"What?" He opened his eyes. Damn woman was still on her back with her legs spread wide before him. He could strangle her. He shoved to his feet and put some distance between them. "Not bad."

"My turn."

"For what?"

"I want to know what it feels like to be in the lock. So wrap those legs around my head, handsome."

The image of Gayle's face posed inches above his cock as he put her in the hold had lust slamming through his body and the aforementioned body part twitching in response. Trying to dislodge the alarming image to rid his body of its even more alarming reaction, he shook his head violently. That didn't work. Fuck. He needed something more physical. He drove a fist into a bag, sending it spinning into the air. That helped—some.

In his peripheral vision, Gayle propped up on her elbows, head tilted at an angle, studying him intently. As though she was seeing more than he wanted her to see. It was unnerving.

"I'm not going to ask," she said softly. "If or when you want to talk about it is up to you, but I'm a good listener, Mac...if you ever need an ear."

The use of his name and not the endearment she'd tagged him with had him shooting a glance at her. Sincerity was etched clearly on her face. She'd seen he'd freaked out and instead of some crazy innuendo, she'd offered him a friend.

There was more to Gayle Matthews than a shocking mouth and a good time.

"Lance hasn't told you about me?" he asked quietly.

"I make it a point not to pry." She pushed to her feet. "I figure when a person is ready to share their darkest secrets, they will. All I know from Lance is you're his friend and you fight. The rest needs to come from you. And when you're ready, I'm willing to listen." She looked down at her body, then started for the door. "I don't know about you, but I stink. I need a shower."

Wow. Not only had she backed off, but she was giving him space *and* letting him save face. Lance was right. She was awesome.

"Hey, Gayle?"

She peered over her shoulder, brow arched.

"Thanks. Not many people would do what you just did."

A soft smile curved her lips. "Nothing to thank. I'm very familiar with the look you get on your face. I don't know what circumstances put yours there, but even crazy Gayle knows when to back off."

She was familiar with the look? How?

As she started for the door again, he couldn't stop himself from calling her name once more.

Why couldn't he just let her leave?

And then he realized he didn't want her to go.

He ran his hands through his hair, unsure how to deal with the sudden insight.

He did need space, but he also needed to know he'd see her again. "What are you doing tomorrow?"

She turned, and again her gaze felt like it was seeing deep into his soul. "I have a race."

Disappointment hit him. A telling emotion of how Gayle affected him, how much he liked being around her.

"Want to come?" Gayle added.

Did he? He studied the woman before him. Her gaze soft. Patient. Kind. "Don't you need to pre-register for those things?"

"I happen to be good friends with the coordinator. I think I can pull a few strings."

He wanted to snatch the offer she gave him without thought. That dangerous reaction pushed him to say, "Let me get back to you on that, okay?

He needed to think things through first.

"Sounds good. I'll see you later, Mac."

He actually missed her endearment for him and hoped he hadn't scared her away from using it. Once the door closed behind her, he sat down on a workout bench, braced his elbows on his knees, and hung his head. It'd been a very long time since he'd actually craved being around someone. He preferred to be alone. Alone meant no one depended on him. That was safe. No risk of failing someone else. He didn't want to invite that back into his life. He'd done it once with tragic consequences.

A creak came from the barn door. "I just saw Gayle— Hey, man, you okay?"

Mac jumped to his feet, rubbing his forehead as he stared at the ground, trying to act like he was searching for something. He didn't need Lance all up in his business. "Yeah. Fine. I had a jump rope. I can't find it."

"It's right there, dude." He turned his head toward his friend. Lance was pointing just a few feet behind him with a classic look of what-the-fuck? on his face. Great. Now Lance thought he was going senile, too.

Mac snatched up the jump rope. "Man, I think I need a nap."

"Zumba wear you out? Did Gayle make you wiggle those hips just a little too much yesterday?"

At the mention of her name, he stiffened. "I don't want to talk about Gayle," shot out of his mouth before he could stop it.

His friend's eyes narrowed. "What happened?"

Well, goddamn. He'd just handed that to Lance on a silver platter, hadn't he? The last thing Mac needed to do was flip the fuck out like he had the other day. He pinned his friend with a warning glare. "*Nothing* happened."

"Bullshit." He fisted his hands on his hips. "What did she do?"

"She didn't *do* anything," Mac bit out between clenched teeth. Anger roiled in his gut at his friend's persistence. Why the hell wouldn't he just drop it?

"Holy shit," Lance muttered, realization dawning on his face as his arms fell slack to his sides. "She's done it. She's gotten under your skin."

"What the fuck, Lance? I've known the woman for a few days."

He didn't want to think about how very deeply Gayle *had* gotten under his skin in that short span of time.

His friend stared at him, then made a sucking noise with his teeth and gave a sharp nod. "Ally would be happy for you."

Fucking hell! He didn't want to talk about Ally either.

"Jesus H. Christ, I don't even know her," Mac roared, fury erupting and completely taking control of him.

Bellowing between fused teeth, he tossed over the bench, sending it crashing to the ground.

"Yeah, and that's why you're going ape-shit." Lance braced his fists on his hips again. "Be honest with yourself, for fuck's sake. You like her."

Mac pointed a trembling finger at Lance. "I'm getting ready to knock the shit out of you." He stormed toward the door. "Leave me the fuck alone, Lance."

"It's okay to move on, Mac." Lance's words reached him just as his hand closed around the knob. "Ally wouldn't want you to hold onto her like you have."

His hand reflexively tightened around the knob, then he spun back around. "You don't think I know that? You don't think Ally and I didn't have late night morbid conversations about moving on if we lost the other?" He took a step forward. "Well, we fucking did. I know *exactly* what Ally wanted for me." But nowhere in any of those talks had there been a scenario of how to move past the guilt of failing her. The thought hit him suddenly and hard. He backed up and yanked the door open. Resentment churned in his gut and he blasted every bit of it at Lance. "So back the *fuck* off."

Chapter Four

What the hell?

As Mac followed Gayle through the gates of the Kansas Coliseum, he surveyed the line of black and orange tents set up around the perimeter of the stadium selling wares and food. Music blasted from two enormous speakers positioned outside a larger pavilion that housed a local radio station. Men, women, and children of all ages milled about, some in crazy costumes, others in regular running clothes. Everyone was laughing and having a great time. Mac, however, was having to take a moment to adjust. Gayle had definitely not been forthright about where she was taking him. This wasn't a race—not any ordinary race, anyway.

He could pinpoint every single person who had already completed the run. How?

A layer of dried mud was crusted on their skin.

The insane woman had brought him to a *mud* race.

Shaking his head, he stifled a laugh. Gayle never stopped shocking him. How in the hell would she top this? She couldn't. There was absolutely nothing she could do or say that would be able to dethrone an obstacle course over a pit of sludge. Nothing.

But he felt no resentment or anger at being misled. The lightness he'd known she'd bring filled his chest. Yeah. Agreeing to join Gayle had been the right decision.

After slamming himself into his room yesterday, the only person he'd thought of as he sat alone on the edge of his bed, head cupped in his hands, was Gayle, and how much he really could use one of her quips to shock a smile out of him—knowing somehow she would drive away the isolation. In those moments, he'd accepted he needed her…at least for now. Though his attraction to her terrified him, she helped bring a lightness back that he hadn't felt in a long time.

He'd called Gayle right then and there and asked if the offer to join her for the race still stood. There'd been no hesitation, just an instant "Of course it does," that had eased his lingering doubts and helped him fall into a dreamless sleep. This morning, when she'd shown up at his door wearing a pair of ultra-bright, pink, running boy-shorts, a purple tank top, and matching striped socks she'd pulled to her knees, he should've known something was amiss. But this was Gayle. If she'd shown up in a freaking tutu, he might have paused for a minute but then brushed it off. His second clue should've been when she suggested he grab a change of clothes. Asking why had only gotten him a smartass, "Do you want to be in sweaty clothes all day?"

Now he had the real answer. What he had on wasn't just getting sweaty. The neon green running shorts and the first sponsor shirt he'd earned as a pro fighter would soon be covered in mud. He didn't give two shits about the shorts. The shirt, well, that was a different matter. Yeah, it was old, but he didn't want it ruined. Unfortunately, the spare wasn't one he wanted ruined, either. He glanced around. Many of the guys had bare, mud-covered chests. Guessed he'd be doing the race shirtless, too.

Gayle peered over her shoulder, one of her pigtails flipping into the air. Those were damn cute on her. They weren't the low ones she had sported the day they'd met. A tail jutted out on each side of her head and was held in place with pink ribbon bows, matching the getup she had on. A smile tried to emerge every time he looked at her.

"I have to find Milton," she said. "He's the coordinator I told you about. He'll have all your stuff."

"Okay."

After five minutes of meandering through the massive crowd of people, a beefy, muscular man with close-cropped black hair, who had to be ten years younger than Mac, came out of nowhere and tossed Gayle over his shoulder, spinning her around.

Mac tensed, then charged forward, prepared to bash the man's teeth in, but then he registered Gayle's delighted laughter. Upside down, she popped the man on the ass, just as she had Mac the other day. Did she smack every guy's ass?

"Milton! Put me down."

The younger man finally put her back on her feet, tugged one of her pigtails, and slung an arm over her shoulder. "Hey, gorgeous."

The radiant smile she sent the man tweaked Mac's gut oddly, and all he wanted was to get her away from this guy. It was also as if she'd forgotten Mac was even there. What the fuck? He cleared his throat, and Gayle glanced over at him. "Oh! Yes!"

Damn. She really *had* forgotten he was there.

"Milton! I want you to meet Mac Hannon."

"What the hell, Gayle! Say it right. This is Mac 'The Snake' Hannon." Milton shoved the hand that wasn't resting around Gayle's shoulder at Mac. "Huge fan! What brings you to Kansas?"

As Mac took the offered hand, he tried to keep from scowling at the masculine fingers dangling a little too closely to a perfect breast, or how the owner of said perfect breast wasn't trying to move away. "I'm helping a friend train."

"Who?"

"Lance Black."

"Never heard of him."

"You will."

Gayle shifted into Milton's side, bringing her arm around his waist and tilting her face up to look at him. "Did you get Mac registered?"

The tweak pinched his gut a little bit harder this time, and Mac worked his neck, trying to relieve the irritation.

"Yep, I grabbed both packets when I saw you coming toward the registration tent. Your bibs and drink tokens are inside." He held out a piece of paper and pen to Mac. "I need you to sign this."

Mac snatched them from him and scribbled his signature on the release form, hoping it would get the man to go away. All the lightness he'd felt was now gone, and it hadn't disappeared until this asshat had shown up and Gayle had started fawning all over the fucker.

"Your heat will start gathering at the starting line in about twenty minutes," the man said. "Have fun, and make sure to stick around afterward."

"Plan to." Gayle rose on her tiptoes and kissed him on the cheek. The sight of those inviting lips he'd been fighting not to take for days, now on another man's skin, had Mac grinding his molars. "Thanks for arranging this, Milton," Gayle said. "I owe you one."

"A favor!" Milton looked at Mac and waggled his eyebrows. Mac swore he felt a tooth crack. "You heard that, right? She owes me one. Woman, I know exactly what I want."

If this asshole didn't get the fuck out of here, Mac was liable to toss him in one of the mud pits. Thankfully, he dropped a peck on the top of Gayle's head, then sprinted off toward the tents again.

Gayle turned toward Mac. "You read— What the hell is the matter with you?"

Since he could actually *feel* the scowl on his face, God only knew what it looked like. He sure wasn't going to express the immense aversion he had for Milton on first sight—nor was he going to examine it. "So this is a mud race. You kind of left out that little piece of information."

"Did I forget to mention it? *Oops*."

"Since this is one of my favorite shirts, looks like I'll be running without it."

"Trust me, handsome, I won't mind."

Warmth spread across his chest, easing the aggravation. It was the first time she'd used her nickname for him since things had gone awkward yesterday…and she hadn't called Milton by anything other than his name.

"I still would've come, you know," he said. "I was thinking about doing the one in Atlanta this year." Though that race was definitely more serious, since it was one of the most grueling mud races anywhere. Costumes were not encouraged. The one today was just a good-time race, which fit Gayle.

"You can line dance, and now you're willing to wallow in mud. You can be such a *stick in the mud*, I just wasn't sure how you'd react." To soften the insult, she stuck out her tongue.

"Take pride, handsome. You've surprised me. Twice. That doesn't happen often."

She started walking toward the tents and he fell into step beside her. "How often do you do these?"

"Whenever one is within driving distance. Rick is usually my mud buddy, but he bailed on me."

"Rick?" How many men did this woman hang out with?

"He's a co-worker."

"You're a meteorologist, right?"

"Yep." As she came to a stop at a table under one of the tents, she dropped her backpack off her shoulder and handed it to the person behind the check-in desk. "If you're taking your shirt off, you're going to want to do it now."

She leaned a hip against the table…waiting expectantly. A rush of heat ran over him. Yeah, he was planning to do this shirtless, but he hadn't planned on doing a strip show right in front of Gayle.

"Come on, handsome. Take it off."

Groaning, he yanked the shirt over his head, wadded it up, and stuffed it into the backpack that sat by his feet, then straightened.

"Holy. Shit."

He glanced at Gayle, who was making it no secret she was gawking, or that she liked what she saw as her gaze slowly appraised every inch of his exposed torso. A part of him wanted to puff out, let her get a really good view, but he was enjoying having her eyes on him a little too much. Instead, he reached down, lifted his backpack, and turned to check it in. The woman behind the table had apparently been in the process of scribbling down something, because now she was bent over a yellow notepad with a pencil still pressed to the paper, frozen…and was openly staring, as well. He glanced around. A lot of women were. Heat crept up his neck. It'd been a very long time since he'd been the object of such ogling — or at least been *aware* he was an object of it.

"My. My. My, handsome. Those abs" — Gayle finally dragged her eyes away from his chest to meet his eyes — "should never be covered up. You really are doing a disservice to women everywhere by doing so."

Despite his embarrassment at the blatant attention, her over-the-top compliment pulled a chuckle out of him. As he handed the backpack to the check-in woman, who had finally stood up straight, a slight caress feathered across his ribcage on his left side. He flinched away.

"Trust," she said. "That's beautiful."

His tattoo. *Fuck.*

Without a word, he hurried past Gayle and out of the tent into the sun. Hands on his hips, he inhaled deeply, disturbed by the way he could still feel the slight brush of her fingertips across the inked skin.

Ally had thrown the word trust around like it was a religion. Trust your decisions. Trust your instinct. Trust it will all work out. Trust, trust, trust. Hell, she even had him putting so much faith in that damn sentiment he'd permanently altered his body.

A load of horseshit was what trust was.

Trust was no damn different than hope — two worthless emotions the human psyche had come up with to try and banish the bad. All it took was finally seeing the truth. He'd seen it. He'd accepted. Nothing could be trusted. Hope was meaningless. No amount of trust or hope would make a lick of difference.

Gayle ran past him and slapped something to his chest, knocking him from his morose thoughts. Automatically his arms came up to grab whatever it was as he looked down. His running bib. Lifting his head, he watched her sprint into the group gathering at the starting line. No awkward moment. No explanations. No puzzling stares. Damn, the woman was amazing.

I'm very familiar with the look you get.

Her words from yesterday echoed back. Was it possible she had been close to someone who had gone through something traumatic? Was that how she knew when to back off?

Either way, she knew exactly when not to push, and he appreciated her for it.

He pinned his bib to his shorts, then jogged to her side. After she attached her number across her stomach, she reached her arms above her head, and arched her back. Mac knew she was stretching, knew for once she wasn't deliberately trying to get a rise out of him...and still she did. The snug purple spandex hugged her breasts, and his fingers itched to reach out and touch her as lightly as she'd touched him.

Fuck, this was getting bad. It was easier to ignore the attraction when she was provoking it, but the awareness of her was becoming constant, evoked simply from her standing there...he couldn't ignore that. And was beginning to think he didn't want to.

"Ladies and gentlemen," a masculine voice boomed overhead, startling Mac out of his alarming thoughts. Thank God. "Thirty seconds."

Gayle bent her leg behind her and grabbed the top of her foot with both her hands. Stretching. He probably should do that. Anything right now to keep from watching her. He followed her lead.

"You're going to love this," she said as she switched legs.

"How long is the course?"

"Four miles and fifteen obstacles."

"Three...two...one." A *boom* sounded, and runners started to sprint down the roped-off section of the parking lot.

Mac hopped from foot to foot, warming up his muscles as he waited for the crowd to thin. Since they were toward the back of the line, their progress forward was slow. Once they got past the bottleneck at the starting line, things opened up, and they were able to set an even pace. He set his stride to Gayle's, making sure to stay beside her. Through the mile jog across a street and into a more tree-thickened area, he found himself anticipating the obstacles, wondering what they would be. Had he known he would be doing this today, he would've studied the course, found out what to expect, made sure there weren't any surprises. Come up with a game plan.

Gayle had taken that away from him. Made him just be in the moment. And there was a thrill to it he'd forgotten he missed. At one time, he used to be a go-with-it sort of guy. What would it be like to be that guy again? Did he *want* to be that guy again?

He sneaked a glance at Gayle. Maybe. At least while he was here.

They came to an open field with tires spread out on it. He and Gayle each grabbed one and sprinted about fifty yards then tossed them onto a growing pile on the other side.

"The first few obstacles are just to warm us up," she warned as they continued down the path.

"Good, 'cause that was lame."

She gave a winded laugh. "Just wait until the mud comes into play."

"That's when the real fun starts?"

"Oh, yeah."

The next obstacle was a wood wall. Easy enough to get

over, since it was like climbing a ladder. Afterward, they awkwardly made their way across a thin rope bridge over a shallow gully, then crept across a rather rickety-looking balance beam. As they approached an arched monkey-bar contraption, Mac noted the large mud pit underneath. Shit was about to get interesting.

"You first," he said. "I'll start when you're a few bars ahead of me."

With his upper body strength, he'd be able to swing across this thing without any issues. But he'd didn't want to just zip past Gayle.

"All right."

She slowly—very slowly—swung from one bar to the next. *Come on, woman.* As she hung from the fifth and sixth bar, he paced along the edge of the pit. She wasn't going to make it.

Monkey bars were hard enough when they were straight across. Put in an arch, and more muscle, strength, and endurance were needed to complete the task. Gayle was using all hers up just dangling as she worked up the momentum to make it to the next bar.

Mac rubbed his mouth, struggling not to start clapping and yelling at her to pick up the pace. Gayle wasn't one of his training buddies. He wasn't at the gym. But the competitive edge ate at him now. Drove him.

When she finally made it to the middle, he wrapped his hands around the first and second bars and quickly monkeyed across. Within seconds, he was beside her. By the way her eyes widened and she gasped, his sudden appearance had startled her. One second she was there, the next she was gone. Right in the sludge below. Fuck, that was his fault.

He glanced down. The sludge came above her knees, and as she struggled to walk, she slipped, landing on all fours. Immediately, Mac let go of the bar. Warm, slimy mud enveloped the bottom part of his leg.

As he mucked his way toward her, worried she was going to be pissed he'd messed up her focus, he said, "Damn it, Gayle, I'm sorry. I didn't mean to make you lose your concentration."

A snicker greeted his words. She lifted her head, and the twinkle in her eyes made something in his chest expand. Holy hell. She didn't give a rat's ass that he'd fucked up her progress. Someone jarring *his* focus would've set him off.

But Gayle was enjoying every single second of this. No frustration. No fierce competition. Just pure joy. He really could learn a thing or two from her.

As he came to stand beside her, he put his hands on his hips. "And here I jumped in ready to save the damsel in distress. But you look happier than a pig in mud."

She tried to push up and slipped, the mud coming up to coat her neck. A laugh burst from her as she held up her hand. "As much as I love to get down and dirty, this damsel could still use your help."

Grinning, he latched his hand around her mud-coated one and yanked her up. After they pretty much had to crawl out of the pit onto flat land, they stood up. Mac surveyed the man-made mud hill in front of them—which had become slicker by the many other racers who had gone over it before them. And the ones slipping over it now.

"This should prove interesting," he said.

"I can tell you from experience, there is no use trying to run up the hill. Slow and steady, handsome." She winked, then started to bear-crawl up the hill by digging her fingers and the toes of her shoes into the mud. When she got far enough that he had room to begin, he followed the path she'd made. Concentrating on the indentions she'd left in the mud, he reached for one of the deep imprints made by her foot. One second his fingers had slipped into the slimy surface, the next, a squealing mass slammed into him and he was sliding down the hill on his back. As he drew to a halt at the bottom, the mass landed across his chest, knocking an *oomph* out of him.

Her muddied pigtail slapped him across the cheek. Breathless laughter warmed his neck as she tried to control the giggles that had overtaken her. One feminine mud-coated hand rested on the naked skin of his chest—a place that hadn't been touched by a woman in many years. The grime didn't hinder the way this accidental touch scorched his flesh, consumed him. Unable not to, he cupped her elbow in his palm, just needing to return the connection.

She lifted her head and gazed down at him, hazel eyes so full of life, happiness in her grin, a streak of mud across her cheek. Everything in him stilled for a brief moment then roared back with a vengeance. He couldn't remember the last time he'd wanted to kiss a woman more.

Ally. Her lifeless face swam before his eyes.

A rough breath stuttered out of him as he struggled to shut down the painful memory that threatened to explode before his eyes, and he released Gayle's elbow.

"Told you it was fun," she whispered, her smile fading just a bit as she sat up and faced away from him.

Mac blinked at the back of her head. She'd seen his struggle, and that made him feel even worse. None of this was her fault. Gayle was beautiful, fun, and charismatic. If he'd been whole, he wouldn't have hesitated with her. But he wasn't, he was broken…ruined.

Needing to get this out of Mac-is-damaged-goods territory and back into funland, he shoved to his feet and held his hand out to her. "Let's try this again. But this time without you being the bowling ball and me the pins."

Laughing, she slipped her hand into his, and he tugged her up. "I make no promises, handsome."

Seeing she was game for letting the awkwardness pass, he exhaled in relief, and they started their second attempt. After the fourth wipeout—all of which were caused by Gayle—the earlier moment was a forgotten memory as Mac heaved to his feet and beat his palm across the fingertips of his other hand, making the universal sign for timeout. "That's it! Timeout!"

At his outburst, Gayle's eyes rounded and she blew air into her cheek, making them puff out. The sight immediately alleviated his frustration, and he chuckled. He wasn't frustrated at Gayle, just the damn hill. Thankfully, they weren't the only ones having issues. Though each time someone finally made it to the top he cursed them to hell.

"I am going up this thing and I'm taking you with me."

He'd wanted to do this two wipeouts ago, but she didn't seem bothered by the slip-and-slide routine so he'd kept his mouth shut. If he took one more trip down this hill, though, he would lose his shit. Locking one hand around her wrist, he started the tedious climb up, dragging her behind him. Every time she lost her footing, he threw his weight forward and tugged her arm to keep the momentum from taking him down. The climb was slow, but finally he made it to within a foot of the top. He braced his body and pulled her up beside him.

"You first," he said.

As she crawled over the lip to flat land, he kept his hand out to shove her over the crest if she slipped. Once she reached the top, he climbed up beside her, and they stood. She immediately lost her footing. Instinctively he snatched her around the waist and yanked her to his body to keep her from making the longest trip yet down that hill. The second the warmth of her hands met his biceps, it registered he was holding Gayle.

Covered in mud, laughing. In his arms.

Life beckoned him.

He pressed his mouth to hers.

Immediately she stilled, her lips softening under his. He liked the way they fit together, liked the tightening of his body. Wanted to embrace it. Deepen it. Just as he was about to cup the back of her head and do just that, a passing runner gave a wolf whistle and Gayle pulled away, studying him…intently.

The reality of what he'd done slammed into him. *Holy shit.* He'd kissed Gayle. Without thought. Though it hadn't been the best first kiss—brief, unexpected—he felt the gravity of this moment to his core. As he stared at her, he brushed his fingers across his lips and swallowed. Gayle made him be in the moment and not remember the failures of his past. Nothing but fighting had done that for him in years. It scared the fucking shit out of him, but he wanted so desperately to grab it at the same time.

Her gaze softening, she squeezed his bicep, a small smile curving her mouth. She simply said, "Okay," then turned and half-slipped half-ran down the mud path.

He wasn't sure what she'd meant by that, but the hushed, reassuring way she'd said the word eased the pressure of the moment, allowed them to continue. And he did.

Obstacle after obstacle came at them after that. They climbed a rope net, crawled through tunnels, and waded through waist-deep mud. When they reached an extremely high rock-climbing wall, there wasn't an inch of their bodies that wasn't caked with mud, which made keeping a grip difficult.

As they climbed side-by-side, Gayle's foot slipped, and

she fell. The whack of her arm hitting one of the hand grips made Mac hiss. He looked down in time to see her hit the ground with enough momentum to roll backward. *Shit.* Worry twisting his stomach, he jumped down and hurried to her side just as she was pushing to her feet.

"You okay?" he asked, scanning her body for any injuries, unnerved by the fear tightening his chest and making it difficult to breathe.

"Wouldn't be a mud race if I didn't fall off the rock wall." Her chuckle and smile made him shake his head at his knee-jerk reaction. "This one always gives me trouble."

She's fine. Chill the fuck out.

"Oh, we've got this." Brushing aside the weird moment, Mac scaled the wall and straddled the top. He reached a hand down. Gayle blinked up at him. He wiggled his fingers at hers and she hesitantly slid her hand in his. As he hauled her up with ease, she squealed. He didn't let her go until he knew she was safely anchored to the top. She turned wide eyes on him. "Holy shit. Did you really just do that?"

Then her gaze swept over his bicep and an appreciative noise passed those sweet lips. "Rick's fired. You're so my new mud buddy. He'd never have been able to just lift me up like that."

Then she slid down the pole on the other side and landed on the ground.

As he followed her down, the appreciative noise she made rang in his head and plummeted to his groin, making him lose coherent thought for a moment as he watched her muddied ass disappear over the hood of a car.

He wanted her. No reason to fight that anymore. But the fear he'd felt for her safety just seconds ago lay heavy in his chest. Wanting her was one thing. Worrying about her was something else entirely, and it made him immediately want to put distance between them.

Gayle jumped up from behind a car. "Don't let me lose you now, handsome. Come on!"

She had no idea there was more to the statement than lagging behind on the race. He was at a damn crossroads and he knew it. If he continued, he'd be starting a whole new chapter in life.

Did he really want to? The future he had now was clear. No heartache. No attachments. No worry.

No real life.

If he allowed people in, then he opened himself up to all of that again. But he couldn't pussyfoot around with Gayle anymore. He wanted her. It was time for him either to go all in and risk it all, or fold and play it safe.

Both were tempting as hell.

Gayle cocked her head to the side and watched Mac stand still. An odd expression twisted his handsome face. A mixture of confusion and pensiveness. She didn't know what was going on in his head, but was wise enough to remain silent as he worked through whatever had triggered this one.

The third one of the day.

She had noticed each and every instant Mac began to struggle with whatever internal demon he was battling. After they had landed in a heap at the bottom of the mud hill, she'd sensed he'd wanted to kiss her. Then this heartbreaking distress had entered his eyes and she'd let him off the hook. After he actually had kissed her, she wasn't sure who'd been more shocked, him or her, but her heart had expanded at the almost awe that widened his eyes. And right there, she'd made the decision that she could be patient. She'd didn't know if whatever he was going through was a fresh wound or an old one, but he was struggling because he wanted *her*. And she did want him. Horribly.

So, she'd give him the time to work through his issues. If anyone knew about having to do that, it was her. Hell, she knew some issues you never really got past, you just found a way to live around them. After she'd lost her longtime boyfriend and her family, it'd taken two more heartbreaks for her finally to find a way to cope with *her* abandonment issues. Why it had taken her so long to realize, was beyond her. The answer had been so simple. Still was.

Leave before you get attached.

The last two years had been the happiest and most heartbreak-free she'd had since the tragedy.

Sam's smiling face formed in her mind for a moment. His dark, unruly hair untamed as ever. His green eyes shining with the love he'd had for her. So damn young. They'd never even gotten a chance to start the future they'd spent years talking about. Her heart squeezed hard once. She allowed her first love to dominate her thoughts for a brief moment, cherishing him even more for being the only man, besides her father, who had unwillingly left her. Then she tucked him carefully back into the past—where he belonged. The only future she had with Sam—or with the family she still desperately missed—was the scientific research she busted her ass to do so, hopefully, one day she could keep their fate from happening to anyone else.

As she surfaced from her demons, she realized Mac still hadn't moved. Racers passed by, giving him confused expressions. When they shot her a look, she sent them a smile, giving them permission to keep going without stopping.

Come on, handsome. Pick the present. If I can do it, so can you.

She understood the war all too well. Saw herself seven years ago reflected in Mac's present inner battle. It was so much easier now to put the past away. Hadn't always been like that—a lot of false starts and heartache had come first. If he was just starting down his road to healing, he had a long journey ahead.

His body shook once. And then he started forward, climbed over the car, and stopped by her side. Even though he smiled down at her, the emotions didn't quite reach his eyes. And there was a new stiffness to the set of his jaw. A sad determination.

"Let's finish this," he held out his hand.

Ah, well.

Taking his offering, she squeezed as a burning stung the back of her eyes. This had been a very difficult decision for him. So many questions filled her, wanting to explode from her mouth, but she pushed them back. After her family died, she'd hated being asked questions, being put on the spot, while the person asking stared expectantly at her. She'd sworn she'd never do it to another human being. Maybe one day Mac would open up to her. Until then, she'd be what he needed.

Someone to bring a little fun back into his life.

That, she could do.

She tugged her hand free, swatted him on the ass, and ran off. A chuckle followed her and she smiled. The distress of the moment had been broken, and they'd veered back onto the happy course. Mac fell into stride beside her. They came to an assortment of ropes hanging from a tree. People were using them to swing across a muddy water-filled pit.

"Ladies first."

Mud caked her hands and the rope from the amount of people who had swung across before her. "We're not making it across the water. You know that, right?"

"Speak for yourself. You look like you could use a good bath, anyway."

She struck an attitude. "Oh, really? Is that a challenge?"

"Sure. Why not?"

She eyed him. "Okay. Whoever makes it across without falling in gets to make the other do something."

"Like?"

"Open game, handsome. The something can be issued anytime, anyplace, anywhere."

His gaze lit with something resembling mischief. "I like those conditions."

"We have a deal, then?"

"Oh, yeah. We have a deal."

Without waiting, she jumped up, wrapped her legs around the rope, and held on. Halfway across, her grip slipped, but she tightened around the rope and landed safely on the other side. She gave a whoop of victory.

She turned to see Mac holding another rope. He jumped up and immediately slipped off, splashing in the water below. He waded out, then climbed up beside her.

"Hey! You let go on purpose," she said in mock outrage.

A wicked smile she'd never seen before lifted one corner of his mouth as a twinkle entered his eyes. "You'll never know."

Then he was the one to take off.

Stunned, she stared after him. A thrill shivered through her body. Whatever decision Mac had made earlier had released a side of him she couldn't wait to get to know.

She took off after him. They came out of the trees and she

saw a billow of black smoke off in the distance. They must be close to the finish line. They hurdled over hay bales, jumped over a fire pit, then belly-crawled under barbwire through thick mud. Holding hands, they waddled their way across the finish line, laughing every time the other slipped. A volunteer handed them each a medal of completion. As they moved off to the side, Mac wrapped an arm around her waist and tugged her toward him. The mud caking their bodies squished between them.

The sincerity on his face made her breath catch.

"Thank you," was all he said.

She wanted him to kiss her again, to pick up from that very brief but extremely electric kiss from earlier, but he released her and stepped back instead.

"Now, where do we go to clean off?" he asked.

"You won't get clean clean, but they have hoses over there." She pointed to an area where a group of people who'd gathered in a huge mudded area were being sprayed with water by volunteers. "It gets the worst off."

"Come on, then." As he started off in that direction, he grabbed her hand.

She let him tug her behind him, her heart fluttering. There was something extremely arousing about his large masculine hand swallowing her much smaller feminine one. Hell, mostly it was just the man. Despite all the baggage he carried, Mac had called to her sexual side the moment she'd bolted around the side of the house and soaked him with the water gun. It was taking a massive amount of restraint to keep from jumping the man. Had he been anyone else, she would've. But if she wanted Mac in her bed, she would have to let him take the lead and go at his own pace.

They reached the group of runners, and Mac maneuvered

them to the middle, then pulled her in front of him. Just because she had to take it slow didn't mean she couldn't egg it on a little, right? Get his mind going in the direction they both wanted it to go.

One of the volunteers arched a hose up so the spray reached where they stood. Gayle faced Mac. Inches separated her breasts from his chiseled, mud-coated chest. Tilting her head back, she let the water sluice over her face and upper body, then ran her palm over her neck and chest. She lifted her head, and the air whooshed out of her lungs at the tight way Mac was watching her. Coiled. Ready to pounce.

His gaze clashed with hers, and the heat there almost seared her to the spot. Yet he did not move. Just observed. Keeping their gaze connected, she let a saucy smile come to her lips and she continued to run her hands over the sides of her face, her neck, the tops of her shoulders, her arms, and the upper part of her chest. She kept her movement PG for those around her, but she had no doubt the thoughts going through Mac's mind were anything but family oriented.

When she had the worst of the mud off her, she bit the bullet and touched his cheek. He jerked but didn't move away, so she took that as encouragement. She washed away the streaks of mud on his face and neck. The entire time his heated gaze stayed fused to hers as his arms stayed by his sides. Her nipples tightened.

Something she'd thought to tease him with had taken a left turn straight to intense. When she finally got Mac where she wanted him—in her bed—he wouldn't be skittish like he'd been since she met him. No, the man would be masterful. Dominating. Even when she thought she was the one in control, she wouldn't be. He'd be.

Sex with this man would be amazing.

"I think you're clean," she said. He wasn't. She hadn't even touched his torso, but she couldn't go there.

"Really? I'd say I'm still pretty filthy." He nodded down to his chest.

The pointed look he gave her ensnared her. It was one of those moments where everything around her faded into the background. All she was aware of was the soulful brown eyes full of heat and promise directed at her, and the way he'd never, not once, during her entire show, taken his gaze off her—and it was too intimate.

She stepped back first. "Nah, you're clean."

A crooked smile came to his lips as he took her hand again and said, "Chicken," then tugged her out of the crowd.

She winked. "Just didn't want to get arrested."

Was it really that, or had she simply spent so many years being the aggressor, that she wasn't sure what the hell to do as the aggressee?

H er hands on his body had been so fucking hot.

As Mac tugged his T-shirt over his head in the changing tent, he could still feel the warmth of her palms sliding down the sides of his neck. It was like the woman had branded him out there, and he'd wanted to buck and thrash with all the lust her searing touch had brought forth.

God, he hadn't felt like that in years.

Consumed with raw lust.

He'd let her see it, too. She'd *needed* to see it. He'd made the decision to go all in, which meant no more hesitation with her, and letting the attraction run free. Over the last few days, she'd watched him struggle. She needed to see there was a man underneath all the baggage. A man who wanted her and *would* take her.

He'd gotten a little insight into Gayle from their encounter, as well. She'd read his intentions clearly, had backed off from his challenge. She was used to having the upper hand, probably felt in control of a situation when she was the one leading the reins. Join the club.

They could prove a very interesting combination.

He looked forward to seeing what that dynamic ignited between them.

After he shoved his feet into a pair of flip-flops, he left the tent in search of her. He found her standing by the refreshment tents. She'd changed into a pair of denim shorts and a pink spaghetti-strap tank. She also wore a pair of matching flip-flops. Dried mud streaked her legs.

She turned and their gazes connected. She smiled. "What is it about a man in camo?"

He glanced down at his camouflage cargo shorts. "And here I thought it was the tat."

"Oh, the tat's hot, too." She ran her hand over his exposed bicep.

Seemed she'd gathered her composure again and was trying to take back the upper hand. He'd let her...for now.

"How about we go grab that beer we earned and something to eat?" he suggested.

Her lips split into a pleased smiled. Yeah, she definitely believed she had the upper hand again. "That sounds great."

Within minutes they were sipping an ice-cold brew. Mac had selected a Polish dog while Gayle had settled on chili. They found a picnic table to listen to the live band. Mac waited for her to sit down, then took a seat beside her, making sure to press his thigh into hers. She froze for a second and shot him a look.

He had to take a gulp of his beer to fight back a chuckle.

This was fun. He liked throwing her off balance. God knew, the woman had kept him on his toes since the moment he'd met her. It was time for him to return the favor.

He leaned over and whispered, "That streak of mud between your breasts is pretty fucking hot."

Her mouth dropped open and her head fell forward to look at her cleavage, then she gave a sputtered laugh and pointed her spoon at him. "You're as bad as I am."

Grinning, he took another swallow of his beer, only to scowl when Milton came and practically sat on her lap. He hadn't liked the familiarity between the two earlier, and he liked it even less now. And yet, it bothered him that he was bothered by it.

"Hey, gorgeous. How was the race?"

"As exciting as ever. What's your opinion, Mac?"

"It won't be my last, especially if Gayle is going to be my partner."

Milton squeezed an arm around her. "Gayle is pretty damn awesome, isn't she? She's run with me on a couple of races over the years. It's always an adventure when she's involved."

Mac tensed. "How long have you guys known each other?"

"What? Two or three years? Gayle taught a seminar a few years ago that I attended. I hung around afterward because I had to get the beautiful professor's digits." He grinned like a fool.

"You guys used to date?" He'd deal with the professor part later.

"Used to? Hell, we still hook up from time to time. What do you say, babe, tonight? Nine o'clock. Your place?"

A fiery stab of jealously pierced Mac's gut.

Gayle slapped Milton on the arm. "Would you stop! His wife of three years is right over there." She pointed to the dark-haired woman handing out beers. "I met them *both* at the seminar."

Milton leaned in conspiratorially. "Did I forget to mention she hooks up with me *and* my wife from time to time?"

"For God's sake, Milton."

He laughed, then stood. "I've got to get back. Glad you *came*, Gayle." He waggled his eyebrows and Gayle rolled her eyes, shaking her head.

"Don't mind him. Milton loves to be shocking. He gets a kick out of people's reactions. He's harmless, though."

Mac dropped the remainder of his dog in the container and wiped his mouth with a napkin. Jealousy. What the fucking hell? Gayle wasn't a permanent. She was a temporary. That was the compromise he'd come to earlier. Keep his distance emotionally, but allow himself to have some fun. Gayle was the perfect person to do that with—but he didn't plan for this to be any more than a good time while he was here. He needed to tell her that, as much as he needed to remind himself, apparently.

"Hey, what's the matter?"

"Can we be up front with each other?" he asked. If she didn't like what he had to say, it was probably better things ended now, anyway.

"I prefer honesty."

"I'm only here for a few weeks while I help Lance out."

"Yeah, I know."

"You've really been persistent in spending time with me, so if you thought a lasting relationship would come out of this, it's not going to happen. I'm not looking for one."

She blinked at him. "Oh my God. Are you serious?"

Her response confused him. "Yeah."

"Why is it when a man pursues a woman he only wants sex, but when a woman pursues a man, she's trying to tie him down?" She leaned forward. "Here's a little piece of news for you, Mac. There are a lot of women out there who aren't looking for anything more than a good time. I'm one of them. I saw you. Thought you were hot as hell and wanted to fuck you. It's that simple."

At her words, he inhaled sharply. God, the woman really did hold nothing back. She'd most likely be the same way in bed. And didn't *that* thought cause his gut to clench.

"I'll forgive this one little slipup of yours because I get the impression you have been out of the dating scene for awhile, and I can see why you took my actions the way you did. But, are we clear now?"

He swallowed. "Perfectly."

She smiled and squeezed his forearm. "Good. Now, what would you like to do with the rest of the day?"

He knew exactly where the day was headed. There'd be no stopping them, and he wasn't going to fight it. "I want to make you dinner," he said. And added meaningfully, "At your place."

Chapter Five

Mac checked the grocery bag for the fifth time to make sure he had everything packed. Fucking nerves. Since he'd returned from the race, the fact that it'd been years since he'd been with a woman for the *first* time had started to get the better of him. He'd been fine until he'd borrowed Lance's truck to run to the grocery store to pick up what he needed to cook dinner. Then reality had given him a stinging bitch-smack across the face. Where?

In the condom aisle.

He hadn't bought protection in over a decade. The wide assortment presented before him had almost made him lose his cool. Glow in the dark? Really? In the end, he'd ended up grabbing a box of extra ribbed. The nerves were temporary, though, a mind-over-matter situation. He always got edgy before he took the walk to face his opponent.

Unfortunately, his need to be prepared had brought forth a serious case of holy-shit-he-was-having-sex-tonight awareness. Made him think stupid-as-shit stuff like, what if he was rusty? Or clumsy?

The hell he would be.

As soon as he saw Gayle tonight, all that raging lust would take control again and he'd dominate the fuck out of her bed. Just as he did in the cage.

Oh, yes, he would.

Damn, he liked this new way of thinking.

While he'd battled his demons on the course, Gayle had become his today—his in-the-moment. She *wasn't* his future—and thankfully she was on the same page with him about that—but she was a symbol of the future he could hope to have with somebody, someday.

Taking Gayle's hand had been the hardest thing he'd ever done. But he'd done it. He'd taken one huge step toward letting people into his life again. It terrified the living crap out of him.

The back screen door squeaked open, then snapped shut. Glancing over his shoulder, he saw Lance step into the kitchen.

"Hey," his friend said.

Other than to borrow his truck, he and Lance hadn't really spoken since last night. Seemed clearing the air with his friend was becoming a constant part of being back in Kansas. "You were right. Gayle's gotten under my skin, and I was freaked the hell out. I was struggling with my attraction to her."

Lance regarded him evenly. "All said in past tense. Something change?"

"Gayle took me to a mud race." Mac exhaled with what may have sounded like resignation, but was anything but. "She has a way about life. She just enjoyed every damn second we were out there. She made *me* want to enjoy it. I hadn't felt like that in a long time, and I kissed her. It felt good. Right. So, yeah, something changed."

He waited for Lance to respond, but all he got was a

squeeze of the shoulder as Lance walked past. Before he walked out of the room, his friend said, "She'll be good for you, Mac."

Staring at the empty doorway, he hoped to hell Lance was right, and this wasn't the biggest mistake of his life. Taking a steadying breath, he gathered up the bags and started the trek across the field.

As he reached the edge of her yard, Gayle stepped out onto her porch and an unfamiliar sensation squeezed inside his chest. A smile tugged his lips. Just like that, the hours of edginess were gone.

"Hey, handsome," she called.

He strode across the lawn, taking in her pale yellow tube-top sundress. The tops of her shoulders were slightly pink from the day in the sun, and her auburn hair hung freely around their slender curves. He trotted up the stairs, and his grin broke free at her bare feet.

"Hey, yourself," he said when he'd unstuck his tongue at the tempting picture.

She opened the door and motioned for him to go inside.

The modest living room was decorated in such non-Gayle colors it took him by surprise. "White walls and beige furniture doesn't seem to fit you."

The house didn't have a Gayle feeling at all. No pictures on the wall. No personality. Even the throw rug on the deep cherry wood floor was just a boring mixture of neutral colors.

A chuckle sounded behind him. "Decorating is overrated." She pointed to her left to another room. "That's a bonus room. I spend more time in there than I do in here."

He craned his neck to peer inside. Laptops and a lot of unfamiliar equipment. "Like a work space?"

"Yeah. I really only use the living room when I have Skylar

here or watch a movie." She motioned to the stairs. "Of course that's the upstairs. Two bedrooms and a full bath up there." As she walked through the living room, she pointed to a door on the left. "There's a half bath down here. This is a much smaller place than Lance's." She disappeared through a doorway at the back of the living room. "And this is the kitchen."

Now, this wasn't so bad. The room still didn't have a sense of Gayle at all, but he loved the polished wood walls and floor. Very rustic. The actual kitchen wasn't huge, just a U-shaped setup with a limited amount of counter space. The stove was positioned so when he cooked, he could still converse with someone seated at the table. He placed his bags on the counter.

"I'm starving. What are we having?"

"Baked courgette and wild mushroom risotto."

The blank expression she gave him had him coughing into his fist to cover a laugh. The woman had no idea what the hell that was.

"Um. Sounds delish."

"It won't take me long. I've precooked everything except the risotto."

"Well get to it, handsome. That chili didn't stay with me long. I'm famished."

"Can't have that."

After she showed him where the cookware was, he went to work heating the chicken stock in a pan, then warming olive oil in another pan. He added the arborio rice with a splash of white wine. While he waited for it to bubble, he was aware of Gayle watching him from the far end of the counter. It'd been a long time since he'd cooked for a woman, and he found he still enjoyed it.

"You know your way around a kitchen," she mused.

"I should. I used to be a chef."

A moment of silence followed. He glanced over at her. She was standing up straight instead of leaning against the edge of the counter. She shook her head. "You're kidding, right?"

"Nope. Used to be head chef at Tuscany in Kansas City."

Her jaw dropped. "That's, like, the most expensive restaurant in Missouri."

"Uh, yeah, I know." He chuckled at her dumfounded expression.

She snapped her mouth shut, then shook her head again. *Holy shit.* Gayle Matthews was actually speechless. He never thought he'd see the day.

"And you let me feed you *my* cooking?" She pressed her palms to her cheeks. "*And* it was cold. I'm horrified."

"If you'll remember, the cold part was my fault." He added the heated stock to the rice. "And even cold, the chicken you made was lovely."

She grimaced. "Yeah, it really compares to the blah-blee-blue you're cooking."

Laughter shot out his mouth. "Courgette and wild mushroom risotto."

"Like I said, blah-blee-blue." She shrugged. "Okay, shock worn off. I'm going to eat this up for all it's worth, and considering how expensive that damn restaurant is, I *know* how much this dinner is worth."

The grin wouldn't leave his lips as he sautéed the mushrooms. Once he had them completed, he added it to the risotto and sprinkled in the parmesan. He then divided the meal onto two plates, turned, and held one out to her. "*Bon appétit.*"

"This looks amazing."

And suddenly he was very self-conscious. He wanted

her to enjoy it, but what if she didn't? He didn't cook much anymore. Just on occasion, like when he'd helped Tommy with Julie. What if he added too much wine or sea salt? "I'm a little rusty. So I hope it's good."

The smile she sent him eased his worries. "This is going to be the best blah-blee-blue I've ever had."

She took the plate and sat down at the wooden kitchen table. He took the chair across from her, watching as she dipped her spoon in and took a bite. Her eyes closed and a low moan came from her.

"Now I am *truly* horrified you ate my chicken."

Relief had him releasing a breath. "Glad you like it."

They ate in silence, mostly because Mac couldn't concentrate on anything besides watching Gayle enjoy his food—which she did with the same relish that she lived life. Each bite came with a cock-hardening moan of appreciation and mumbled words of praise. Would she be just as vocal in bed? The idea made him shift in his seat.

After she took the last bite, she dropped the spoon in the bowl. "Handsome, that was delicious."

"I could tell." He sent her a cocky smile.

"What in the world would ever make you leave the kitchen?"

All the hot and bothered feeling he'd had over the last few minutes instantly turned to a block of ice. "I wanted to focus on fighting."

Not a lie, but not the whole truth either.

She tipped her head. "How's that going for you?"

"Best decision I ever made." That wasn't a lie.

"Don't you miss being a chef?" she asked.

"I miss cooking for others. Not necessarily the working in a restaurant part."

There, a nice balanced response. He could do this.

"Well, you can cook for me anytime."

When she stood and reached for his plate, he said, "I'll get the dishes."

"Nope, you cooked. I'll clean." She took the dishes to the sink. "Do you want anything to drink while I do this? I have spiced rum in the liquor cabinet just waiting to be opened."

Alcohol sounded good. "Yeah, I'll take one of those."

As she added coke to a shot of rum in a tumbler, he leaned against the end of the counter, and when she offered it to him, he sipped while she started washing the dishes. His gaze traveled over her body, lingering on the swell of her hips. She reached for one of the pans and he noticed a dark bruise on the back of her arm, right above her elbow. "Did that come from today?"

She twisted toward him, a question on her face.

He nodded toward the bruise. "Your elbow?"

She tilted up the arm in question. "Oh. Yep. I think I got that one from the wall I slid down. Got a nice big bruise on my thigh, too. Don't tell me you don't have any injuries?"

"A couple of scrapes."

"It's that fighter's body of yours. It's used to taking a beating, and something as simple as a mud race isn't going to damage it."

Eyes on her discolored skin, he pushed off the edge of the counter and moved until he stood directly behind her. He ran his fingers gently over the bruise and the curve of her elbow as he lifted his gaze to look down at her. A shiver quaked her body.

"Don't forget the one on my thigh," she whispered, turning into him. As she tilted her head back and looked up at him, the invitation in her eyes was unmistakable.

"Where is it?" He reached down to run his fingers over her knee.

She dragged the hem of her dress high up her thigh. A dark bruise about the size of a fist stood out against the creamy skin. He trailed his fingers over it, loving the feel of her smooth skin. He wrapped his arm around her waist and tugged her to his chest. With mouths inches apart and her hands on his biceps, they gazed at each other. It was the most intimate embrace he'd been in for so long, he took a moment just to enjoy the feel of her soft, curvy body pressed into his.

Then he ran his palms over her hips, cupped her ass, and lifted her those mere inches to capture her lips in a kiss so opposite the one earlier in the day, it could've been given by a different man—and in a way, it was. Unlike before, he was no longer struggling. He'd made his choice. And now it was time to claim his reward.

Her arms wound around his neck, her breasts flattening against his chest, and he swept his tongue past her lips into the warmth of her mouth. A groan erupted from deep inside him. She tasted so good—a mixture of the food he'd made, and something more, something uniquely Gayle.

Her flavor was intoxicating, addicting. Hauling her up his body, her gorgeous legs instantly wrapped around his waist, bringing her center to rest on the rigid strain inside his jeans. He took the few steps needed to press her back into the counter. As he ground his cock against her, he moaned into her mouth. Holy fuck, that felt good.

He propped Gayle in the corner of the counter and ripped his mouth away to look at her. Lips swollen, eyelids heavy, breathing rough. All from his actions. God, she took his breath away.

Now he wanted to hear her. Tugging the tube top down,

generous breasts bounced free, nipples puckered into tight, perfect tips. He circled one with his tongue and was rewarded with her sharp, uneven gasp. Fingers cleaved through his hair, holding him there. As he sucked one nub deep into his mouth, he worked his hands under the skirt of her dress and found the elastic band of her panties. He tugged them over her legs and let them drop to the floor.

Now it was time to see exactly how uninhibited Gayle was.

He'd never shied away from sex. Seemed four years of celibacy hadn't changed that. He wanted her open to him, wanted to be confident she had no modesty when it came to bed games. He raised his head, gaze locked with hers, as he lifted one of her legs and planted her foot to one side of her on the counter. When he reached for her other leg, a naughty smile curved her lips—and froze him in place.

Gayle slowly lifted her leg herself, spread her thighs, and placed her other foot on the other side of the counter. Mesmerized, he watched her grasp the fabric of her skirt hanging between her thighs and slowly draw it up to her stomach. And she was exposed. Pink, wet, with a narrow strip of hair.

"Fuck, woman," he growled, unable to take his eyes away.

"Have a taste, Mac."

Oh, yeah. She was definitely just as free sexually as she was with life. A thrill shot through him straight to his cock, hardening it even more.

Lowering his head, he took his first sample, the equivalent of a nibble, but it was enough to wrench a moan from her. Needing to coax more of those delicious sounds out of her, he sucked her clit into his mouth and circled it with his tongue. His actions didn't go unrewarded. Listening to her was so fucking hot, it spurred him to increase the aggression of his mouth and tongue, and to thrust fingers deep inside her. As she came against his lips, the harsh moan of her orgasm filled him with pure male satisfaction.

He placed a gentle kiss on her swollen clit and then lifted his head.

Yeah, he could listen to Gayle's bedroom noises all fucking night.

And that was exactly what he planned to do.

Gayle kept her eyes locked on Mac's wet lips. For a man who had been so hesitant, he sure as hell wasn't hesitant in the bedroom. Shooting her arm out, she fisted his shirt and yanked him forward, fusing her mouth to his in an aggressive kiss that made it clear they were far from done.

Letting go of the shirt, she trailed her hands down his chest to the hem and tugged it up. He broke away long enough to pull the shirt over his head and toss it on the floor. A few seconds of fumbling later, his shoes, pants, and boxers were off, too. He lifted her off the counter and put her on her feet. While he tore through a grocery bag, she shimmied out of her dress, letting it pool around her feet. He came back with a box of condoms and she smiled, then took his hand and led him out of the kitchen.

She liked a man who came prepared.

He didn't ask any questions, just let her take him. The delicious man had tasted every inch of her and she planned to return the favor in turn. When they reached the couch, she pulled him to stand in front of her and tapped his pecs with her fingers in a gentle shove. Not that it would've taken him down, but he fell back against the cushions in a comfortable position.

Chuckling at his easy willingness to play along, she lowered to her knees between his spread legs. "For a man who can be so predictable, you keep surprising me."

A cocky smile turned up those amazing lips. "Got to keep a woman guessing."

"That you do, handsome. That you do."

She lowered her eyes to the thick, long cock jutting proudly from his body. As she ran the tip of a finger over the velvety skin, it jerked. "Would you like to feel my mouth on you?"

"Oh, fuck, yeah."

God, he was going to be one hell of a lover.

Gently she cupped his balls, massaging them in her palm as she slowly slid the head of his cock inside her mouth. The groan followed by a roughly muttered, "*Fuck*," gave her incentive to keep going. She took each inch of him in, then pulled back, over and over, increasing the speed with each bob. His breathing became choppy, and she jerked her head up.

No coming for the man. Not yet, at least. Her mouth wouldn't be the only place his cock would penetrate first. She moved her way up his body and nipped at his hips, kissed over his drool-worthy abs, circled her tongue over his nipples, and sucked on his throat before finally getting to his lips. Delving her tongue between them, she straddled his pelvis, his cock sliding against the back of her ass.

"Condoms?" she asked against his mouth.

A foil package was shoved into her hand. She gave a hum of appreciation, then tore it open and worked her hand between their bodies, sliding the rubber over him.

"Fuck, just having you wrap your hand around me feels so

fucking good."

"You just wait."

She lifted up, then slowly took him inside her. Closing her eyes, she moaned in pleasure as the man stretched and filled her. *Jesus*. She took a moment just to enjoy the feel of him, then she opened her eyes. And she started to ride. His fingertips bit into her hips as she moved her pelvis in a rhythmic motion. *So good*. It felt so damn good. She leaned her forehead against his, increasing the speed of her hips. It wasn't enough. Not deep enough. Not fast enough. A frustrated moan stuttered past her lips.

Quick as a snap of his fingers, Mac flipped her on her back. His arms anchored beneath her knees, keeping her legs spread wide and pressed up close to her chest. He took control, pounding into her. How deep he got, how fast he thrust, how hard he took her, made uncontrollable sounds of pleasure escape her mouth. She bit her bottom lip, trying to mute them. Even hushed, they poured out of her. She couldn't keep her responses contained because he dominated her body, yanked them from her. She fought against the urge to let every moan, groan, and "Oh, God," rip loudly into the air.

She loved sex, enjoyed the hell out of it, but this overpowering carnal need was new—and a bit terrifying.

When he reached down and touched her, she came instantly, and the cry that pushed to erupt with it was smothered by her clamped teeth, the decibels chopped in half. Above her, Mac jerked, a guttural growl rumbling out of him, his eyes clenched tight. Breathing heavily, moments later, he lowered and braced himself on his elbows.

"Holy shit," he whispered as he kissed her.

Holy shit was right. The man had just rocked her damn world. Sex with Mac had been a whole new experience, and she was giddily thankful she had a few more weeks with the man. Because *this* kind of sex, she could get used to.

A computerized music beat broke into Mac's sleep as Gayle stirred beside him. Lifting his head, he watched her fumble for her cell phone on the end table. He rubbed his hand down her side and settled back against the pillow, thinking about the amazing night they'd shared and how utterly sated he felt. An intense training session didn't wear him out this well.

"Hello?" The huskiness of sleep roughened her voice, and he found it so sexy he nipped her bare shoulder. She squeaked and swatted at him, but then she sent him a grin. A round of morning sex, then a nap, sounded like a great idea. He rained kisses over her skin.

"Really?" Her body tensed, and he lifted his head, concerned. "Wichita Falls, Texas. Got it."

Flinging aside his arm and the covers, she hopped out of bed, revealing her beautiful naked ass as she scanned the floor, then glanced toward the door with a frown.

She was looking for her dress. It was downstairs where their clothes had been discarded in the living room.

She darted to her dresser and started yanking out garments. "It's just shy of seven. If we leave within the hour we can be down there a little after lunch. With the late spring, it's been quiet this season. Maybe we'll get some footage. I need to have something to give to Peter soon, or I'm worried he's going to pull the funding."

Season. Footage. Funding. What was she talking about?

He lifted up on his elbow and watched her. There was an excited animation to her movements. What the hell was going on?

Balancing the cell on her shoulder, she shimmied into underwear and black shorts. "Yeah, meet me here. I've got to get some things ready, then we'll hit the road."

She tossed the phone on the bed and yanked on a shirt almost simultaneously.

"Who was that?" he asked.

"Rick," she said as she gathered her hair in a ponytail and secured it with a band.

Why was she rushing around like a mad woman? He rubbed the heel of his palm against his eyes. "Your co-worker?"

"Yep. There's a storm system forming down in Texas. The first of the season that has the potential to bring tornadic activity."

At the mention of the violent natural disaster, every muscle in his body petrified. His heart squeezed painfully. He sat up straight. "Gayle, why are you so amped over a storm system?"

He feared he already knew the answer but prayed he was wrong.

"Damn it. I need a bra." Distracted, she went back to dresser and tugged one out.

"Gayle. Why?"

As she worked a bra on under her shirt, she scrunched her nose at him. "Potential tornadoes, handsome. Why else would I be excited about possible tornadic activity? I can't chase if the atmosphere isn't right to spawn twisters."

Chase?

A roaring filled his head. His mind, his body…his heart protested against the repellant information. She grabbed a pair of hiking boots, perched on the end of the bed, and laced them on.

"Are"—He had to swallow hard against the chokehold her words had locked in around his throat—"you saying you're a *tornado chaser*?"

"Technically, we're called storm chasers, but yeah, the goal is to catch a tornado."

Oblivious to his blossoming horror, she hopped to her feet and gave him a peck on his dazed lips. "We're heading to Texas, so I'll probably be gone a few days. Let yourself out, okay? I'll see you when we get back."

Then she was gone.

Just like that.

As if she hadn't just given him the worst mindfucking of his life.

Woodenly, he pushed aside the covers and stood on numb legs. How had this happened? *Why* would this happen—to him? *To him?* He stumbled his way downstairs, dazed, and jerked on his clothes. Hearing Gayle rummaging around in the bonus room, now knowing what the equipment was used for, his stomach heaved. He couldn't look at her, couldn't be in the same room with her. Silently, he let himself out the back door.

As he made his way to Lance's house, the stupor her admission had caused faded, and the ugly darkness he knew as life took hold.

Why was he so goddamn stunned? This was the way shit worked. Four years of depending on nothing, on nobody, and he'd gotten along just fine. Then that woman had come in and fucked it all up. And as soon as he opened himself up again, what happened? Life coldcocked him hard right in the face, then stood over his dazed body and said, "You stupid motherfucker."

He couldn't argue.

Only a stupid motherfucker would spend years keeping his distance from everyone, only to unknowingly fuck the one woman who actively sought out—who actually *chased after*—the destruction that had shattered his life.

What were the odds? How was that even *possible*?

Of all the women in the goddamn world, the one, the only one, he'd responded to sexually was a fucking *tornado chaser*.

Mac stepped into the house and froze. Lance was sitting at the kitchen table, reading the newspaper and eating a bagel. Had he known all along? Of course he had.

Mac released the door, letting it slam shut. *Motherfucking asshole.*

His friend jumped as his head shot to the side. Dropping his bagel on a napkin, he shoved the chair back and stood. "Jesus, man? You're pale as a sheet."

"Did you know?" was all Mac could get past his clenched teeth.

"Know what?"

"About Gayle."

"I need more details, bro. You're not making much sense." Lance took a cautious step forward. "What about Gayle?"

"She chases tornadoes."

His friend jerked back as if struck, then immediately shook his head. "No. You've got to be mistaken."

"Mistaken? She's headed to Texas to chase a system right this minute." Fury overtook Mac and he fisted his hands, baring his teeth. "And she was fucking *excited* about it. People will die, but she's over the goddamn moon about the possibility of catching video footage. It's fucking *disgusting*."

"Shit," Lance whispered, and swallowed. "Did you—"

"Yes. I fucked her last night," Mac cut him off, not wanting to hear his friend, wanting—no, *needing*—someone to blame.

A pained grimace contorted Lance's face and he hung his head. Lance knew. And he understood the magnitude of how severely this had fucked Mac up. Good.

"I let her *near* me. The only woman I've been with since I left this fucking place is a goddamn adrenaline junkie, and her fix of choice destroyed my fucking *life*." Mac pointed accusingly at his friend. "You *told* me she would be good for me."

Lance lifted his head. Compassion and worry shone from his eyes, causing Mac to flinch. He'd had enough of that goddamn sympathetic expression to last a fucking lifetime. It was why he didn't let people in.

"I would never have encouraged it had I known, Mac. I swear to that. She moved in six months ago. Tornado season has just started. All she ever mentioned was being a meteorologist and that she had her PhD. That's it."

It didn't matter. What was done, was done. "When is this fight of yours?"

Lance blinked. "A month."

"That's all you've got, and then I'm the hell out of here." He stormed toward the door. Just before he left the kitchen he turned and leveled Lance a deathly glare. "Keep that crazy, reckless woman away from me, do you understand? I won't be held responsible for what comes out of my mouth if you don't."

CHAPTER SIX

Three days later, Gayle turned the steering wheel of the SUV into her driveway. She spotted Mac standing on Lance's front porch and her stomach jumped. She devoured the sight of him in black training shorts that couldn't hide the strength of his thighs. The sleeveless, neon green fitted shirt hugged his chest and displayed the Celtic tattoo on his bicep beautifully. She couldn't wait to trace those inked black lines again. It was insane how much she'd missed the man. She waved at him, but all he did was give a fierce scowl and stand motionless as a statue as she drove into the barn behind her house.

"Was that the guy?"

She glanced over at Rick, who looked as exhausted as she felt. "Yeah."

"Well, you sure had the curmudgeon description down. Dude looked all kinds of cranky."

She gnawed on her bottom lip. He'd had time to think again. She'd tried not to worry about it while she was gone, but unease over him having second thoughts about their little *fun* arrangement kept invading her mind—and Rick had noticed. He'd pestered the crap out of her about why she was so distracted until she'd finally caved and told him about the handsome fighter who was visiting next door. Rick's cryptic sigh, followed by, "What does it matter, you'll only keep him around for a few weeks before you move on, anyway," was accurate, but still hadn't kept the man from dominating her thoughts...as he had her bed.

After they climbed out of the truck and stored the gear away, Rick helped her carry the electronics into the house. "Peter's not going to be happy, is he?"

Gayle made a face. "Nope, but we can't control a storm system. He's just going to have to get over it."

"You don't think he would pull the funding, do you? I'm enjoying getting a regular paycheck for once."

She chuckled softly. Like he needed it. She'd met Rick almost eight years ago at a frat party at the University of Alabama in Huntsville. Though he'd had no interest in atmospheric science, he had a BA in painting and art history. When she'd started chasing, he'd asked if he could join her because he wanted to try capturing Mother Nature on canvas. And, boy, could he ever. His paintings sold and sold well. He'd been driving for her ever since—without pay. But then, she hadn't been getting paid, either, at first. When that had changed, she'd made sure Rick got a little bonus, too, for the loyalty he'd shown her.

"He better not pull our funds. Not if he wants to flaunt Dr. Gayle Matthews as chief meteorologist for WKKS News."

That PhD had given her a hell of a bargaining chip when Peter had approached her with the job offer. She'd never held one iota of interest in being on TV. But video footage she'd captured last year of an EF-3 tornado that had hit a small town in Oklahoma had garnered national attention. Peter Gates,

General Manager of WKKS News, had approached her days later and asked about her credentials. He'd offered her the job of chief meteorologist on the spot, which she'd promptly turned down. She was very happy with her cushy professor position, and had an understanding with the University of Kansas that she did not work during active tornado season so she could conduct her ongoing field research. But when Peter's offers kept getting more and more interesting, she'd quickly realized what he was truly after—her title as PhD in atmospheric science and her new national recognition. And so the bargaining had begun.

The final agreement was that she would work for him as his chief meteorologist, he would provide her with a decked-out SUV with all the weather crap she needed to continue her research, and she would take tornado season off from the station so she was able to dedicate her time solely to chasing and her research. All the video she caught would be owned by WKKS, as long as it was clear that any footage necessary for her research could still be used by her. She couldn't care less about the videos, really. The raw data was what she was after. The science.

So, now she had the best equipment money could buy instead of what she could acquire each year on her meager salary—and no freaking tornado season to use it on. The universe was no doubt having itself a real good laugh at Gayle's frustration.

"We'll just keep watching the maps and the numbers," she told Rick as they put the laptops and other gear on her kitchen table. "We're only a couple weeks in. Things are bound to pick up."

Hopefully, somewhere out on the miles of flat desolate land. Those were her favorite chases—with only the beauty of Mother Nature spread out before her—and the draw of her research. Once populated areas were affected, though, her research took a backseat to lending a hand where needed. People always came before data. Thankfully, those instances were few and far between.

She inhaled and turned to look at Rick. "Go home. Get some rest. You know the drill."

He saluted her. "Aye, aye, boss lady. You do the same."

He let himself out the back door. She walked to the window and peered out at the house across the way. Lance and Mac were heading for the barn. Yeah, she needed to rest. A chase was always exhausting, even if it was a big fat bust like this one had been. Three days of traveling all across the Midwest pursuing promising data, and not even a measly funnel had peeked out from the dark clouds. She could hear Peter's outraged blubbering now. The downside of doing her research under someone else's thumb, especially a person who had no inkling about weather, was starting to surface. Real storm chasing wasn't like in the movies. If Peter gave her too much grief, she'd tell him to take his high-tech gadgets and stuff them. She'd been doing just fine on her own. She could do so again, if need be.

She eyed the phone. Nah. He could wait.

First she had a fighter she needed to see.

She strode across the field, opened the barn door, and stepped inside. Silently, she moved off to the side as Mac and Lance were grappling on the mat. She couldn't tell what they were doing. Lance was trying to bend Mac's arm in a direction it definitely wasn't supposed to bend. Mac finally slapped Lance's shoulder and he released him. Both rose to their feet.

"Better," Mac said. "We need to work on that a little more, but you're getting the hang of it." Mac's eyes flicked to where she stood, then flicked back, and he stiffened. A fierce frown tightened his lips.

Lance looked over his shoulder and grimaced when he saw her. That wasn't like Lance at all.

Unease made her swallow. What had happened?

Not one to cower, she smiled and strolled farther inside. "You guys getting your sweat on?"

Lance moved forward, running a hand through his hair, casually stepping between her and Mac. "Uh, yeah. Been going at it pretty hard the last couple of days."

She glanced around Lance at Mac. "Hi, handsome."

If anything, Mac's scowl became even scowlier. Wow. She'd *thought* she'd seen him transform into the fighter a few times when he was trying to deal with her antics, but she was wrong. Way wrong. The man before her right now was intimidating as hell, and if he'd been the one she'd met on that first day, there would've been no way she'd have been so bold as to ask him out. A handsome but grumpy curmudgeon she could deal with...but a lethal, looked-like-he-could-snap-a-tree-trunk-in-two fighter, no way, *nuh-uh*.

Why was all this hostility suddenly directed at her?

Lance took her arm and steered her toward the door. She gaped at him. He was trying to make her leave. What the hell?

"I was going to come by your place in a little bit and see if you'd mind watching Skylar for a couple of hours. I have a voluntary pickup scheduled."

"Sure. No problem," she said, yanking her arm away and turning back toward Mac. "Why don't you come over and hang out with us?" she asked him.

"I don't think so." His hands tightened into fists at his sides.

"Why not?" His attitude was starting to piss her off, but

she managed to ask nicely.

"Mac." There was a cautioning rumble in Lance's voice that made Gayle shoot a glance at him.

That did it. "What the hell is going on? *I* couldn't have done anything. I haven't even been here."

It was like she'd taken the cap off a shaken bottle of soda. Mac advanced on her so fast she almost retreated, but she held firm, notching her chin up in defense.

"You're all about living in the moment," he mocked, his voice getting a little louder, a little more cutting, with each word. "Throwing caution to the wind, having no regard for safety. You take life for granted. You embrace danger." He raised a finger and jabbed it at her. "You don't give a good goddamn about the wellbeing of others."

Every word hit her like the blast of a rifle, ripping away at her bit by bit.

The last time she'd felt this shell-shocked, she'd just learned she'd lost everyone she loved.

But unlike the time before, pain didn't engulf her. Anger did. And as the stunningly cruel words sank in, that anger grew. "You don't know a *damn* thing about me," she said, slowly, calmly.

"Oh, I know plenty. You're a fucking catastrophe waiting to happen. Reckless. Impulsive. Careless—"

"Bro," Lance interrupted with a stronger warning note in his voice. "You need to step back."

"Bat-shit crazy." An unmistakable shadow of disdain darkened Mac's eyes. "You get off on risk-taking, no matter who will get hurt, and it makes me sick."

Lance raised his hands in a calming gesture. "Everyone needs to take a timeout."

"Fuck. You." She flipped him off with both hands, then

spun around and slammed out the door.

Lance's, "Fucking not cool, man," followed her out into the field.

Fury vibrated through her entire body. She took life for granted? *Didn't care for the wellbeing of others?* Screw his judgmental ass. If he wanted to jump to conclusions on how she chose to live her life, then so fucking be it. She didn't owe *anyone* an explanation.

"Gayle. Wait!" Lance called after her.

She kept striding. Fuck that.

His hand finally latched on to her arm and whirled her around. "Listen, I'm sorry about Mac."

"Don't you dare apologize for that dickhead."

Lance groaned. "I warned you. Mac has some serious baggage."

"*Everyone* has baggage, Lance. What that man has is serious"—she tapped her finger to her temple—"*mental* issues that could really use a good dose of shock therapy."

She started to spin again, but Lance stopped her.

"I'm trying to explain, Gayle, if you'll stop for a goddamn second. He's been to hell and back—"

She jerked away from him. "Aren't you hearing me? I. Don't. Care." She stepped forward and pounded her chest with her finger. "*I've* been to hell and back. *I've* had to pick up the shattered pieces of my life and learn to live again. And I have *never* judged someone like that because of my *baggage.* He—"

Lance's eyes went wide. She snapped her mouth shut. Tears threatened to form and she blinked them back furiously. *Damn it.* She never talked about the past. No reason to relive it when nothing would change it.

"Gayle, I had no—"

She lifted her hand in front of his face. "I am *not* doing this. I made peace with my past a long time ago. You just keep that prick away from me. I don't give a flying fuck what he's been through. I don't care how horrific his story is. He's just showed me his true colors and I want no part of him. Anytime you need me to watch Skylar, it will be at my place. I don't want to be anywhere near that judgmental bastard."

Mac cringed as the barn door slammed against the outside wall and Lance came barreling back inside.

"What the *fuck* was that?" Lance got right up in his face and pushed him a step backward with his body. Mac didn't object, letting his friend have his anger. "Gayle is a good person and she sure as fuck didn't deserve that shit from you."

"I don't want to be around her, Lance."

"Well, you sure as hell guaranteed that by being judge and jury over *her* life."

Things had gone a lot further than Mac had intended. But the moment he'd looked up and saw Gayle standing there, his chest had tightened…and not in anger. The disgust and fury that had swamped over him for still feeling something when he knew what she did for a living, and that she was nothing more than an adrenaline junkie, came pouring out in words before he could stop it.

The abject terror he'd felt over the last few days when he thought about her within touching distance of a tornado had made him crazy. The fear she created inside *him* because *she* willingly put herself in danger was overwhelming.

Jesus. If he felt this powerfully in the short amount of time he'd known her…it just plain pissed him off. The whole fucking thing pissed him off big-time.

He *couldn't* care for this woman. It would kill him.

He needed to keep his distance. Needed to make sure she kept hers.

He'd wanted her anger. Anger was safe.

"You want to know what I just learned?" Lance continued. "That woman you were just an absolute prick to has been through something, too. Something real bad."

Mac jerked up and looked at his friend. "What do you mean?"

"Well, let's see. Raging pissed off woman says she's been to hell and back and she had to pick up the pieces of her life and learn to live again, but she has never judged anyone the way you just did."

A painful knock to the gut stole Mac's ability to breathe. She'd been through something so bad she'd had to learn to live again? No. Lance must have misheard. Gayle didn't come across as haunted at all, much less broken and mended.

"Did she say what it was?"

"Yeah, no," came Lance's sarcastic reply. "But did you *hear* what I said, Mac? Did you hear the difference?"

What was Lance getting at?

His friend groaned and slapped both hands over his face. "You're fucking pathetic, dude." He lowered his hands and stared at Mac. "She learned to *live* again."

"I've had to do that, too."

"No. Gayle truly lives. You are just here. Marking time. Big difference. *But*, Gayle made you smile and laugh, Mac. She brought you out of the shell you had erected around yourself. *She* made you live." Lance took a step forward. "And you just treated her like a pile of dog shit. She may be a storm chaser, hell, I don't know. But I think the two of you have a lot more in common than you realize." He swept his arm toward the barn door. "Look at her. Gayle has been able to find peace with whatever it was she went through. Maybe she can help you do the same."

A feminine voice called Lance's name from outside, and he glanced toward it. "That's Piper. Skylar's here and I have to go. Gayle is watching her while I'm gone. It should only take a few hours. I suggest you do some really hard thinking and figure out a way to make amends with that woman, because you know what? I *was* right. She would be good for you."

With that, Lance stormed from the barn, the door slamming against the outside wall for a second time. Mac stared after him, then slowly lowered himself to the weight bench, linking his fingers between his knees. What *had* happened to her? There were so many ways a person could travel to hell, have their life shattered. The idea that someone could've hurt or neglected her made him shudder.

And yet, she still embraced life with gusto. She hoped and trusted. Laughed. Smiled. And gave of herself freely.

What he'd done by going off on her was the equivalent of pulling the wings off a butterfly that'd just flown from its cocoon.

She deserved his words of remorse…and gratitude. She *had* made him smile. She'd made him live again—however briefly.

The problem was coming up with the right words to express it. The only people who knew his whole story were the ones who had witnessed it. Not once had he ever verbally shared the horrors of that day with another living soul. He didn't know if he was capable of doing it now. Or ever.

How long he sat there trying to put together the right way to share the darkest, bleakest, most horrific day of his life, he wasn't sure. But suddenly a crash of thunder shook the structure surrounding him and he lost the ability to breathe, to move, as he was thrown headlong back to the moments just before a ferocious mass of twisting air had annihilated his life.

Gayle folded her arms across her waist as she gazed out the window at the storm cloud darkening the sky. Lightning brightened the grayness, and another boom of thunder quaked the glass. Wind swayed the tops of the trees. The forecast had called for isolated storms today, and she was definitely in the mood for a storm. Rain dinged off the glass panes, then the skies opened up and deluged the window with water. Inhaling, she closed her eyes and let the soothing sound flow over her.

God, she loved a spring storm. A cleansing of the earth and the smell of freshness afterward. If only the storm thrashing inside her would cleanse and refresh her the same way.

Almost forty-five minutes had passed since she'd left Lance standing in the field by the barn. Twenty minutes ago, he'd dropped off Skylar and tried to "talk" again. She'd instantly shut him down. Mac no longer existed as far as Gayle was concerned, and she resented the tight, angry emotions she'd been left with because of that awful man.

It makes me sick.

Well, right back at you, asshole.

To *hell* with him. Yeah, she was unconventional. Did things the way she wanted to and didn't apologize for it. She had her reasons. Damn good ones. She'd gambled on love too many times and lost. Forever didn't exist.

Thunder cracked again, and a sniffle sounded behind her. Gayle twisted around. Skylar was sitting on the couch with her face buried in her hands.

Shoving aside her own problems, Gayle hurried to the child's side and knelt in front of her. "Sweet pie, what's the matter?"

The little girl lifted her head. Tears brightened her eyes. "I put Bacon down to hug Daddy, and then I left him there."

Ah. Bacon was Skylar's stuffed pig, and she was extremely attached to it. Most likely, Lance had hustled her right over here as soon as Piper dropped her off. "He's in the house, right?"

The little girl nodded.

"Then he's going to be fine."

"What if he's scared? I've never left him alone in a storm before."

Meaning Skylar was a little fearful of this storm and wanted her comfort object.

Gayle swallowed. "M-Mac is there to take care of him." God, it was hard to even say the man's name.

"*Nuh-uh.* He's still in the barn. Daddy said so."

"But that was twenty minutes ago. I'm sure he went inside as soon as he realized a storm was coming." She brushed the blond curls back. "Bacon will be fine."

Skylar crossed her arms stubbornly. "What if he isn't? What if Bacon is alone and scared because I left him?"

Never argue with an eight-year-old. There was only one solution…and she would only do it for Skylar. "Listen, sweetpie, this is just a regular thunderstorm. Not even close to one of those really bad ones we sometimes have. But there is still lightning and it's pouring, so we can't go out in it right this second. As soon as the worst passes, we'll run over and get him, okay?"

Skeptical eyes watched her intently. "Promise?"

"Cross my heart," she said, doing the finger motion over her chest.

"Okay. As *soon* as it stops raining."

"Yes. Now let's find something to do so the time passes quickly."

After she ushered Skylar into the kitchen and settled her down at the table, Gayle made them each three ants on a log. As they ate the celery, peanut butter, and raisin snack, she watched the cloudburst through the open back door. Strong, but not severe. A nice torrential downpour with cracks of thunder and flashes of lightning. The wind gusted here and there, but it was more of a robust breeze than damaging squalls. The humid air had already cooled, leaving behind the fresh, clean smell she loved directly after a storm.

Wouldn't be long now. By the time she had tossed away their napkins, the rain was giving its last bit of nourishment to the ground. She opened the screen door, gazing up. Blue skies were already peeking through the dark clouds. "Come on, let's get Bacon."

As they walked across the saturated field, she hoped she could get in and out without coming face-to-face with the asshole. Honestly, she hoped to hell she somehow managed to get through the next few weeks without seeing him ever again.

As they trudged past the barn, she noticed the door had blown open. Why wouldn't the dick lock it after he left? Lance had a lot of expensive equipment in there.

"Skylar, you go on in and get Bacon, okay? I'm going to lock up the barn for your dad. I'll meet you at the back door."

"Okay." The little girl ran into the house, the screen door slapping closed behind her.

Sighing, Gayle approached the door. As she started to shut it, a furious grunt came from inside the barn.

She poked her head inside and froze. Straddling one of the practice dummies Lance used to train, was Mac. Sweat coated his entire body, dripped off his chin, matted his clothes to his skin, and slung off his wailing arms as he beat the dummy into oblivion. He suddenly jumped off it, grabbed it by the neck, and hurled it against the wall. An enraged bellow followed, then he stood there taking in huge gulps of air, clenching and unclenching his fists.

What the hell? She cautiously stepped inside, making sure to keep some distance from the enraged stranger before her.

"Mac?" she said softly.

His head snapped around and he stared at her—no, he stared *through* her. Her stomach knotted painfully at the vacant look. This wasn't training. This was something else entirely.

He's been to hell and back.

She'd told Lance she didn't care how horrific Mac's story was, believing there was no excuse for his behavior. But now… There was no sign of the Mac she'd spent time with, laughed with. This man…this man was caught in some mental hell. She swallowed, her heart breaking for him when just moments before she'd wanted to strangle him with her bare hands.

"Mac," she repeated, a little more forcibly.

A shudder quaked his body as the tension expelled from him in a quick rush. Blinking, he glanced around, his eyes landing on the dummy across the room. He held out his hands, staring at them. Raw, bloody scrapes covered both knuckles. Gayle pressed a hand to her mouth. How long had he been beating that thing?

His gaze snapped to hers and every muscle stiffened as the haggard lines on his face drew into a deep scowl. "Get out."

"I've already seen it, Mac. I can't unsee it even if you send me away."

A muscle jumped in his clenched jaw and he jerked his chin up.

"How often does this happen?" she asked.

"Never."

"Then what triggered this?"

"I don't want to fucking talk about it."

"Tough shit." She nodded at his hands. "You need to clean those up. Come on. I'll make some coffee while you do."

She made it to the door before she heard him move behind her with a string of angry mumbles. At least it was just resentment bringing on this anger. She knew what the resentment stemmed from—having someone catch him at the mercy of his emotions. Rick had caught her one time. Though she hadn't been raged out like Mac had just been. She'd been in sobbing hysterics. There had been some throwing, though. And fury at who she'd lost.

As soon as they walked into the kitchen, Skylar bounded up to them with the pale pink pig clutched to her chest. "Bacon was fine."

Gayle forced a broad smile for the child. "I told you he would be." She glanced at Mac. A sheen of sweat coated the gray pallor of his skin. The adrenaline was fading now. "Hey, Skylar, why don't you go up to your room to play a bit? I think we'll stay over here until your daddy gets home."

"Can I play Skylanders?"

"You betcha."

"Awesome. Daddy never lets me play." She raced from the room.

Worry shafted through Gayle as Mac collapsed into a chair at the kitchen table, resting his elbows on the wood and burying his face in his hands. She hurried into the bathroom and grabbed the first aid kit from the cabinet. As she stopped at the table, she slid it in front of him. He lifted his bowed head and glared at the box.

"All right, handsome." She banded her arms around herself, still shaken from what she'd witnessed. "Time for you to open up."

His jaw clenched. "I *said* I don't want to talk about it."

"And I said tough shit. Consider it penance for being such a buttmunch."

He remained stubbornly silent. Damn it all to hell.

"Listen. I've known there was something going on with you, but I didn't pry because I don't like anyone prying in my business. But when I find a man beating the crap out of something in a mindless rage, I need to know what the hell triggered it and why."

"I thought you said you were going to make coffee." There was still an angry bite to his words. *Hmm.* So anger was his coping mechanism. Suddenly, a whole lot of her encounters with him made a whole lot more sense. What had she done before to set it off? Clearly, there had been so much more underlying that exchange.

She held her ground and hiked an eyebrow. "I'll make the coffee when you start talking."

He slowly turned his head and glared at her with all the scary fighter he had in him. Before, it had made her hesitate. Not now. It was a mask. A façade to keep from dealing with deeper issues. She was sure of it.

She kept hers stubborn and pointed. A standoff. A battle of wills. She would win this one. The man desperately needed to talk.

For a full minute, they both refused to give. Finally she

said, "I always get what I want, handsome. I can do this—All. Day. Long."

"Fine. You want to know my whole life story, here you fucking go. Did you know I grew up in this flat, hellish land?"

Ignoring the anger behind his words, she ambled over to the coffeepot and started the process to fulfill her end of the deal. "No. I didn't. Was it here in Cheney?"

"No. Emerald fucking Springs. You would know about that place, wouldn't you?"

She froze while putting the lid back on the coffee grounds and briefly closed her eyes. *Oh, God, no.* "When did you move to Atlanta?"

"When do you think?"

Pressing her fingers to her mouth, she stared down at the canister. The timing was there. She pulled her hand away from her mouth, flicked the machine on, inhaled deeply to compose herself, and turned to face him. "You were in the EF-5 tornado, weren't you?"

He stared straight at her. He didn't need to confirm it. Behind the hostility, the answer was etched clearly on his face. Tortured. Traumatized. God, the whole town had been destroyed. People killed…

"I wasn't where I was supposed to fucking be," he said, anger vibrating his voice.

She swallowed and quietly pulled out mugs. What did he mean by that?

"I was in a restaurant that wasn't mine, helping some friends. Not knowing that decision would be the worst fucking decision I'd ever make." He shook his head. "The tornado struck and while I was trapped under a goddamn refrigerator worried about *myself*, my home was being destroyed."

"Tell me."

"The restaurant was full for early dinner. Full. We scrambled, trying to get everyone tucked in somewhere. I was the last one, but there was no more room. So I crawled under the sink, wrapped my arms around the pipes, and started praying. The roar. I'll never forget the roar…the screams, the glass shattering. The fierceness of the wind as it literally destroyed everything around me. I got pinned, until Lance found me and pulled me free." His face contorted in pain before he wiped it away with a murderous scowl. "It was my day *off*. I should have been *home*." He paused for a heartbeat. "Because I wasn't, my wife was killed and I was left to find her."

His wife. Mac had lost the woman he loved. Stunned, Gayle sank into the chair across from him, unable to form words.

Mac shook his head, and she knew he was seeing the agony of the moment all over again. God, how she wished she could ease his pain. But how could she, when her own still felt just as fresh?

"She was ten weeks pregnant." He stared straight ahead, but the anger was gone from his voice. Instead it was filled with detachment. Monotone. She wasn't sure which was worse.

God, a wife *and* a child. *Fuck*. That was worse. A lot worse.

Gayle took a shuddered breath as a tear slipped down her cheek. She quickly dashed it away. "Jesus. I'm so sorry, Mac." And she was. More than he could know.

Needing to touch him, comfort him in some way, she cautiously took his hand in hers, grateful when he didn't yank away.

"I left Kansas a month later and haven't looked back once. Not until Lance called. How the hell do you say no to a man who saved your life?" Mac stared off across the room. "He didn't do me any favors by pulling me out that day."

She understood that train of thought, though she was

long past her own death wish. But in the beginning there had been many, many months when she'd struggled with her grief, and she'd also wondered if she would be better off dead. Not knowing how to move forward, with a future so uncertain.

He took a deep breath, tugged his hand from hers, and scrubbed his face. A moment of hurt pinged her chest, but she let it go. People wanted comfort in their own way. Mac didn't seem to want any. The fact he let her hold his hand, even briefly, was a small miracle.

"The first crash of thunder today brought every damn memory raging back. It's being back in the fucking place. It's just one miserable reminder after another of the worst day of my life." He suddenly glared at her, and there was an accusation in his eyes she didn't understand. "And you *go after* those things. How can you deliberately get close to a tornado? Be so damn excited about the possibility of one forming? Don't you understand the pure devastation those things bring to people's lives?"

Ah. So that was his issue with her.

Not her unconventional lifestyle but that she chased tornadoes. Okay, not the first time her job had gotten a bad reaction…though never quite to this degree before.

But how would he react when he found out *why* she did what she did?

"Oh, I understand." She gave a sad smile. "All too well."

He frowned, his anger and accusation slowly giving way to uncertainty. "What?"

"Seven years ago, I lost my parents, my sister, and the man I'd been dating since my senior year in high school to an EF-5 tornado."

She didn't bother with the details. Now wasn't the time. This was about him. She just wanted him to know she truly did understand.

Mac sat up, staring at her. "Lost them…to a *tornado*?"

"I was finishing up my master's in atmospheric science at the University of Alabama in Huntsville when it happened. Weather has always fascinated me, but I had never chased until the year after they died." She sighed, and at his silent query, she explained, "I needed to know…how tornadoes worked. Why they happened. I wanted to further tornado research so others didn't have to die the same way as the people I loved. I've dedicated the last six seasons to doing that. Facing them head-on helped me a lot in dealing with what had happened. Maybe you should try it."

He jerked back. "Fuck, no. I have no desire ever to experience one of those bastards again. No way would I deliberately seek one out."

Lifting her palms, she said, "Just a suggestion. I get it. But if you change your mind, the invitation is there."

"I won't be taking you up on it. What you do is fucking crazy."

He's seen even more than you have. The reminder calmed her and kept her from responding to the insult. "What I do has helped a lot of people, Mac. You may not understand it, but don't belittle the research I've invested the last six years of my life in, simply because of your past."

He stared at her for a moment, then swallowed and gave a jerky nod. "Fair enough."

Her feelings still smarted from his attack earlier that afternoon, but knowing the events that drove him had pretty much wiped away her anger.

"So, can we call a truce?" she ventured.

A long pause followed, then he said, "This…this thing between us…it's not happening. It can't. Not like the other night."

The renewed hurt that pierced her chest surprised her. "Because I'm a risk taker?"

He exhaled. "I can't start caring about you, Gayle. I can't go through that horror again. And you've got to admit, with your job, the chances are pretty good."

Caring about her? She frowned. She really hadn't considered that night as anything more than she'd enjoyed with other men. She simply liked sex. But the implication of Mac's words tweaked her chest in an odd way. The understanding smile she offered him felt fake, strained. "Fair enough," she parroted his words. "But can we be friends?"

"We can try."

Try. At least the warning was there this time, right? She wouldn't be blindsided. She'd make sure not to get too attached. Make that, at all. With the emotions his struggles had stirred in her, she was at risk of starting to care about *him*. She had such a damn soft heart, wanting nothing more than to support and comfort when something bad was going on with the people she called friends.

But men tended to trample all over women like her. Thankfully she had learned her lesson, had learned to keep her distance and reserve her compassion for those who truly appreciated it.

He'd warned her, and she planned to heed the warning. The man may have gone through hell, but if he couldn't get past her job to see who she really was beneath all that, then they had no possibility of any kind of real friendship.

Oh, yeah. She would tread very carefully around Mac Hannon.

CHAPTER SEVEN

Standing with his feet spread in front of the screen door in the kitchen three days later, Mac scowled as he watched Gayle and a dark-haired guy stuff plastic containers in the back of a souped-up Nissan Xterra. The black SUV was wrapped in the WKKS News weather team logo with a radar image in the background. The bumper on the front was not a stock bumper, but the kind of sturdy grill that protected the headlights, usually seen on vehicles for off-roading. An assortment of antennas protruded from the roof along with a whole bunch of odd-looking equipment.

Her tornado hunting vehicle. The guy had backed it out of the barn behind her house about thirty minutes ago.

A storm system must be brewing somewhere. Fucking fantastic.

Shaking his head, Mac turned away, closed the inside door, and strode through the kitchen to collapse on the living room couch. He threw his arm over his eyes, blocking out the late evening sun. In the days that had passed since Gayle had found him in the barn, they hadn't really had much interaction with each other. Friends was definitely not the path they were on. It was more like they tolerated each other's presence. For him, he didn't care for the raw and exposed consciousness he had when he was around her. She had seen him lose control. Every time he saw her, he was reminded of that.

"Hey, man," Lance asked, shaking Mac's foot. "You awake?"

"Yep," he responded without removing his arm.

"I just got a lead on a repo I've been hunting for a few weeks. I'll probably be gone most of the night."

"K." Lance's presence loomed over Mac and he heaved a sigh. "What?"

"You want to come with? I invited you down here, and I just keep leaving you by yourself."

"Nope. And you invited me here to help you *train*, which we did this morning and for the past three days. I'm fulfilling my end of things. I don't need company. Go earn your money, Lance."

"But after—"

"*Go.*"

Lance hovered for a while longer, but eventually his footsteps faded down the hall. Seconds later, the front door closed. His friend had been acting like a fucking helicopter mom since Mac had told him about the other night. This was exactly why he never confided his personal shit to people. They got all weird afterward.

Even the damn training sessions with Lance had been tense, as though his friend thought Mac was fragile or something and wasn't putting all his strength into it. How was the jackass going to prepare for a fucking fight if he didn't go at training 100 percent? It took Mac laying one on him hard for Lance to finally snap out of his kid-glove approach.

Why didn't people understand Mac didn't need anyone? He was totally fine being alone.

He shifted to his side and stared at the coffee table. Tires crunched on gravel as the SUV drove around the house toward the front. So they were off on their exciting, action-packed tornado adventure. Worry for Gayle built in his chest. No. He didn't care...*he didn't.*

What he cared about was getting some sleep, which had eluded him since the barn. He closed his eyes again.

A low rumble of thunder sounded in the distance, and his eyes snapped open. His entire body stiffened. The windows were now dark instead of bright from the afternoon sun. Well, at least he had successfully escaped into the oblivion of sleep for a while. The lack of nightmares was just a testament to how exhausted he was.

Slinging his legs over the side of the couch, he sat up blinking. What had woken him up, anyway? A brilliant blue flash lit the room. His breath seized in his lungs. Another streak of lightning brightened the darkened area.

Trapped. Heavy. Couldn't breathe. Complete darkness except for the strobe of lightning. Screams. So many goddamn screams.

Fuck! He flicked on the lamp on the end table so the bursts of light weren't as palpable. He worked his neck from side to side, trying to rid his body of its increasing tension. Just a storm. That was all. He would not let his mind fuck with him.

A deafening crack rattled the walls.

The scrape of the car as the bumper slipped closer to his head. Desperation to free himself. Lance suddenly there.

Cold sweat beaded on the clammy skin of his upper lip. Trembles quaked his hands as the airway in his throat seemed to shrink. He sucked in a whistling inhale and jerked to his feet.

Don't think. Don't think. Do something. Anything.

The TV.

Lightning flashed twice as a clap of thunder immediately followed.

His destroyed home. Nothing left. Bellowing her name. Frantic. Terrified.

Roaring his fury, Mac grabbed a throw pillow and hurled it into the hall. Cursing, he strode to the large flat screen, his strides stiff, awkward. Another bright strobe made him stumble away from the windows.

A pile of debris. A bloodied hand. The white gold wedding band and encrusted engagement ring sparkling in the sunlight.

He knotted his hands in his hair, squeezing his eyelids closed. No. *No! Don't remember.*

The bushes outside began to scrape against the glass as the winds picked up. He snapped his head up, and his breath strangled as he stared at the branches flattened against the windowpanes by the howling wind.

The slim fingers remaining motionless. Not even a twitch. He paralyzed with fear. The realization dawning. The refusal to believe.

White dots danced before his eyes. He sucked oxygen into his lungs, then hurried to turn on the television.

The growing violence of the weather outside beckoned him into oblivion—into the past—and, *goddamn it*, one trip back into hell this week had been enough.

He forced himself into the kitchen, yanked open the fridge, and grabbed a beer. Another violent crack shook everything around him.

Flinging rubble off her. Lifeless blue eyes. Fence post jutting from her chest.

He jerked and dropped the bottle on the floor. Glass and

beer exploded all over the hardwood floor. Motherfucker! He fucking hated this.

He grabbed a kitchen towel and dropped it on the spilled beer, then snatched a new bottle from the fridge, twisted off the top, and took a long guzzle as he watched white lightning splinter across the sky.

Dead. His wife. His child. Dead.

His throat closed, the brew getting stuck on its way down. Choking, he cupped his mouth as the beer spewed out and over his fingers. Some wet his shirt, the rest plopped onto the floor.

Fury took over and he launched the bottle against the wall. The loud crash of the glass shattering, the beer gushing, gave him a momentary sense of relief. He heaved deep inhales, fists clenched tight at his sides.

The heavens opened up and torrential rain smacked against the windows, rattling the panes. The wind howled. The limbs beat the glass.

He failed. Failed to protect her. Failed to protect his child. He failed them both.

Just as he lifted his arm to hurl another bottle, a loud pounding had him shuddering out of the memories. The noise came again, and his gaze snapped to the door. He flung it open to find Gayle standing on the top step. Drenched hair clung to her face and droplets of water dripped off the tip of her nose and chin. A sage-green tank top molded wetly to her skin, while her khaki shorts dripped water down her legs to her muddy bare feet. A shiver racked through her, knocking him out of his stunned stupor.

"Gayle!" He moved out of the way to let her by. "What the hell are you doing running around in a storm like this?"

Another shiver went through her as she stepped inside

and held up a cup, also dripping water. But she smiled. "I was making cookies and realized I was out of sugar."

What the fuck? He glanced at the monsoon outside. "And it couldn't wait? What the hell are you doing here anyway? I thought you left."

"No, not yet. As for the sugar, thought I'd be able to make it here and back before the sky opened. Guess I was wrong." She sent him another smile. "So. Sugar?"

He stared at her and realization dawned. "I don't need babysitting, Gayle."

"What are you talking about? *I* need sugar."

He lifted an incredulous brow at her, which she returned in spades, then shook the cup at him. "Sugar, Mac. *Please.*"

He'd give her mad props, she was damn convincing, but no matter how much she wanted to deny it, he didn't believe her trek through a downpour and crazy wind was because she wanted to bake any damn cookies. He took the cup from her and went to the cabinet. After he dried it out and filled it with sugar, he turned back to find her with her arms wrapped around her body, shivering.

He put the cup on the counter. "You're going to be stuck here for a while. Let me get you something dry to put on."

The fact she didn't argue was just more proof she'd come over here for him. What was she worried about? He'd tear up Lance's house? His eyes cut over to the pool of beer and shards of glass on the floor. Meh. Maybe she had a reason to be concerned.

After he tugged a T-shirt off a hanger, he snatched a pair of jogging shorts out of the drawer. The shorts probably wouldn't fit her, but he took them anyway and handed them to her. Mumbling thanks, she disappeared into the downstairs bathroom. The storm was still raging outside, but just having her here seemed to calm the horrific images that had tortured him.

When she returned, a weird sensation crackled under his ribs. His black Zac Brown Band concert T-shirt was huge on her. Pretty much swallowed her whole. The hem reached right above her knees, while the sleeves were below her elbows.

She was the most gorgeous sight he'd laid eyes on in a long time.

She held his shorts in her hands. "Um. Yeah. These came to my shins. And as much as I'd like to look like Kid 'n Play, it's not really the time of year for costumes."

Taking them back, he chuckled. It felt good. Real good. The last time— *Wow, holy shit*. The last time he'd laughed was the night they'd slept together. "Somehow, I didn't think they'd fit."

A crash of thunder shook the house and he went rigid.

"Why don't we find something to occupy ourselves?" Gayle suggested.

"How long is this storm supposed to last?"

She studied him for a moment, then sighed. "There's a long line of them coming in. Could be hours."

"Is there a chance—Is that why you were packing your SUV earlier?"

"I don't chase at night, Mac. It's dangerous. Rick and I are watching developments, preparing just in case. But this system… One can never be certain, but conditions are not really favorable for tornado formation. Doesn't mean we won't see a few crazy intense storms come through, though."

"Great."

She moved around him into the kitchen, then stopped abruptly. "Wow. Somebody had a party in here." She glanced at him over her shoulder, a look of mock disappointment twisting her face. "I'm hurt I wasn't invited."

Even though she was making light of it, embarrassment burned his skin. He'd lost control. Again.

She seemed to sense his discomfort because she turned to face him. "Mac!" she said in a commanding tone that compelled his head up instantly. The intense way she regarded him took him aback.

"It's *okay* to be angry. Do *not* feel bad about it." She held his gaze for a moment, then returned to the broken glass and beer. "I'm going to get this cleaned up."

"I'll get it."

Without comment, she handed him the broom, and he got to sweeping.

She left the room for a few moments and returned with an armful of towels. "I'll put these in the wash after we wipe all the glorious beer you wasted off the wall and floor."

Mac felt the first tugs of a smile. Ten minutes later, she walked out of the laundry room next to the kitchen, folded her arms, and said, "Now what do we do?"

Tapping a finger to her lips, she surveyed the room. "You know what?" she muttered, then squatted and opened a cabinet door. "Aha! Yeah."

She held up a bottle of vodka. "What do you say, handsome? Want to get smashed?"

His eyebrows flew to his scalp. "Seriously?"

"Hell, why not?"

When was the last time he'd gotten a really good drunk on? It *had* been a damn hell of a week. "I believe in the fridge Lance has lemonade he made for Skylar."

Her eyes rounded. "Was it homemade?"

"I…think so."

She started glancing around like a madwoman. What was

she looking for?

"Hell, yes!" she exclaimed as she put the Vodka bottle down and came back with a lemon in each hand. "Ever had a lemon drop?"

Shots? She wanted to do shots? "Years ago. Like, culinary school years ago."

"Ever played Never Have I Ever?"

A drinking game? "Again, years ago."

"Wanna?" A playful twinkle lit up her eyes that he couldn't resist.

"Shit," he muttered with a defeated laugh. He was going to fucking regret this.

"Awesome!"

She went to work gathering everything, and within a few minutes she had two shot glasses, a plate of lemon wedges coated in sugar, and the bottle of vodka sitting out on the counter. She'd also put her iPhone on the deck, and fun, upbeat dance music drowned out the noises from outside.

She poured the glasses full of the liquor, and asked, "Do you remember the rules?"

"Refresh my memory."

"I say something I've never done, and if *you've* never done it you don't have to drink, but I do. If you *have*…bottoms up."

"Ladies first."

She leaned forward, a mischievous look coming to her face. "Never have I ever fought in a cage."

A shocked laugh burst out of him. He shook his head and reached for the shot, eying her over the rim. "You play dirty."

She leaned back, smiling with pleasure. "Thank you."

He tossed the drink back, then bit into a lemon wedge. "Never have I ever gone to a traditional university."

Giving a nod of reluctant approval, she took her shot.

"Now that we have the gimmes out of the way, let's make this interesting." She leaned forward again. Resting her elbows on the counter, she laced her fingers together and studied him. "*Hmm*. Never have I ever…gone streaking."

The random confession immediately brought a memory of him doing just that in his early twenties, drunk out of his mind. Ally had been horrified, but it was something they'd laughed over for years. A smile came to his lips now. The liquor burned on its way down.

"Never have I ever bungee jumped," he countered.

Her nose scrunched as she lifted the tiny glass to her lip. Wow. The woman had bungee jumped. He shouldn't be surprised. She raced tornadoes. They tossed a couple more never-have-I-evers at each other, where Gayle had to take both shots. Because, no, he had never gone to a bridal show, but she *had* entered a wet T-shirt contest. Crazy woman.

Eyes slightly glazed, she studied him silently for a long moment, then inhaled deeply. "Never have I ever gone on vacation somewhere tropical."

His honeymoon. Two full weeks on the sandy beaches of Aruba. At the memory, warmth filled his chest. As he focused on Gayle, he almost laughed. She was swaying slightly in her seat. He tossed back the shot.

"Never have I ever been interested in weather." Poor woman was two shots up on him.

She slammed the little glass down, and slurred slightly, "Never have I ever had sex in a strange location."

"Really? Not once?" Well, that was just…sad. He and Ally had gone through a phase where the whole idea of doing it somewhere where they could get caught was exciting. Man, he hadn't thought about this stuff in a long time. He'd forgotten…

Hell.

He snorted softly and lifted his gaze to Gayle, realization dawning once again.

She gave him a lopsided smile. "You're onto my game, aren't you, handsome?"

Awe filled him. She'd made him think of the good—remember the good. "You really do play dirty."

She gave him a smug look, then her mood switched to a very unlike-Gayle seriousness. "The past isn't all bad, Mac. You can't repress the good memories and focus only on the bad. When is the last time you thought about your wife with a good memory?"

The question stunned him silent for a moment. "How do you—"

"I've lost people I love, too, remember?" she interrupted.

Yes, she had. "A very long time. How did you know what to say to trigger the memories?"

She shrugged. "The streaking, I gambled on. You just seem like you would've been the type. I was wrong about the bridal show. Thought since you'd been married, you'd been dragged to one. The other two I just kept the subject broad enough so almost anything could fall under it."

"We eloped, ran off to Vegas. Got married by Elvis." Another smile came to his face. Damn. It felt awesome to think about her without fighting. To actually smile as a good memory came to the surface instead of allowing the bad to dominate his mind. He returned his attention to Gayle. "The sex one. Were you being serious about that?"

"Oh, definitely." His jaw dropped, but she swayed forward, an impish smile curving her lips. "It just depends on your definition of 'strange location.'" She winked. Then she jumped off the stool. "I love this song!"

The song was Bruno Mars' *Runaway Baby*. Mac watched

her dance around like a Muppet. The warmth he'd felt revisiting memories of his wife filled him again while watching Gayle. She really was amazing. Warm. Caring. Forgiving. Why hadn't some man snatched her up? Were they all idiots in this state?

In the field she was in, there had to be a lot of guys who were thrill-seekers like her, who wouldn't hesitate to jump in an SUV and race straight into a hell that included flying houses and raining farm equipment, as though it was a bright sunny day.

Why did it bother him thinking of Gayle being with someone like that?

He had no future with her. He would never live in Kansas again. She would never leave. And the idea of being involved with a woman who willingly sought out the thing that had destroyed his life—it was incomprehensible. He would never open himself up to allowing a tornado to destroy him a second time.

No, making sure to keep Gayle firmly in the friend zone was the only way it could ever be between them.

Sudden brightness behind Gayle's eyelids made her stir. Something tightened around her waist, bringing her closer to a hard wall. Blinking open her eyes, she winced against the dull ache in her temples and the cotton of her mouth. Damn vodka. She'd do it again in a heartbeat, though, if it brought back the softness that had relaxed Mac's typically stern face. Giving him that had meant a lot to her. He'd spent so long dwelling on the bad. He needed to remember the good.

Lifting her head, she studied the broad chest she was using

as a pillow. Lord, when had she fallen asleep? She was such a damn lightweight, and doing that many shots back-to-back had hit her like a ton of bricks. She remembered dancing, the liquor scolding her for it, and running to the bathroom before she lost it right there in the kitchen.

She closed her eyes. Well, at least Mac had been distracted.

As she started to sit up, a squeeze on her hand stopped her. Her gaze shot to where it lay on his chest with his hand covering hers. She surveyed their positions. He was sitting up, with his head leaned back against the cushion, while she was nestled under his arm, his palm resting on the swell of her hip. How was she supposed to get up without waking him?

Slowly she slid her hand out from under his. Swinging her legs over the side of the couch, she eased to the edge and watched him. The urge to caress the stubbled cheeks was almost overwhelming, but she kept her hands to herself.

She'd almost not come to the house, had almost turned back, uncertain for the first time about what she should or shouldn't do when it came to him. The skies opening up had pushed her forward. When he answered the door, his face had been alarmingly pale, his eyes haunted.

If he'd been here alone...

She shook herself. She didn't even want to think about how this house would've ended up.

A crash of thunder shook the house. Even in his sleep, Mac's body tensed and he mumbled, "No."

Gayle froze. Should she wake him?

Lightning brightened the room again, followed by another *boom* of thunder. A low moan came from him and he started to fidget, as if trying to escape an unseen menace.

"Mac," she whispered, touching his face to disrupt the dream.

"No," he moaned softly.

Stomach knotting at the sorrow in his voice, she took his face between her palms and whispered his name again.

"*Ally*." A broken plea so full of distress, tears immediately sprang to her eyes.

Ally. That had to be his wife's name. Obviously, the man was more traumatized by how she'd died than he let on.

Suddenly, he jerked, and his eyes popped open. While he took a moment to register his surroundings, she scooted away and fought to get herself under control, close to crying. He'd lost so much. Been through so much. Even more than she had. Yeah, she'd had to learn to live life without her family and Sam. Though she and Sam had been planning to get married after she finished her MA, she'd been living in Alabama while he stayed in Kansas. The long-distance relationship had never been an issue for them. As it was, she hadn't gone to bed with Sam every night. Hadn't seen him every day. The distance hadn't lessened the excruciating pain caused by the silence of her phone after his death. The ache to receive just one more "Good morning, sunshine" text from him had been poignant.

And then there was her family and the emotional black hole left behind in the house she had grown up in. She'd only returned to her family home a few times a year since going off to college, but even so, the house had never been the same again, after.

But to have a person who was an intimate part of your daily life ripped from you—Gayle swallowed. It was hard to imagine. And to add to the agony, Mac had his own nightmarish experience to relive over and over again. She had been saved from all that.

Hell, she'd never experienced a tornado in the way Mac had. Not even close.

When he finally focused on her, she was sitting on the end of the couch farthest from him. She forced a playful smile on her lips, "Hey there, handsome."

She used the nickname intentionally. Anything to make him believe she hadn't picked up on his nightmare. Those were for him alone. She wasn't sure how often he had them, but having that kind of nightmare was hard enough to deal with, without knowing someone else had witnessed the ordeal.

She should know.

Shaking his head, he pushed up. "Don't think I've woken up to that before."

"Really? Never? A sinfully sexy man waking from his slumber is so...*rawr*." She clawed her fingers toward him, putting as much playfulness as she could into the sound and gesture, even though she didn't feel frisky at all. She was relieved when a small smile twitched at the corners of his mouth, and the sadness faded from his gaze.

Silence fell between them, and she sent up a silent *thank-you* when her cell phone rang. Considering it was two in the morning, it could only be one person.

Even though taking this call in front of Mac was probably a bad idea, she couldn't ignore it.

"Time to roll?" she asked as soon as she had the phone pressed to her ear.

"Yeah, it is. It's big, Gayle. We're looking at our first potential mass outbreak over the next few days."

All the ingredients needed for the formation of supercells had been brewing for a while, now. They'd known it would be any minute, which was why they'd gone ahead and loaded the SUV that afternoon.

"All right. We need to be on the road by seven am."

"10-4, boss lady."

As she hung up, she had a hard time looking at Mac. She wasn't ashamed of what she did. Quite the opposite. She took pride in helping people, and in the information she fed to the National Weather Service. But after seeing how affected he was by the storms, it was difficult to meet his eyes.

"Do you need to leave?" he asked just as another clap of thunder boomed above them.

She made herself face him. "No. I don't have to be back at my place until right before seven."

Nodding, his gaze slipped off to stare at the wall as his nose scrunched. At length, he said, "I saw you packing earlier and heard a vehicle drive away. I'd thought you were already gone."

"Just preparing. We knew this was coming. That was probably Rick you heard leave."

Mac never took his eyes off the wall, odd expressions contorting his face. Deep-in-debate-with-himself expressions. What was going on in that mind of his? She remained silent. After a minute, she started gnawing on her bottom lip, after two, she finally asked, "What are you thinking?"

He slowly turned and regarded her for the span of a heartbeat. "I'd like to come, too."

She stiffened. "Say that again?"

"You did say I could join you on a chase. Correct?"

"I did," she said cautiously.

"And we both know you didn't come over here for sugar, Gayle. If you hadn't come over here, I'm not sure what this night would've done to me. I'd already started to go to some bad places before you showed up. But you knew just how to distract me over the last few hours. Now I think maybe you're right and I need to face this head-on…so I can move forward."

Crap. Yeah, she had said that. But she'd been thinking more

the baby-steps approach. A couple of smaller chases with rope tornadoes out in open fields. Hell, she'd actually been hoping to take him on a few of the many, many busts they went on. Let him see for himself that every time she headed out, she didn't lasso a tornado and ride cowboy style on its destructive back. Most of the time, they didn't even see a drop of rain, let alone an event. The damn driving was more of a danger — some of the amateurs out chasing were downright reckless on the road.

The system today, however, had the potential to spawn powerful wedge tornadoes, which meant they were going to see more real action. While predicting the precise location where a twister might touch down wasn't exact, the intense storms they'd encounter would be much worse than the ones he'd experienced so far this week. He hadn't had a great reaction to those. Something bigger might push him right over the edge.

"Mac." She inhaled, then blew it out between her lips. "I don't think this chase is right for you."

"Why not?"

How did she say this without it sounding like she was calling him a coward? She wasn't. Not in the least. The anger was worrisome, though. Mac being trapped inside the small confines of an SUV with multiple storms surrounding him was the equivalent of tiptoeing through a minefield.

"This is a giant trough. We'll be following it through a few states. We're going to be gone for days."

"Lance won't mind. In fact, I'm pretty certain he would encourage it. I can check with him, though, if you want me to."

Ugh. Okay. Different approach. "We spend a lot of time in the SUV. And with a huge system like this, we're seriously looking at fifteen, maybe eighteen hour days. Wouldn't you rather go on one closer to home, so you're not bored out of your mind?"

"I'll take a book. I wanted to get in some reading while I was here, anyway."

All right. Upfront and honest it was. "Mac. This is a *dangerous* system. A high-risk front, with the potential to form high-precipitation supercells."

"I don't know what any of that means."

"Supercells are what make the tornadoes. Which means that all that"—she swept her hand to the window and the storm still raging outside—"is nothing compared to what could possibly happen with the huge storms the front could breed. I... I don't think you're ready for that."

Grimacing, she waited for him to get angry, but he calmly studied her as if he was really considering her words, and, boy, she hoped he was.

"I understand." He nodded, but her relief was short-lived. "I'd still like to go."

She suppressed a groan and slapped her hands on her thighs. She'd tried. "Okay. You're a grown man. You can make decisions for yourself. But there is one rule, Mac."

"What's that?"

"I'm the boss. You do what I tell you to do. And if you throw one piece of my equipment, I don't care how big and strong you are, I'm going to throw you. Got it?"

"Got it."

"Oh. And pack light."

CHAPTER EIGHT

Mac sat in the backseat of the SUV, watching a small Oklahoma town speed by as they raced to the western corner of the state.

The skies were clear with nary a cloud.

Hard to believe they were only an hour away from where a system was supposed to wreak havoc on the land.

Maybe this had been a bad idea.

A really bad idea.

The longer they drove, the more his gut started to clench with doubt. Earlier this morning, after Gayle had hung up the phone, it'd seemed like the logical choice. His nightmare had been disturbingly vivid as he'd tossed aside the rubble and found Ally's lifeless body. For the hundredth time in four years.

When Gayle had received a call from Rick at that exact moment, Mac took it as a sign from the universe. Lance had all but shoved him out the door, telling Mac not to worry about him, just go and heal. So the decision had been set in stone.

But now he wasn't so sure this was the right method to go

about it. What if facing this shit fucked him up worse than he already was?

Shaking his head, he blocked out the mental negativity. He'd made the decision, and he would stick with it.

He turned his attention away from the road to the front seat. Rick, Gayle's chasing partner, was driving. When she introduced them before they left, Mac had noticed the guy was around her age and definitely not bad-looking from a dude's standpoint. A worn red ball cap covered his dark hair, and he kept it pulled low over his eyes. He wasn't necessarily muscular, but he also wasn't lanky like a stereotypical lab rat either, more along the lines of an average, burly guy who did blue-collar work. Women tended to dig that.

More than once Mac caught himself watching Gayle and Rick's interaction to see if there was, or ever had been, anything more between them than storm chasing. So far, the only thing he'd picked up on was a friendship with the occasional sarcastic, but good-natured, insult.

Gayle sat on the passenger side; her hair was gathered to the side to hang over one shoulder, as she jotted something down on a notepad. All kinds of equipment, ranging from cameras to GPSs to tablets, surrounded her. He felt like he was in some kind of fucking aircraft. A laptop mounted on the center console between the seats pivoted in her direction for easy access. She spent a lot of time on the thing, looking at maps and radars. She'd explained that one of the gizmos on the roof was a satellite internet connection, so she was always up-to-date with the latest weather information. There were a shitload of transmitters and radios, too. Why she needed so many, he had no clue. But every damn one of them was on, emitting a constant low hum of static in the car, a startling screeching voice shattering the silence on occasion—though *he* was the only one who jumped. Big fearless cage fighter, his ass. Fuck.

He hadn't contributed to the conversation much over the last four hours. How could he? Gayle kept tossing around a bunch of words he didn't understand. Things like dry lines, outflows, and wind shear were complete Greek to him.

As they got closer to their destination, they'd started passing more weather nuts on Interstate 35. One right after another. How could he tell? Every damn one of them blazed their intentions on the side of their vehicle with some clever tornado chasing slogan.

"Looks like we're in for a chaser convergence," Rick said with a tight laugh.

Gayle scowled as she glanced up from the laptop to peer out the windshield. "Damn, that just means more yahoos to worry about."

Intrigued by her reaction, but again having no clue what language they were speaking, Mac leaned forward. "What are you two talking about?"

"Chaser convergence. Systems like this bring in weather chasers from all over the country. That's why we're seeing so many of them." She pointed to the passing cars. "The towns are going to be packed with yahoos."

"What's that?"

She sent a mocking smile at him. "A yahoo is what you think I am, handsome. A thrill-seeker. What they really are is amateurs without proper equipment. They clog up the roads something awful, don't know the etiquette of chasing, and put themselves and others in danger. I really wish they'd just stay home." She returned her attention back to the laptop with a scowl.

Mac asked, "And what you do *isn't* dangerous? Why is one

danger okay and not the other?"

She slowly turned her head toward him. Irritation was written all over her face and took him slightly aback. Other than when he'd been a complete dick to her, Gayle was always carefree. Guess that didn't apply to questions about her job. Then again, she'd been tense all morning. Not really herself. Was this how she got while out hunting these monsters? He wasn't sure how he felt about this new side of her.

"I'm not claiming I'm safe at all times. It *is* Mother Nature. Everyone in this car can attest that her fury is unpredictable."

Rick muttered a, "Hell yeah, we can," which earned him a nod from Gayle.

"However," she continued. "I take *every* precaution to stay safe. I don't take stupid risks just to get a better view. I will back off, even if it means I miss the storm." Her speech was gaining speed and power as it went, just like one of her storms. "Yahoos don't. Most of them have watched way too many documentaries on the Discovery Channel, think chasing looks *so* awesome, and have no regard for the actual danger. All they do is get in the way of those of us doing actual scientific research!" The last was said in a high-pitched burst of frustration.

Okay, then.

Thoroughly slapped down, Mac lifted his hands and sat back. "My mistake."

Gayle went back to tapping on the damned laptop and jotting stuff in a notebook.

A tense silence enveloped the cab. Another thirty minutes down the road, she looked up, took the pencil out of her mouth, and said, "Rick, take the next exit. This is a perfect location to stop and get something to eat before things pick up this afternoon."

She looked over her shoulder at Mac. He expected to still see some lingering annoyance, but she sent him a soft, *real* smile. "Ready to stretch your legs?"

"That'd be nice." She really hadn't been kidding about the driving. And he'd forgotten his damned book.

"There won't be any fine dining over the next few days, handsome. We're on a fast food and convenience store snacks diet."

At the exit, Rick veered off the interstate and they rolled into a town so small if Mac blinked he'd have missed it. Rick pulled into a truck stop and jumped out. "What's everyone want? I'll grab it."

"Just make it easy and get three burgers, three fries, and three sodas," Gayle said as she climbed out the passenger's seat. The other man trotted off.

Mac also got out and stretched. Muscles thanked him as he lifted his arms over his head.

Gayle went to stand by the bumper, head tilted up to the sky. Though he appreciated the nice view of her legs under her worn, ripped jeans, he had to admit he'd rather see her back in his clothes again. He sidled up next to her. The clouds were thickening, even he could tell that, but they were sporadic, not the dark, angry thunderheads he always associated with a brewing storm. How the hell could she tell a tornado might happen today but not on some other random day?

"What do you think?" he asked as she continued to gaze upward.

She was quiet for a long moment, then met his eyes. "Are you really ready for this?"

The uncharacteristic tension he'd noticed in her since this morning suddenly made sense. She wasn't concentrating on tracking the forecast. She probably hadn't even been irritated by his question earlier—okay, maybe some—but usually she was so unflappable he had a hard time seeing past the cheery mood she exuded to any underlying frustration.

Today she couldn't hide it. Because she was worried about *him*.

Damn. "You really didn't want me to come, did you?"

"Not on this one." She gave a soft laugh, but it seemed hollow. "You were pretty adamant, though." She sighed. "Mac, I have a job to do. You might not understand what I do, but I don't just go after these things for the adrenaline or some sick thrill. I'm gathering data, as are a lot of other research-oriented chasers, so we can *help* people. Things are going to get scary. Intense. In your eyes, I'm going to make some stupid decisions."

"I can handle myself, Gayle."

She studied him for a minute, her doubt shining back at him loud and clear. "Can you?"

Then it hit him. She truly regretted bringing him along. And man, that hit the ego pretty hard. But he had to respect her bluntness.

She continued, "I will pay for a rental car right now so you can go back to Cheney if you have any reservation whatsoever about going through with this. Believe me, I won't judge you, Mac."

He *had* been having doubts, but hearing her express worry over him raging out brought out his stubborn streak. "Listen, as much as I'd like to be a fearless Spartan warrior and charge straight into battle, I'm not. I'm also worried about what I'm going to see, how it's going to make me feel. But that's *my* deal. I know what I'm getting into. Your warnings have been heard. You do your job, and I'll take care of me. Okay?"

She caught her bottom lip between her teeth, drawing

his attention down. Swallowing, he averted his gaze off to the field across the road. The last thing he needed was the damn attraction to Gayle to come roaring back just as a fucking tornado roared up. One thing at a damn time, for fuck sake.

A resigned exhale came from her. "Okay. I won't say anything more, then."

A few minutes later, Rick joined them and handed each of them a white paper bag. After they got back in the truck and dug into their food, Gayle looked up the latest weather information.

Mac watched her go to multiple tabs on the laptop. Since he was here, he might as well learn a few things. "What exactly are you doing?"

Without looking up, she said, "Each one of these programs gives me the data needed to calculate which area has the highest potential for supercell formation."

"What kind of data?"

"Wind flow patterns and temperature, which can cause moisture, instability, lift, and wind shear. What I'm doing now is trying to pinpoint the location where the activity will start. The CAPE is higher about forty miles west."

"Cape?"

"Convective Available Potential Energy which is—" She glanced at him, chuckled, and waved her hand dismissively. "Never mind. That's getting too technical."

Most likely she added the last part because he was squinting at her with a what-the-fuck-is-coming-out-of-your-mouth stare. He had no clue there was so much science involved in this stuff.

"In weather-for-dummies terms, the higher the number, the more likely a storm will be severe." She traced an area on the screen. "This area here is very unstable, which is good for us. We also have agitated cumulus clouds developing on the satellite, which means storms are going to start firing along this line soon."

He studied the black and white image. The clouds looked like pulled cotton—not really very menacing.

"Rick, let's stick with the main routes, stay out of the convergence for now. I'm hoping most of them will be drawn farther south into the panhandle, which is also looking very promising. We'll end up bottlenecking soon enough. Let's avoid them for now."

The other man nodded, put the SUV into drive, and pulled back onto the road. As they drove through a very rural part of Oklahoma, Gayle kept a close eye on the data.

"Got a couple of cells finally forming on radar, Rick. Take the road coming up on your left. We need to veer south."

The excitement vibrating in Gayle's voice made Mac swallow. She leaned over and turned the volume up on NOAA weather radio.

"The National Weather Service has issued a severe thunderstorm watch for portions of western Oklahoma until 9:00 p.m. Those storms can produce winds over seventy-five miles per hour and large hail," she told him.

Mac glanced out the window. The clouds were definitely thickening and darkening in the distance. He tried to block out the constant updates from the weather radio and gibberish filtering in from other chasers on the CB until the word "warning" caught his attention.

"*Radar indicates a thunderstorm moving northeast at twenty miles per hour capable of producing heavy rain, damaging wind, and large hail. People in the warning area are advised to seek shelter.*"

Gayle glanced over her shoulder at him. "We're right on top of this sucker. You ready? Because things are about to get real."

No. No, he was not. He gave a jerky nod anyway.

Tension crept into his body and he spent the next few minutes fighting it back. Just when he thought he had it under control, Gayle let out a breath, and said, "Oh, God, it's beautiful. Look at it!"

Certain it was a tornado, he stared at the headrest in front of him and inhaled deeply, then he made himself look out the window. Air gusted from his lungs when a twisting mass was nowhere to be found. What was she talking about? Then he glanced into the distance and his mouth dropped open.

What. The. Fuck? In all his years in Kansas, he'd never seen anything like that. Maybe because he'd never really paid attention. Maybe because he'd never been out in the open when a storm was brewing. But there was *nothing* beautiful about the sci-fi monstrosity of a cloud they were approaching now.

"Pull over," she said, slapping Rick on the arm.

He parked behind a line of other vehicles. Gayle jumped out with her camera and stood on the side of road, taking pictures. The wind was blowing so hard her clothes pressed tight to her body. He made himself get out and go stand beside her. The strength of the wind stung his eyes, and he had to put his hand in front of his face to ward off the worst of it.

"What is that?" he yelled.

She lowered the camera. "That's what we call a mothership supercell."

Yeah, it definitely looked like a prelude to a flying saucer bursting forth. Fucking eerie. The huge, circular cloud with protruding rings hovered above them in a black mass of menacing raw power. Seriously. This was shit they put in movies to scare the hell out of people.

What kind of horrific memories would that storm trigger?

He pushed the question away. That was the whole point of doing this. Take the power of the storms away from his past.

As she chatted away with her explanations, he didn't like the positive way Gayle spoke about all this storm shit. It turned his fucking stomach.

After she snapped a few more pictures, they returned to the SUV. She immediately grabbed the hand microphone off the ham radio, pressed the button, and said, "This is Gayle Matthews. Storm chaser and meteorologist for WKKS News. I have visual on a rotating wall cloud moving northeast along Sam Brown Road in Mint, Oklahoma at an estimated twenty miles per hour."

Lowering the mic, she studied all her equipment for a few moments. "There's a road about half a mile down on the right."

That's all she needed to say. Rick nodded and pulled back onto the road behind a few other cars that were also leaving. Mac was a little taken aback as those vehicles turned onto the same side road. He guessed he shouldn't be. They were using the same stuff Gayle was, so it would lead them in the same direction.

"Who were you talking to?" Mac asked.

"National Weather Service for this area. They use trained spotters to confirm the exact location of severe weather, so they can get out advanced warnings to the public." She fell silent as she stared pensively up at the cloud the SUV seemed to be following.

About five minutes later she said, "We have hook echo."

Tensing, his gaze flew outside the window. He'd lived in Kansas long enough to know a hook echo indicated possible rotation of a tornado on radar. Within minutes, rain pelted the windshield. Wind shook the SUV. Mac grabbed hold of the sides of his seat and clenched every muscle in his body.

"Turn left, stay behind the line," she told Rick. A moment later, the rain stopped. "Funnel!" she shouted.

Mac glanced outside and sure enough a thick, whirling black mass extended from the cloud halfway down to the ground.

She quickly lifted the mic and identified herself. "I have visual of a funnel cloud moving northeast along—" A second later, she said, "Scratch that! Debris ball spotted. We have confirmed touchdown. Cone-shaped tornado is on the ground." Then she repeated the info, which he quickly learned she did each time she spoke to the authorities.

Gayle clicked off the mic. "Take a right on this road and get next to it."

Next to it? Mac's heart walloped his chest. The increased blood flow went straight to his head and white dots danced before his eyes.

The roar…growing louder and louder as it churned closer. The rattling of the kitchenware. The impact. Glass shattering.

Closing his eyes, he slowly inhaled two calming breaths, then exhaled.

It will have control of you no more.

Once he felt the tension release, he opened them.

Fucking horrible mistake. Instead of staying in the distance, the monster in front of them was spinning closer and closer, growing larger and more menacing by the second. His grip on the seat tightened as his mind bellowed to scream at Gayle that she was a fucking lunatic. Grinding his teeth against the urge, the swirling beast held him paralyzed. It felt like he could literally reach his hand out the window and touch the damn thing. In reality, it was probably the length of a football field away. Which was too fucking close by a mile. Wind gusts shook the car like an angry mother.

"Tornado is shifting to an easterly route and gaining momentum," she told the National Weather Service. The concern in her voice didn't go unnoticed.

The debris ball was huge, littered with dust and occasionally something larger. Right now the tornado was in an open field, but he saw the shift in direction Gayle had mentioned. Instead of going off at an angle and keeping to flat land, the change kept it on a straight course—and that looked like a town up ahead sitting innocently in the tornado's destructive path. Fuck. Memories of his own destroyed past threatened to overwhelm him again, but he forced himself to stay in the present. Pressing the heels of his palms to his forehead, he silently repeated, "Shift motherfucker, shift."

"Trajectory continues easterly, headed for the populated area of Mint."

As they took a right onto another road following behind the twister, the sound of sirens filled the car. A cluster of homes came into view and the town's water tower stood proud in the distance.

The tension in the SUV thickened. Unable to look away, Mac knotted his fingers in his hair, transfixed on the beast and the defenseless town below it. His heart was pounding so hard he thought it might crack a rib.

"Tornado is shifting again. Toward the northeast." Excitement laced every word.

About thirty seconds later, the tornado sideswiped a small farmhouse, taking off some siding and shattering the windows. Rick slowed the car. Mac swore. A barn and a fence took considerable damage, but that was it, then the tornado moved back into open fields. The town had been miraculously saved from a direct hit. A few minutes later the tornado started to shrink, until it was thin rope, and then it disappeared completely. Mac's heartbeat started to slow in relief and he managed to peel his fingers from the edge of the seat. *Holy fuck.*

"Tornado has dissipated."

She repeated, then hooked the mic back on the side of the radio and collapsed back against the seat with a heartfelt, "Thank God."

Awe rose in him as he stared at her. "Gayle, with all this equipment, why the play-by-play?"

She turned her head. "We have made amazing progress with radar and such, but the one thing we do not have is something that tells us when there's an actual touchdown. Still need human spotters for that."

He blinked, and she turned back to the monitors. "Another tornadic storm brewing twenty miles east."

Holy shit. The woman really *did* help people.

Stretching, Gayle groaned as her muscles sighed with pleasure. They'd logged over fifteen hours in the SUV yesterday before they'd called it a day. Unfortunately, the rest of the afternoon had been a bust. She either focused on the wrong storm, or got there too late and missed the action. At least Mac was getting a realistic view of what storm chasing was—long hours in a car, bad food, and endless waiting.

Someone suddenly grabbed her arm and pulled her to the front of the SUV. She squealed. Yanking her arm free, she whirled around. Rick. And he was furious. He'd been a grumpy butt since they'd left this morning. "What in the hell is your problem?" she demanded.

"I've been trying to get you alone all damn day," he muttered harshly, glancing off in the direction Mac had headed. "But *he's* always around. Hovering."

"He went to the bathroom. You can speak freely, Grasshopper."

Rick's lips pinched together. Oh. Good Lord. He was in a right foul mood.

"I'm not staying another night in a room with that man, do you understand? I do the driving. I need sleep."

Not expecting that, Gayle frowned. "What happened?"

"He fucking moaned and tossed and turned and kept calling out for an Ally all goddamn night. Gayle, I didn't sleep at all."

Damn it. "Okay. I'll figure something out."

"You better. Caffeine is only going to get me so far."

"I hear you. I'll take care of it."

Rick gave a terse nod, then slammed himself behind the driver's wheel, chugging his super caffeinated beverage, furious eyes locked on her. She sighed, running her fingers through her hair, as she squinted off into the distance. Her heart went out to Mac, but Rick was right, the driver needed to be well-rested.

They'd stopped at a motel last night, and she and Rick got separate rooms, as always. Without anyone saying anything, Mac had automatically assigned himself to Rick. She'd thought briefly about trying to get him to stay with her, but the man had looked beaten down.

Though they hadn't encountered any more tornadoes yesterday, they had been through some nasty storms. Each one had taken its toll on him. She'd watched the mental battle he fought. She didn't know what memories went through his head during these storms, but he couldn't hide the clenched eyes and locked jaw...or the haunted look when his eyes popped back open. He was reliving a lot. Despite that, he had kept to his side of the bargain. He never let the anger take control. Though she would probably have to fix the seats from his strong fingers digging into them.

Because he didn't go to his outlet, she'd hoped he was so emotionally exhausted he'd just pass out. Apparently, all that had happened was his demons had come out to play while his body had been at rest.

How in the hell would she convince him to stay in her room tonight?

At least she still had a few hours to figure it out. It was only two o'clock. Storms were just starting to fire. She'd think of something while they were on the road.

As she turned, Mac came out of the convenience store. He'd taken her advice and brought only comfortable clothes to wear, which for him was his workout attire. Too bad he hadn't brought along his tight workout tops she loved to ogle, but opted for cotton T-shirts instead. Massive bummer, but the T still strained against his muscles and was more of a tease to what lay beneath than an all-out show like his other shirts.

Just watching the man walk toward the car was hot. Maybe it was the relaxed swagger of his stride. In fact, he'd been pretty relaxed all morning, but that could be because they'd been traveling and hadn't encountered anything. Not that they usually did until the afternoon. He suddenly looked her way and smiled, and her breath caught.

The guy was simply yummy. And having once had a taste of him, it was very difficult to stay in the friends zone now that he'd put her there. From what she could tell, she was *strictly* there now. She hadn't received one hint of attraction from him since she'd returned home three days ago. She couldn't really blame him, though. The man was going through a traumatic readjustment four years in the making. How could lust compete with all that?

Still, that didn't keep her from wanting to touch him. And badly. She ached to at times. Somehow, she kept her hands to herself and kept a friendly smile plastered on her face.

He sidled up beside her and leaned against the SUV. "Where is the next chase target?"

"Very good, handsome. Getting down with the lingo." She grinned. "About an hour away. You ready to head into Texas?"

"Yes, ma'am," he drawled and pretended to tip a hat at her.

Chuckling, she said, "Get in the car, cowboy."

As Rick drove, Gayle worried over her data. Though they had only encountered one tornado yesterday, the main reason was because of her decision to stay away from the chaser convergence—for Mac's sake. If she'd gone with the pack she most likely would've seen a whole lot more, since yesterday thirty-one tornadoes had touched down throughout western Oklahoma and the Texas panhandle.

With the continued instability of the atmosphere, the slow-moving system would likely spawn even more tornadoes than yesterday. Now it was just a matter of getting to the right area.

Thirty minutes later, rain was coming down in sheets, making the wipers pretty much useless. Gusts of wind swayed the SUV. Multiple large red cells filled her radar as thunderstorms triggered along the line. The radio updates issued severe thunderstorm warnings and, so far, nothing had indicated anything escalating—but that could change in seconds.

"Gayle. What the fuck?"

Counting to five, she reined in her patience with her partner. "What do you want me to do? The storms are everywhere. I've at least got us in the rain, right?"

Rick grumbled from the driver's seat.

"You got something to say, say it."

He turned his head toward her then looked back out the windshield. "Why this system? Why not a more isolated one? But no, we had to come to this one."

Gayle counted—again—knowing he was only irritable from lack of sleep. Normally, he loved this. "I want to get off the interstate. There's a big storm approaching from behind us, and I don't want to get caught in traffic."

It was one of her biggest rules. No interstate during a storm. Ever.

Rick glanced over at her for a second like he didn't agree, but nodded and took the next exit, which brought them into a very rural area of Texas. This, she was comfortable with. This had escape routes. This wouldn't lead to them being trapped bumper to bumper like a sitting duck.

Ten minutes passed—the air thick with agitation. Thunder crashed in the distance as the storm drew nearer.

"If we take this road coming up on our left, it will lead us to a main road a few miles down that goes into Cater. We need to stop and reassess."

Another rumble of thunder sounded. She glanced back at Mac, who had been awfully quiet. Though his skin was slightly pale, he definitely looked better than he had yesterday driving through the storms. The car started to bounce. She snapped her head forward to see they had drifted off the road. Rick was shaking his head and doing weird squinting things with his eyes. "Rick!"

He jerked up straight, hands tightening on the wheel, and

righted the car.

"Pull over, right now," she ordered.

"I'm fine."

"Pull over this damn second!"

Jaw clenched, he did what she asked.

She opened her door. "We're done. I'll drive, and we'll find a place to stay for the night."

"But—"

"We're. Done."

In something that could be unpredictable, she did her damnedest to be safe. She sure as hell wasn't going to get injured or killed because her driver had fallen asleep. If Rick had known everything to look for, she'd have let him man the data, but he didn't. For six years, he had been the driver while she did the maps, videoing, and everything else.

As soon as she stepped outside, she was drenched. She ran around the front of the SUV, passing Rick on her way, then jumped into the driver's side. When he closed his door, she put the car in gear and pressed the gas. The tires spun in the mud, but the car didn't move. A moment of disbelief had her pressing the accelerator again with the same results. She stared out the windshield, the reality of the situation crashing into her.

Stuck.

They were officially sitting ducks.

She slammed her hands on the steering wheel. "Damn it!"

Rick, who had already fallen asleep, jerked upright again. "What?"

"We're stuck."

"The hell we are."

"The hell we're not."

Thunder boomed overheard and lightning suddenly lit up

the darkened late afternoon sky.

Shoving open the driver's side door, she hopped out, the torrential rain chilling her to the bone. Mac cracked his door open, and she shook her head at him. The what-the-fuck expression he gave her would've been comical if this weren't a seriously bad situation. His door opened wider. She pinned him with a death stare that immediately made him recoil—probably because he had never seen this side of her.

"I'm the boss. Stay in the fucking car," she yelled over the pounding rain.

The door clicked shut. Smart man.

Before she dealt with him, she had to figure out how much trouble they were really in. As she rounded the back of the SUV, she groaned, knotting her fingers in her sopping hair. The rear passenger-side tire was sunk axle-deep in the mud. Damn it. She never should've told Rick to pull over. A brain fart on her part from the shock of him falling asleep behind the wheel. These Midwest backroads became mud pits once the rain started. She'd seen tons of vehicles get stuck by running off the road or simply by pulling over. She *knew* that. God, this was a *huge* fuck up.

Being caught with storms surrounding them was a nightmare situation. What were they going to do?

Something hard pelted the top of her head, followed by another and another. Wincing, she looked up. The swirling grey whirlpool above her made her stomach plummet. *Oh, God!*

Thunder crashed as she raced to the driver's door and yanked it open. "Get on the CB and see if there is anyone around here who can pull us out."

The paleness of Rick's face increased her agitation. She darted a glance at Mac, who was watching intently. *Stay calm. Do not let on something is wrong.*

She simply lifted her brows in a questioning manner at her partner as nickel-sized hail showered her back and bounced inside the car. Swallowing, Rick slightly nodded toward the laptop, which he angled toward her so she could see. At the kidney bean shape on radar, everything in her stilled. High precipitation supercell. She inhaled a shaky breath and swallowed. "We've got to get the hell out of here."

Rick was out of the car instantly. She glanced at Mac. A lightning bolt streaked toward the ground in the distance. The thunder grew louder. It was time to see if he was really ready for this, because shit was about to get real ugly.

"I need you to get out of the car." But he didn't seem to be paying any attention to her. Seemed to be staring at her forehead. "Mac. I need you to get. Out. Of. The. Car."

"Why the *fuck* are you bleeding?" he said between gritted teeth, eyes still locked above her eyes. She touched the area, wincing at the tenderness. As she brought her hand away, watery red coated her fingertips.

"I got clocked with a nice-sized piece of hail. No big deal. Now get out of the car." A gust of wind blew her upper body farther into the interior. "We are in a deadly situation right now called the bear cage. A tornado can drop any second. Get out of the fucking *car*."

Every bit of color leached out the man's skin, but he moved.

The bear cage. No one but the chasers who drove armored vehicles went into the bear cage. There could be a tornado on the ground right now and she wouldn't know it because of the amount of precipitation falling. With rain-wrapped tornadoes—worst case scenario, everything bad that could happen, happened.

And it was happening.

The wind whipped by her, the rain stinging as it hit her exposed skin. Hail bruised her body. Holding her hands in front of her face, she pushed to the back of the SUV. Mac and Rick were already trying to lift it out by the bumper. It wasn't going to work. Rick should know that, but panic was driving him now. In lesser precipitation, the wheel would've been stuck. In this, it might as well be cemented in.

Water poured into her eyes and mouth as she frantically searched for something, a piece of wood, anything with traction. The ground was so muddy she slipped a few times, landing hard on her butt or side. Just as she made her second trip onto her rump, everything stopped. Like a switch flipping, the lashing downpour, the hail, the wind—everything cut off.

No!

"Run!" Terror squeezing her throat, she struggled to her feet. "It's coming! It's coming! In the ditch. *Now*."

A churning rumble, sounding like a train in the distance, reverberated behind her. They had seconds. *Seconds*.

She sprinted past the two men, diving into the ditch a few feet away from the SUV, which was dangerous in and of itself. Lying flat, she covered her head. She felt movement around her, then a large body covered her, pressing her farther down. Strong arms wrapped around her head. Mac. His breath warmed her cheek as he shielded his own face against her.

The rumble grew louder as the wind became fiercer. From the drop in pressure, her ears popped. Debris swished by. One second the sound grew deafening and then it became fainter and fainter. And suddenly they were being deluged with rain and hail again.

Everything had happened in less than a minute.

Mac eased off her and collapsed back on the ground on his butt. Rain water sluiced off his nose and chin as he stared straight ahead, breathing heavily. He didn't seem to feel the hail pelting his body.

She pushed up on her knees and reached out a hesitant hand, wanting to touch him but unsure if she should. "Are you okay?"

His gaze flicking to hers briefly before returning straight ahead, he gave a short nod. She glanced around and saw Rick, pushing up, soaked and muddy, but fine. *Thank God.*

Uncertain what to say to the man sitting unmoving in the driving rain, she rose and went to see if the SUV had been damaged. The vehicle was still stuck in the mud, of course. Thankfully, the antennas and Doppler were still intact. Which meant the tornado hadn't been very strong and had most likely just sideswiped them. Man, talk about a close call with major luck thrown in.

She reached inside and tugged the microphone for the CB. Thank God it still worked. She put out a call for help, then rubbed her mouth and glanced over at Mac again. He hadn't moved out of the muddy ditch, though he was on his feet now. The rain had lessened considerably and the hail had stopped, but he still looked like he was being shelled by the storm. A haunted gleam had hollowed his eyes. Deep lines of pensiveness grooved his face. He was standing only a few feet away, but he was *not* here.

A chasing crew pulled up and she refocused on getting the car freed. Within minutes, their Jeep had winched the SUV out of the mud. As they drove into town, soaked, muddy, and shaken, no one spoke.

In the six years of chasing, that was the closest encounter she'd had with a tornado. With the unpredictability of weather, she'd had close calls before, but nothing like this. She glanced into the backseat. Mac was staring out the window, just as distant as before. He hadn't spoken a word since he'd asked why she was bleeding.

She had a sinking feeling that coming on this chase was not going to help him. She feared it was just going to make everything worse.

A low moan made Gayle's eyes snap open and she sat up in bed. Mac was thrashing on the other bed, his sheets tangled around his legs. She shoved aside her covers and rushed to his side.

"Mac," she whispered.

His body immediately calmed, and she breathed a sigh of relief. A quick glance at the clock showed it was a quarter after three. It had taken time for his unconscious mind to gather up the energy to torment him. They'd been in bed for hours.

After grabbing a pizza and getting the motel rooms, she'd just looked at Mac and said, "You're staying in my room tonight." There'd been no argument. He'd picked at his slice for a while, then excused himself and took a shower. Afterward, he'd gotten into bed. At a loss as to what to say or how to help, she'd taken a shower herself and done the same. Lights had been out by nine.

As she turned to crawl back into her bed, another soft moan sounded, followed quickly by another sorrow-filled *No*. His head turned on the pillow. Soon he would be calling out his wife's name, and Gayle wasn't sure she could listen to the agony in his voice again.

Climbing up on the mattress, she perched on her knees beside him. Tenderly brushing back his hair, she shushed soothingly. His brows furrowed as a groan filled the room.

"No," he murmured.

She leaned in closer. Keeping her voice calm, comforting. "Mac. *Shhh*. It's okay."

"Gayle!" that tortured voice whispered. "Please. No."

Lungs locked, she sat up ramrod straight, staring down at him. She hadn't heard him right. She couldn't have heard him right.

"Gayle. Please." And just as before, the plea was filled with such agonized beseeching it filled her own chest with pain.

But this time he was dreaming of *her*. No. It must only be because he'd heard her talking to him in his sleep.

"No!" Then he jackknifed up, chest heaving. Sweat coated his forehead as he stared straight ahead. She froze.

He slowly turned his head toward her. They came nose-to-nose, and she had the hardest time breathing.

"Thank God," whispered past his lips. Then his hand snatched her around the neck, and his mouth crushed onto hers. Shocked, she gasped, bracing herself on his exposed biceps.

One second he was holding her head captive as he delved deep into her mouth, the next, her back was bouncing on the mattress where he'd tossed her down, his body covering hers. One masculine leg shoved between her knees as he kissed her aggressively. There was desperation in the way he moved, gripped her, thrust his tongue between her lips—as though making a determined effort to banish the demons from his mind.

It didn't matter that his actions were spurred on by whatever horror he'd witnessed in his dreams, her body reacted the same. Her nipples tightened. and her clit throbbed to life. He worked his hand between their bodies and hooked his fingers in her panties, dragging them down her legs, his mouth moving furiously on hers.

She wanted him with a severity she couldn't understand—

but not like this. After the emotions wore off, he'd regret this, possibly be furious it happened. Ripping her mouth from his, she turned her head away and shoved at his chest. "Mac. We can't. You're not thinking clearly."

"Shut up, Gayle. I'm clear." As if to prove his point, he grabbed his wallet off the nightstand, opened it, pulled something out, then flipped it in front of her face to see.

A condom.

"Do you see how clear I am now?"

Okay, then. She nodded.

"Good."

He yanked her panties off the rest of the way and moved fully between her legs. Lifting up, he stared down at her, and she *saw* how clear he actually was. The distant, haunted gleam from before was gone. Pensiveness gone. Those had been replaced with a feverish lust completely directed at her.

"I just had the most God-awful nightmare. And I need to be inside you. Hear your gasps. Hear your moans. Hear you coming." He touched a finger to her. "And you're already wet and ready. I need to feel your life, Gayle."

He quickly ripped open the wrapper, sheathed himself, then thrust forward. At the sudden fullness, she arched, crying out. Embedded to the hilt, he closed his eyes and groaned. "That's it. Make those noises for me. Let me hear you."

He buried his head against her neck as he slowly withdrew and pushed back. He continued the steady pace, his harsh breath heating her skin. She let out small stuttered gasps and cradled the man in her arms and her body.

"Gayle, you feel so good." His lips pressed into her shoulder, then a light nip of his teeth. He thrust a little harder, a little faster.

She wanted him deeper. Spreading her legs, she grabbed

his ass in her palms and drove him forward. He pushed up on his hands, towering above her as he increased his pace.

Knowing he was watching her was an aphrodisiac. Closing her eyes, she relinquished all control and allowed the feelings he created inside her to tumble out into the open. Moans, gasps, muttered words of pleasure. She held nothing back. Didn't quiet herself, didn't care if she woke the entire motel, she gave him what he needed—by simply expressing what he truly did to her body. There was no falseness, no exaggeration. Just an uninhibited response. To him.

"So goddamn beautiful," he said, his voice strained. "So fucking full of life." Sliding his hand over her mound, he circled her clit. The sensations inside tripled. "I want to watch you come."

With that explosive combination, she came fast—long and loud. He took a harsh breath and his steady pumping faltered. He braced his hands on the mattress as he thrust hard three more times, his body quaking, then he collapsed to his elbows with a sated groan.

Still breathing hard, she placed a kiss on his shoulder. "Are you okay?"

Gratitude—and something else she couldn't quite name—warmed his eyes as he brushed her hair back. "I am now. I needed this. I needed you."

He kissed her and shifted his body so she turned onto her side, then he spooned behind her. He wrapped an arm around her waist, and she stroked his forearm. Wow. She'd had sex before. Thought she'd understood what it was just to kick back and enjoy the act. The first time she'd been with Mac, she realized she'd held a part of herself back.

Tonight she'd set herself free.

And most likely free to have her heart crushed in the process.

Chapter Nine

From the moment he'd woken this morning to find Gayle already dressed in khaki shorts and a pale green tank top, her hair pulled back in a ponytail, sitting cross-legged on her bed tapping away on her laptop, Mac had noticed a new tension in her. No doubt it had to do with the unexpected turn of events last night. But after he'd woken from the nightmare to find her beside him, safe and alive, he couldn't keep from reaching for her, much less stop what happened afterward. And he didn't regret it. Not for a second.

The terror of yesterday's events had catapulted him into the moment and with its stranglehold had kept him from sinking into the past. As she'd run past him screaming a tornado was coming, he had not been paralyzed with fear—instead he'd been pushed into action. Compelled to protect the woman he'd grown to care for.

Last night, for the first time, his nightmares hadn't revolved around finding Ally, they'd been about losing Gayle. Definitely things he was going to have to think about...but one thing was clear, a corner had been turned.

As the day wore on and they drove the five hours north toward the intersecting borders of Oklahoma, Texas, and Arkansas, her shoulders had grown even more rigid. Once they made it over into Arkansas, they'd camped out in the parking lot of a truck stop for the last three hours. Gayle became obsessive over the laptop and her assortment of different radars and numbers. A few minutes ago, she and Rick had released a weather balloon into the air.

And that was when the mood in both of them had changed. As usual their technical speak went over Mac's head. Something about separate things converging, cap levels eroding, and a bad feeling. But it was then he finally realized Gayle's withdrawn attitude didn't have anything to do with last night.

Something was brewing. Now.

Something horrible.

"Okay. Why the hell are we sticking around here?" he finally asked.

Everything about today was off. After the long, hurried drive to get here, they just sat on the hood of the SUV and watched the sky. No one talked. Every minute that crept by in the edgy quiet increased Mac's damn stress. Two storm chasers not excited about the chase and having "bad feelings" was seriously fucked up.

Gayle studied him, almost as though trying to decide if she was going to let him in on the secret or not. Her shoulders slumped. Fuck. She'd decided to tell him. Now he wasn't sure he wanted to know. "We're waiting, Mac."

"On what?"

"The explosion."

That sounded...bad. "Can you be a little more specific?"

She shifted on the hood until she was turned toward him.

"About an hour ago, the Storm Prediction Center issued a PDS. Particularly Dangerous Situation. The SPC only issues a PDS when the elements are ripe for very severe weather or major tornado outbreaks."

"How could it possibly be worse than yesterday? And yet, you guys have never been this tense before. Why?"

"These types of storms—" She inhaled. "Emerald Springs was a PDS."

Mac reared back and his stomach twisted sickeningly.

"It might not happen," she quickly added. "It all depends on how things play out. But, yeah, it could get a lot worse than yesterday. And if it does, we're in the epicenter of where it'll go down."

"Shit," he muttered, the hair actually standing up on the back of his neck.

As if she could read his thoughts, she said, "I'm sorry Mac." Regret burned bright in her eyes. "But I can't leave you behind. Not this time. And I can't send you off. You're safer with us."

Not an hour later, cells started to light up the radar with reds, greens, and oranges. She took particular interest in one about eight miles south. "Let's go," she told Rick.

As they reached the darkened edge of the storm, the high tower looming above them made Mac swallow rising panic. For two days, he'd seen these clouds, watched them spawn tornadoes, but even he could see this one was different.

Lightning billowed within the darkened clouds, lighting them up from the inside.

"Storm is moving northeast. Two more cells forming toward the north. Stay with it, Rick."

For thirty minutes they trailed the storm deeper into Arkansas. Mac stayed mute, refusing to disrupt Gayle's concentration, especially with her continually muttering, "I don't like this."

The ominous feeling grew with each passing minute. A few seconds later, Gayle mumbled a vehement curse. "The cells are converging. We have a rotating core."

"Fuck," Rick muttered.

"What does that mean?"

She glanced back at him, her lips pressed tight. "Fucking huge, violent storm that's trying to become even bigger by inviting more storms to the party."

After she gave the NWS an update, she said, "We need to move in."

Tornado warnings for the city of Makersville, Arkansas, started streaming out of the NOAA radio.

As she stared at the storm, she twisted her fingers together. Watching her distress tugged at his gut. He wanted to take her in his arms and tell her everything would be okay. But that wasn't a promise he could make. Her worry did show him how much she cared about the safety of others.

Her eyes widened and she fumbled for the mic on the ham and started talking. Mac looked outside.

Not one, not two, but three tornadoes were on the ground.

"Holy fucking shit," he muttered.

She released the mic's button. Without looking away from the tornadoes, she said, "You know what to do."

Mac wasn't sure who she was talking to until Rick accelerated from the creeping pace they'd been keeping to breakneck speed. *Away* from the tornadoes.

Gayle brought the mic back to her mouth. "The vortices are converging into a single vortex."

Say what? Mac twisted to stare out the back window. The three tornadoes were now one and it was growing. In little over a minute, it'd widened to what had to be the length of a football field. The one they'd seen the first day was a fucking baby in comparison.

"Why are we leaving?" Honestly, he'd rather keep the damn thing in sight.

"We have a very large wedge tornado on the ground headed northeast," she said into the mic, but she was looking at him. "Less than ten miles outside of the town of Makersville, directly in the tornado's path." She glanced at Rick. "Fifteen minutes before it hits."

Rick pushed the SUV faster.

"What's going on?" Mac asked, confused. Weren't they speeding away from it?

Neither one answered. Less than six minutes later, they raced into the town of five thousand people. Even though the warning sirens were blaring everywhere, and a large dark cloud towered behind the town, people were still milling about. It didn't really surprise him. The sirens went off a lot this time of year—so often, they became easy to ignore. Gayle grabbed a megaphone he hadn't seen before, rolled down her window, and eased her body out through it to perch on the sill.

"Take cover *now*. Monster tornado coming," she repeated as Rick reduced his speed to a crawl and inched down the road, weaving around any traffic in the way. As they passed a police cruiser, she waved it down. The cop lowered his window and she quickly told him what was happening. He got on his megaphone and did the same, taking off in a different direction.

Mac wasn't sure if it was the presence of a storm chaser vehicle or the crazy woman yelling at them, but folks started moving. People already driving on the roads started taking side streets to get out. As the SUV reached a less commercialized area, Gayle slipped back inside. "Get us out of here, Rick."

He floored the gas and flew through town just as the tornado made impact on the other side. Rain pelted the windshield, quickly followed by golf ball sized hail and wind so strong it made visibility zero. Thunder boomed as crazy-intense lightning struck the ground.

"We're in the core. Get us out!" Gayle whipped around to look out the back.

It was the fear in her eyes and her voice that terrified Mac the most.

"Put your seatbelt on," he ordered. When she didn't move, he yelled, "*Now*, goddamn it!"

As she fumbled with the belt, the glass in front of her went *crack* and shattered into a spider web of cubes as debris slammed into it. Screaming, she flinched away, flinging her arms up to protect her head. In one swift motion, he released his belt and lunged forward, covering her. Something else bounced off the broken windshield, and a deluge of water and hail assaulted his shoulders and back. He curled himself tighter around her.

Seconds later, the torrent ended abruptly.

Mac eased back, shaking off the sluicing water. Gayle lifted up.

Rick exhaled, his fingers white around the steering wheel. "We're out."

Mac sat in his seat, the quaking in his hand making it difficult to snap his seatbelt back on. The image of Gayle screaming and protecting her head was seared in his mind.

"Are you okay?" Gayle asked. "That hail was the size of canned hams."

"Nothing worse than I've taken in the cage." He tried for a smile at her joke, but by the doubtful once-over she gave him he knew he'd failed. In truth, his shoulders and back stung like hell. And if he hadn't put himself in between Gayle and Mother Nature, it would've been her sweet curves taking the beating instead of his hard fighter's body.

As Rick circled around, Mac was transfixed by the black swirling mass maybe half a mile away that slowly churned through the heart of Makersville. Slim fingers brushed against his. He glanced down to find Gayle's hand reaching through the seats and he latched on to it. As she held up the video camera to document the destruction, he saw tears rimming her eyes as her lips moved around words he couldn't hear.

She was praying.

Rick crept the SUV along. Every once in a while a brilliant flash of blue light lit the air or the inside of the tornado, which was eerily stunning. Flying out from the massive debris ball surrounding the vortex, paper and other light objects swirled around their vehicle. Memories assaulted him of being trapped, helpless, in pitch black darkness. The deafening roar of the fierce winds. Shattering glass, loud crashes, and booms as walls toppled and the roof tore away. The violent sounds becoming muted from the air pressure clogging his ears. The overwhelming smell of natural gas and fresh cut wood. Airborne dirt and debris pelting his skin. Terror-filled screams of the patrons in the freezer, certain death was imminent. He heard it. Felt it. All over again. Like he never had before.

People were going through that right now, right in front of him. He turned to the woman beside him still mumbling a prayer. Her actions had no doubt saved lives today. And could have cost her hers, too.

It took the twister ten full minutes to eat a path through the town. Ten minutes of terror for the people trapped under the destruction left behind by the swirling demon. Ten minutes of terror for those hiding, waiting, and praying for mercy as it crept closer. Mac rubbed his face. Ten minutes of abject horror for him to live through, as well. Helpless. Stricken. Flooded by terrible memories.

As the monster neared the edge of town, the momentum keeping it together slowly unraveled, and it started to lose strength. By the time it moved back out onto flat land, it was less than half its original size. A few minutes later it was gone—as though it hadn't just destroyed an entire small town.

"Go," Gayle whispered to Rick. "We can't leave. We have to help."

A sumo wrestler might as well have sat down on Mac's chest from the heaviness suddenly compressing his lungs, threatening to suffocate him. *Search and rescue.* As the SUV turned back into town, the path of destruction left behind took Mac's breath away.

"Oh God." Gayle pressed her hand to her mouth.

The town was simply gone. Asphalt had been ripped up. Stores completely leveled. Vehicles looked as if they had been picked up and crushed in a giant's hand. All that was left of trees were denuded stumps, the tops completely torn away. Timbers were speared into windshields. A piece of fence was impaled deep into the side of a standing cement wall.

It was Emerald Springs all over again.

Rick maneuvered the car around the wreckage until he reached the worst of it. Horror, sorrow, and empathy bludgeoned Mac as he surveyed the houses that had been wiped off their foundations, piles of rubble everywhere.

Oh God, these people. The shock. The fear. The grief. Emotions clogged his throat and he squeezed his hands into tight fists, digging his nails into his palms. His trauma happened in the past. This was happening to people right now, this minute.

Fires had started from gas line ruptures. Cars were perched precariously on rooftops. A crib lay broken on a lawn. A pained groan pressed out between his desperately clenched teeth.

Gayle squeezed his hand again. "I'm so sorry, Mac. I wanted to save you from this." Her sentenced ended on a smothered sob. "There are people trapped. We have to help."

"Absolutely," he managed.

He felt the same way. Felt so much respect and was in awe of her because of her compassion. But that didn't stop the demons that had tormented him for the last four years from completely overtaking him.

Rick stopped the car. As Gayle opened the door, screams for help punched him in the gut, hitting him harder and with more power than any heavyweight fighter ever had. A man stumbled out into the road, blood coating the left side of his face. Gayle immediately hurried over to him, put her arm around him, and helped him sit down. Rick came up to the man and handed him a water bottle. Where he'd gotten it, Mac had no idea.

But the sight of the two of them helping reached deep inside Mac. He hadn't been able to help Ally. No one had been able to help her. She had most likely been taken from this world before she'd even hit the ground. But he could help someone now.

He opened the door and climbed out. From where the tornado had demolished a line through the heart of the town, he could see for miles in each direction. People were slowly emerging from damaged buildings on the perimeter of the tornado's path and were making their way over to the destruction that lay before them, while others were crawling out from under rubble and climbing out of storm shelters.

The cries for help went through him like knives. He met

Gayle's devastated but determined gaze, gathered strength from her, and leapt into action. A young teen was pinned by a collapsed wall. Mac lifted it and she crawled out, sobbing. Other than a few scrapes, she was relatively unharmed. A miracle.

Ambulances, police cruisers, and fire trucks slowly made their way through the debris. But there still weren't enough rescuers. As he helped the girl to one of the EMTs, he felt a tug on his shirt. He glanced down. A small girl, maybe around the age of three, with blond hair and blue eyes. Blood ran from a cut on her forehead, and her clothes were soaked and caked with dirt. But it was the innocence in her eyes that knocked him hard in the heart.

The blond hair and blue eyes reminded him so much of Ally. And she was right around the same age as their child would've been… His heart wrenched painfully as he squatted in front of her.

"Hey, sweetie." His voice was thick with repressed emotions and he had to clear it.

"I can't find my mommy." Tears welled in the child's eyes as her chin started to wobble. She touched the knot on her forehead. Her little fingernails were painted a cheerful pink, such a contrast to the devastation around them. "M-my house is all gone, so is my m-mommy. I want my daddy."

He didn't know if he had the strength for this. "It's going to be okay," he soothed, seeing the shock of whatever she'd been through was wearing off. "I need you to be brave for just a little bit longer so we can find your mommy. Okay? Do you know where your house was?"

Taking hiccupping breaths, the little girl looked around, and he could tell she wasn't sure. How could she? Everything was leveled. Then she pointed a tiny trembling finger down the road a bit. "That's my room," she said, then burst into a wail only a terrified child could make. "Mr. Alligator!"

The child's distress tore at him, and he gathered her up in his arms, as he glanced over at the one pink wall still standing about forty yards away. The tiny body convulsed against his chest as she sobbed for everything she had lost. God, he hoped he found her mom. Maybe he would…just like he found Ally.

He squeezed his eyes closed. He couldn't let his mind go there. Not now.

When he opened them, he made eye contact with Gayle, who was hurrying over. She stopped in front of them and gently touched the child's back. The little girl lifted her head. Wetness streaked her face as she took shaky inhales.

"Hey there, sweetie. I'm Gayle. What's your name?"

"S-Sophie." She scrubbed her eyes with her fists.

"She can't find her mom," Mac said, and Gayle shot a glance at him. They stared at each other for a moment.

"What's your mom's name, honey?"

"B-Brandi."

"I'll go find her," he said.

Gayle inhaled, then a sympathetic smile came to her lips as she held her arms out to the child. "Honey, why don't you come with me? I have something in the car I think you'll like."

Sophie went into Gayle's embrace and hugged her tiny arms around Gayle's neck.

"I'll have an EMT look at her bump, too," she whispered to him, then she headed to the SUV. After she opened the trunk, she put the little girl down and pulled out a plastic container, set it on the ground, then lifted the lid. When Sophie swooped in and yanked out a teddy bear, hugging it tearfully to her chest, he wanted to tug the woman beside her to *his* chest.

Inhaling deeply, he started making his way to the area

where Sophie's house used to stand. If her mom had been sucked from the house by the vortex, there was no telling where she could be, but he hoped that wasn't the case. He hoped, God, *he hoped*, she was just somewhere under the rubble.

But Ally had been under the rubble...

A cold sweat broke out across his skin, and his footsteps faltered. Breathing seemed an impossible task. Starry dots formed before his eyes, and his vision tunneled as the image of her lifeless body formed in his mind.

No! He shook himself.

He forced himself to keep walking. As he passed a mound of wreckage, a muffled whimper came from underneath. Flinging large slabs of wood off the pile, he eventually uncovered an elderly man. Another guy hurried over to help the man out and Mac moved on. Seconds later, he heard a low whine. He shoved aside two mangled bicycles twisted together with some yard ornaments and uncovered a terrified, drenched terrier. The dog trembled as it cautiously stepped out. He picked up the animal. A woman about fifty yards away burst into tears and came running. "Minnie. Oh, my God. Minnie!"

She took the pup from his arms, then grabbed Mac in a strong embrace, her heartfelt sobs muffling her, "Thank you, oh, thank you!" but not the relief and happiness.

Four more times he was stopped by muted cries for help. Two of the people were in critical condition. Volunteers helped ease them onto a ripped-off door and a piece of plywood and loaded them on the back of a truck to rush to the hospital. He also found a father and son huddled together in a closet, the only remaining room of their home.

When he finally reached Sophie's yard, he scanned the

area. Déjà vu almost brought him to his knees as four fingers caught his attention. Barely visible, muddied, and sticking out between two pieces of house debris. They were slender with nails painted bright pink.

His entire body went numb.

He couldn't do this. He couldn't face it. Not a second time.

The fingers twitched. Just a flick.

His heart stuttered, and he stumbled in a rush over debris to reach her. He hurled bricks, branches, and pieces of furniture away like a madman. Then she was there. Blond like the little girl. Injured badly, but alive.

"Brandi?" he asked.

She coughed. Tears welled in her desperate blue eyes, overflowing down her cheeks. "M-my d-daughter?" she managed to ask.

"Sophie is fine. She's with my girl—" Stunned, he shook himself. "Friend. She's with my friend. Are you injured?"

"M-my…ribs."

"Okay. Don't move. I'll fetch help." Glancing around, he motioned to an EMT a little distance away, who hurried over. Then he looked for Gayle. She was nowhere to be found. Panic climbed his throat. Frantically, he searched over the destruction and finally saw her about thirty yards away digging through wreckage of a building. The tightening eased.

He spotted the little girl, too, and had to smile. She huddled with a group of other kids on the street, each clutching a new stuffed animal. They all still looked scared, but were no longer crying. "While they get you ready to move, I'll fetch Sophie."

As he went to stand, Brandi's hand caught his. "Thank you. I don't think I will ever"—she took a shallow breath—"be able to repay you."

Giving her fingers a gentle squeeze, he shook his head and

said, "You've helped me more than you will ever know."

As he walked across the debris-strewn lawn to get Brandi's daughter, his heart felt lighter and freer than it had in years. Gayle had been right. He'd needed to face this. And he hadn't just faced the most traumatic day of his life. He'd relived it. Every emotion, every memory, brought to the surface, flaying him alive, making him bear witness to the destruction—but from the outside this time. It gave him the chance he hadn't been given four years ago. He'd helped. Even though it wasn't his wife under the rubble this time, he'd been able to do the one thing that had bludgeoned him with guilt since her death. He'd been here to save someone's life. And he'd spared a daughter, and a husband, from living in the pure hell he'd been forced to live through for four years.

He'd desperately needed to banish his inner demons, and today, because of Gayle, he'd finally done it.

He had a lot to thank that woman for.

Exhausted both physically and emotionally, Gayle sat on the edge of the bed. It was a damn miracle they'd found two motel rooms, because of all the displaced people and rescue workers descending on the town. Thank God, because she didn't know what she'd do without a safe place to tame the emotions roiling inside her.

She, Rick, and Mac had worked well into the night. Though most of the town had been leveled, there'd been only five fatalities. More could tally tomorrow. But considering the catastrophic damage and the homes without storm cellars, she knew the death toll could've been so much worse.

The destruction was devastating, showing how powerful

this tornado had been. She'd found a roof tile embedded in a wall, and a kitchen fork driven so deep into the trunk of a debarked tree she hadn't been able to wiggle it out—she was pretty certain this one had been an EF-5.

As she yanked off her hiking boots, a searing burn scorched her palms and she gasped. Mac immediately spun around. "What?"

She gently pressed her tender palms together. "Nothing."

After what other people had lost today, she didn't have the right to complain about a couple of blisters. He knelt before her and tried to take her hands.

She tugged them away. "I'm fine."

"Baby, let me see."

Sighing, she held them out.

"Jesus," he hissed. "What happened to your gloves?"

"They only lasted about three hours."

Open blisters exposed raw bleeding skin. A cut ran across one palm from a piece of twisted metal she'd lifted off a young woman. Since she kept up-to-date with her shots, she wasn't worried about tetanus.

"Yours can't be any better," she mumbled at his horrified look.

He showed her his palms. He had a blister or two, a scrape here and there, but nothing like hers. "I fight, Gayle. My hands are used to taking a beating."

"I suppose they are." Tears pushed to be set free and she blinked, easing out a long breath.

The traumatic events of the day had festered all the emotions she normally kept carefully suppressed, and she was close to breaking down. Not surprising. She always had a really good cry after days like today. She couldn't do it in front of Mac, though. She was so proud of him and the way he'd dealt with everything, she wouldn't let her weakness bring him down. "I'm going to take a shower."

"Fine, but as soon as you get out, I want to treat your hands."

She attempted a smile. If it made him feel better...

After she closed herself off in the bathroom, she awkwardly stripped and stepped under the steaming hot water, thankfully without too much pain. But as soon as she started lathering her hair with shampoo, her palms ignited in fire and she almost cried out. Trying to massage the soap in, let alone get it out, proved futile. Anytime she curled her fingers, intense throbbing heat pulsated through her hands. Soap slid down her forehead, stinging her eyes, too. She was close to losing it completely.

"Mac!"

"What's the matter?" came from behind the curtain an instant later, filled with concern.

That's all it took. The day's emotions engulfed her all at once, and a sob bubbled in her throat. She pressed her lips together, fighting to keep it contained.

"Gayle?"

When she didn't respond, he jerked back the curtain. All she could do was stare at him, tears blurring her vision as water from the overhead spray flowed down her body.

"Baby, are you okay?"

The sweetness of his words tore away at the last of her control. The dam burst.

She covered her face with her palms, no longer feeling physical pain, as sobs heaved out of her. Strong arms engulfed her, and she was dragged forward, her cheek meeting saturated cotton. The man had stepped into the tub with her, fully clothed, shoes and all.

Taking comfort in his embrace, she leaned into him, sliding the backs of her fingers up his back as her body shook from the force of her emotions.

What was she doing? After everything *he'd* been through today, everything he'd had to face, the memories that had resurfaced... She tried to pull away, reaching up to swipe at her eyes. He'd been so damn brave, and here she was being a—

He tightened his grip around her, refusing to let her go. "Gayle, you put the Man of Steel to shame. Let me be strong for you for a change."

She hesitated for a brief moment, then she let go and buried her face in his chest and allowed herself to be weak for once, allowed herself to seek comfort from someone else— allowed herself to cry in front of someone. Really cry.

When she finally lifted her head, he didn't say a word, just reached around her and squirted the shampoo in his palm. He turned her and massaged her scalp until there was a good lather. After he rinsed her hair, he did the same with the conditioner.

She faced him again. He gazed down at her for a moment, then cupped the back of her nape and took her lips with his. She searched for the hem of his saturated shirt, but he gently knocked her hands away and peeled it over his head. The wet fabric plopped heavily onto the tile, followed slowly— excruciatingly slowly—by waterlogged boots, jeans, and boxer briefs.

It was just the respite she needed to finish taming her chaotic emotions. As she watched him undress, a different kind of emotion filled her—need. Need and desire for this amazing man who'd put everything on the line today. She shuddered out a final breath, letting go of the pain, her heart swelling instead with love.

When he finally straightened, she looked at his beautiful, powerful body, and the ugliness of the day receded. With him, she felt totally nurtured and safe. And, God, how she wanted to touch him.

"I want to wash you," she said.

"Yeah, I want you to wash me, too, but I'm not going to let you do it with those hands." A wicked grin gradually curved his lips. "How about you watch instead?"

She mirrored his smile. "I'm intrigued."

He grabbed the bar of soap and ran it provocatively over the wet skin of his chest and abs and tossed the bar back down. He then started sliding his hands down both his arms, his chest, and his well-defined six-pack, deliberately tantalizing her. Watching his strong fingers roam over his sudsy body was a huge turn on.

She caught her bottom lip between her teeth as those fingers delved lower. He wrapped one hand around his cock and started stroking. He had her so mesmerized by the action, she didn't see his other hand reach out and tweak her nipple. She gasped.

"Someone likes watching me."

She didn't look away from his working hand, but she did smile wider. "Oh, yeah. I like watching your cock get hard."

His arm shot out and yanked her to him. "My hard cock would like to be deep inside you."

He left her for a brief moment to dig protection out of his sopping wet jeans, then his mouth was on hers again as he lifted her up. Wrapping her legs around his waist, she looped her arms around his neck, but kept her hands dangling free. He pressed her into the damp wall and, in one motion, embedded himself inside her. They groaned into each other's mouths. Bucking into her in a fast, hard rhythm, he massaged one breast while gently rolling her nipple between two fingers. Moaning, she leaned her head back. His lips immediately went to her exposed neck, sucking, biting, and kissing.

"Jesus, Mac," she stuttered out.

When his mouth closed around her nipple, sucking deeply, and his hand stroked between her legs, she came apart instantly. She expected him to join her. Instead, he slowed the aggressive motion of his finger to just a gentle rub of her clit as he thrust. He buried his face in her neck. "Fuck, woman, I can't get enough of being inside you."

Then his fingers resumed their skillful dance. This time her orgasm was stronger, longer, and loud. Mac thrust forward, and his body tensed against hers. "Fuck," he bit out. "Fuck."

A massive quake shook his frame, then his muscles slowly relaxed. When he finally lifted his head, a lazy smile curved his mouth. He kissed her gently and put her back on her feet outside the tub, not letting her go until he was sure she had her footing. After he got out, he snatched a white towel off the rack, gently dried her, and wrapped the towel around her body, tucking it closed between her breasts.

"I'm going to dry off. I'll be out in a minute to treat your hands." He kissed her again, then sent her out the door with a soft pat on the rump.

Smiling, Gayle padded into the room, grabbed an oversized T-shirt and panties, and slipped them on. There was a lot to be said for having someone special. Someone who understood what you were feeling and didn't hesitate to give of himself. Someone you could trust.

Her smile faded. Those were dangerous thoughts. She *didn't* have Mac. She needed to remember that. He would be gone in a matter of weeks.

"Sit down on the bed," he said as he strode in from the

bathroom, a towel wrapped around his waist.

Perplexed by her thoughts, she did as he asked, watching him pull on a pair of checkered pajama bottoms and grab the first aid kit.

He knelt before her and she studied the top of his head, trying to sort out her feelings. She liked him. A lot. There was no doubt she could very easily fall for the man. And that scared the hell out of her.

Relationships and Gayle Matthews did not work. She'd accepted that three years ago. If it wasn't death that separated her and the man she'd allowed in, it was her job, or her immaturity, or her seriousness, or her goofiness, or her commitment. Seriously? Could the reasons be any more bipolar?

The end result was always the same…he left.

And Mac would, too. Even if he weren't already leaving town.

She had to protect her heart from him. First, there wasn't a part of her that believed for one instant he would stay in Kansas, and there was no way she'd ever move away. Second, at the mud race, he'd told her he wasn't looking for anything serious. Which led her to believe he only wanted to test out the waters, since he hadn't dated since his wife died.

She couldn't blame him. He deserved to date. To have fun and enjoy the single life after the solitude he'd sentenced himself to the last few years. She studied him for a moment, really studied him. And saw that he did look less haunted. He was smiling now, laughing. He needed time to reacquaint himself with that happier man, become comfortable with him again. Have a few good experiences to offset the bad. And then maybe he could find the right woman and be able to love again.

Mac was capable of endless love. He'd already proven

that. When he loved, he loved with his all.

As he worked the antibiotic ointment into her palms, then carefully wrapped them with gauze, she ran her fingers over his hair. He deserved a woman who would fill the huge void Ally had left behind when she died.

Gayle wanted that for him with all her heart.

But she wasn't the one to do it. She just couldn't see them working long-term. There were too many obstacles.

But that wasn't going to stop her from enjoying the man while he was here.

"There," he said as he taped the end of the gauze down and sat back on his haunches.

She grinned at her wrapped hands. "Should I bring my fists up to protect my chin?"

"That'd be pretty fucking hot, actually."

"*Huh.* I'll have to remember that when I can bend my fingers without cringing in pain."

He sat beside her on the bed. "I wanted to ask you about the teddy bears. That was so nice of you. It meant a lot to those kids."

"I started carrying them after seeing my first destructive tornado." How would he react when he found this out? At the time it hadn't felt appropriate to blurt out she'd chased the very tornado that had destroyed his life while he'd been reliving it in his head. "I started chasing six years ago, but it wasn't until about four years ago that I actually saw an EF-5 rip through a town." She looked away.

He stiffened beside her. Yeah, he got her implication.

"You were in Emerald Springs."

She nodded. "I followed it straight into town and jumped out immediately to help. I'll never forget, as the people emerged, how stunned they were. Especially the ones who'd ridden it out inside a house. Like they couldn't believe they had survived and were questioning how that had happened."

"I know the feeling," he murmured with a sigh.

She touched the bandage he'd so tenderly wrapped around her hand. "The children were all panicked and crying, and I remember seeing a little boy who was completely distraught over a stuffed puppy. His mother explained to me he'd had the puppy since he was eight months old, slept with it every night. It hit me then that while this was difficult for the adults, it was even worse on the kids. They don't have the ability to make sense of what happened. How can they, when even as adults, we can't?"

"I take it he didn't find the puppy."

She smiled. "No, he actually did. Dirty and missing an eye, but he found him. Ever since, though, I've carried around the box of stuffed animals in the SUV. These kids have lost everything, especially their sense of security. I figure I can give them back a little of that feeling with the teddy bears. Something to start over with."

"You really do a lot of good, Gayle. I see that now."

The praise made her uncomfortable, and she gave a slight shrug. She didn't do it for glory. She did it because it was the right thing to do. Lots of chasers did what she did. "I can't imagine what they've been through. I have never gone through what these people—what *you*—have experienced. I have no idea what it's like to crawl out of the rubble, or open the door to a storm shed and see everything familiar to me gone."

"But you lost your family in a tornado."

"Yeah, but I wasn't with them. I was away at college. It was—" Closing her eyes, she inhaled deeply, controlling the pain that immediately surfaced. Seven years later, and it still hurt to talk about it. "It was my birthday, and they were driving down to surprise me. They got caught on the interstate. Had nowhere to go, nowhere to hide. They were stuck. The damn tornado ripped right through my family and my high school sweetheart."

His face was wreathed in empathy. "Hell. I'm sorry."

She swallowed the lump of emotions stuck in her throat. "I often wonder what they were thinking in those final moments. I know they had to be terrified, but were they thinking of me, wishing they'd taken a different way, stopped for lunch…?" Her voice broke and she pressed her lips together.

She tried not to think about that day too often, but days like this made it hard for the memories to stay repressed. Amazing how she was the one sitting here so helpless, and Mac seemed to be so strong after what he'd gone through. But, after one of these big twisters that leveled towns, it sometimes took a few days to collect herself. It was like the past came roaring back and all the questions that had haunted her the last few years refused to leave until she could get back into her routine and tuck them away again.

"I wasn't even aware they were killed until two days after the tornado." Her vision swam with unshed tears.

Mac's hand found her lower back and rubbed circles, but he remained silent, for which she was thankful. For the most part she dealt with these moments alone. It felt good finally to get them out.

"For two days I was hurt and angry they didn't remember my birthday. I left some nasty voicemails I can never take back, but I thought they were safe, thought they'd just forgotten me." She stared straight ahead. "Twenty people died in that storm. It didn't level any homes or hit any towns, but it crossed a busy interstate and took twenty people's lives. I even watched it on TV, having no clue my family and boyfriend were dead."

"Jesus, I'm sorry, Gayle." He tugged her to his side and kissed the top of her head.

"They were all I had. We were close, too. Sam and I had dated since high school, and somehow had made a long distance relationship work when I went off to college. I was so lost afterward. My home—the place where I'd grown up, had celebrated birthdays, Thanksgiving, and Christmas—was still standing, but the day I returned it was just a shell. The people who'd made it a home were gone." She pulled away to look at Mac. "I suppose if you think about it, our reactions weren't so different. I sold our house. I haven't been back to my hometown since. I threw myself into my studies like you threw yourself into fighting, and I started chasing the season after they died. I'm determined to further tornado research and, in the process, if I have the chance to save one life directly in the path of Mother Nature's destruction, then I'm going to save that life. Nobody should have to die like that. The people I loved shouldn't have died like that."

She laid her head on his chest, and he was silent for a long time.

Then he whispered, "No. No one should."

CHAPTER TEN

The next afternoon, Mac was using a chainsaw to cut through a tree that blocked a street. After the tree trunk split in half, he released the lever and let the engine idle as he searched for Gayle among the volunteers and displaced homeowners. He found her, standing with an older woman, picking through a pile of wreckage. He'd checked her whereabouts a lot over the course of the day. He needed her within sight at all times… although it bothered him how much he stressed over her well-being. A little worry was healthy, but this was borderline obsessive. He ran his arm across his forehead, wiping off the sweat.

The morning and most of the afternoon had passed fairly quickly. Rick was hauling debris to the side of the street, while Mac was helping wherever someone needed him. Gayle had mostly hopped from person to person doing the thing Gayle did best—making them feel special while helping search for whatever missing items they hoped to find in the rubble.

Just as he was about to go back to sawing again, a ginger-headed man with rounded glasses came striding toward him with the little girl from yesterday in his arms. She was still clutching the teddy Gayle had given her, her face buried in its fur. The man didn't say anything. Just put the little girl down, then grabbed Mac in a bear hug.

He didn't question the man, knowing he had to be the husband of the woman he'd freed yesterday. He clapped the man on the back and let him hug his fill.

When he released Mac, he stepped back and picked up the little girl again. "I'm Dennis King. You saved my wife."

Mac gave him a compassionate smile. "I'm thankful I could help."

"I was at work. I was on the phone with Brandi as it hit. I thought I'd lost them both. Never felt so helpless in all my life. When I saw the neighborhood…the house"—the man swallowed heavily—"th-thank you." He looked as though he might break down any second.

"You're more than welcome," Mac said, then gave him a moment to regroup by glancing over at Gayle.

She had stopped sifting and stood watching him. A sad, encouraging smile came to her lips. No matter what, she was always strong for everyone around her. Last night had been an anomaly for her—a moment of weakness he might never see again, because that wasn't who she was. She was strength and dominance wrapped up in a small package. He'd never be able to forget what she'd shared with him last night, or the connection he'd felt with her on far more than a sexual level. Two people who'd had to learn to move on after losing those closest to them, and in such a similar way. Only someone who had gone through it could understand. It was a rare thing.

"How is your wife?" Mac asked the man when he seemed to have gathered himself.

"She had to have surgery. Her hip was completely crushed.

She broke a couple of ribs, too, and sprained her wrist really badly, but her prognosis is good."

"I'm glad to hear that," Mac said. He smiled down at the little girl, who was carefully studying the bear. "How are you doing?"

She looked up, her face somber. "I miss my momma."

"I'll bet she misses you, too, a whole lot. I see you still have your teddy bear."

She hugged it tight. "We get to sleep in the big bed with Daddy at Nana's."

He suspected the little girl would probably have many nights sleeping close to her father. The man knew what he'd come close to losing and would be forever changed because of it.

"So, you're staying at your nana's."

"Nana made me cupcakes for dinner. We took some to Momma."

The father smiled down at her. "She loved them, didn't she, pumpkin?"

The girl brightened a little as she nodded.

"What do you think you'll do now?" Mac asked him, glancing at the empty place where the man's house once stood.

The guy stared out over the flattened land. "Rebuild. Brandi and I met here, got married, and made a family here. Neither of us can imagine living anywhere else."

Would Mac have done the same thing if things had ended differently? That hadn't been his path, though. His path had led him—

Again his eyes found Gayle. She was chatting with the older woman now, who was actually laughing.

He didn't exactly know what place she was meant to have in his life...or what she should be to him. Maybe nothing more than the person who brought him back to life and helped him move on. But he would always have a connection with her, especially after this experience. And somehow, he didn't find that connection as frightening as he once did.

"I wish you and your family all the best," Mac said.

"We wish the same to you."

"Daddy, look. It's Gayle."

"Want to go say hi, sweetie?" The little girl nodded, and the man looked at Mac again, sincerity etched in every cell of his face. It reached deep inside Mac. "Thank you. If there's ever anything…"

Mac smiled and shook his hand, then the man strode off toward Gayle. She gave him a warm smile that squeezed Mac's chest. The man lowered his daughter, and Gayle squatted and returned the hug Sophie flung at her, then said something animatedly that banished the somber little face and earned a genuine smile from the girl.

Gayle would make a great mother one day.

But how would she ever be able to juggle family life with her dangerous profession? Though Mac had seen the true benefits of her storm chasing, he was also acutely aware of the risks. Carried the bruises on his back from the hail yesterday as a reminder. If he hadn't been there, the hail could've seriously hurt her or worse. How could she continue putting herself in danger if she got pregnant? Or with a family back home waiting for her?

Why did the very idea twist his stomach?

And which part of it didn't set well with him? The idea of a family worried sick over her every time she headed out to chase a storm? Or the thought of her family not including *him*…?

Nope. The last thought didn't set well with him, at all.

However, he was *not* staying in Kansas. And no matter how he may or may not feel about Gayle, he wasn't prepared to live the life of a chaser's spouse, or even significant other.

A special friend with benefits? Sure. He was definitely up for that.

But anything more...there was no possible way.

CHAPTER ELEVEN

Groaning, Gayle shuffled into her house and closed the door. *Finally.* They'd stayed out an extra two days helping the little town with cleanup and had just driven back home this afternoon. After almost a week of living in the SUV and run-down motels, eating fast food or whatever they could grab at a convenience store, she was ready for a long, hot bath with a big glass of wine and her own bed—where she planned to sleep for the next forty-eight hours.

Hopefully.

She and Mac had fallen into a routine the last few days. They'd return to the motel, shower, and then make love before she fell asleep with his warm body curled behind her. Mac had slept peacefully since the tornado, no nightmares, no calling out, and because of that, she'd awoken each morning still wrapped in his arms. She'd gotten used to it. It would be weird being back in the real world, with he over at Lance's and she at her own home.

It was better that way, though. Mac was getting under her skin in a major way, and her time with him was ticking down.

If she didn't watch herself, she was going to be in for one hell of a rude adjustment when he left.

Too bad those reminders didn't stop her falling straight back into his arms every time he touched her. She loved having him touch her. Anywhere. Everywhere. Loved how her body responded whether they were taking their time or going at it like two people who were never going to fuck again.

Her nipples tightened thinking about how he took her—over and over. She couldn't remember a time when her body anticipated a man the way it did him. Was ready for him as soon as he walked into a room.

Maybe it was her age.

She'd heard the older a woman got the more her libido went into overdrive. And, damn, her libido was definitely in overdrive for that man.

She tugged her small suitcase up the stairs, went into her room and straight into the bathroom. After turning on the faucet and adjusting the water, she made her way into the kitchen and poured a glass of wine. Wandering back to her bedroom, she put her iPod into the deck and sifted through her song collection until soft classical music filled the air. She really wasn't in the mood for lyrics right now.

As she slipped into the claw-foot tub, the hot water welcomed her. Sighing, she leaned her head back against the rim and closed her eyes.

No thinking. No memories. Just the symphony of Canon in D soothing her as it always did. No matter how negative a mood she was in, the opus of violins swept it away with peace and calmness. After her family died, she'd spent months listening to it repeatedly, not understanding why it seemed to be the only thing that helped. It wasn't until her grief became manageable that the reason had hit her. Every night for as long as she could remember, Pachelbel's Canon had played softly in the background during family dinner. Listening to it made her feel connected to them—still to this day.

The classical piece had played four times before she got busy shaving her legs and scrubbing her body. Feeling truly clean for the first time in days, she belted a terrycloth robe around her and started to go back downstairs. Halfway down, a delicious scent made her mouth water.

He hadn't.

A small smile threatened and she bit her bottom lip, trying to keep it from blossoming. As she crept toward the kitchen, the aroma became stronger. When she stepped inside, she found a freshly showered Mac standing at her stove, cooking away. The sight was beautiful. His face was drawn in concentration as he flipped something in a pan. She leaned against the doorjamb, watching him. If he was as masterful in the cage as he was in the kitchen, he must surely win every fight. She looked forward to watching him in the cage one day.

He'll be gone before you get the chance.

The reminder stung but, knowing the truth of it, she pushed off the frame and moved closer to him. This thing between them was temporary. She'd been lucky to get even this much. He'd completely shut her out before the chase; at least now she was getting to spend time with the man.

And she was used to temporary. Comfortable with it. She would enjoy all the stuff they shared, right up to the end.

"*Mmm*, nothing hotter than a man cooking."

He sent her a half-cocked smile. "You like this, *huh*?"

"You better watch it, handsome, or I'm going to make sure you burn whatever it is you're concentrating so hard on over there."

"Hard is right. But not over the potatoes."

When she reached his side, he turned his body toward her and she wrapped her arms around his neck. The evidence of his arousal pressed into her belly. "Oh. Yes. Very hard," she whispered.

"Woman, you're going to be the death of me." He gave her a swift kiss and smacked her ass. "Go away. I can't focus when you're so close. I need to feed you first."

She sashayed around the counter and did his bidding. "What are we having?"

"We've had nothing but crap for the last week. So, I thought a good home-cooked meal was in order tonight."

"Handsome, the last thing you cook is home-cooked meals. Julia Child couldn't whip together the meals you make."

He grinned. "Go ahead and continue stroking the ego. I don't mind."

She waggled her brows. "That's not all I'd like to stroke."

"Stop," he said, pointing a spatula at her, but amusement and heat warmed his eyes.

"Fine." She mock-pouted. "I'll behave. For now." He flipped some kind of potato patty. "Seriously, what are we having?"

"Roasted chicken with chardonnay and fresh herbs, potato galette and asparagus with brown buttered breadcrumbs."

"Ah, so another blah-blee-blue."

A chortle came from him. "Yeah, that."

"Well, if it's as good as the last time, I can't wait."

Mac worked over the stove for a while, then asked, "What are you doing tomorrow night?"

She rested her chin on a hand. "Sounds like I'm spending it with you."

His gaze darted to her, then he *tsk*ed softly, shaking his head. "You don't even know what I'm about to ask you."

"Doesn't matter. I'm game."

He studied her for a moment. "You really don't back away from anything, do you?"

The smile she gave felt more strained than usual. He was actually dead wrong. Mac had the ability to break her heart. She'd had enough heartbreak to last a lifetime, so she was deliberately backing away from that possibility—and fast. Keeping things light and sexually charged was all she would allow herself to give him.

She shrugged. "Just call me curious. If you're wanting me to do something with you, I'm intrigued enough to want to go."

"There's a fight tomorrow night. It's a local MMA circuit. Lance signed up about two months ago to fight, and honestly, I'm itching to get back inside the cage, so Lance is going to see if they'll fit me in. Not sure yet if they will, but either way, we'll get to see some fights."

"Why wouldn't they let you fight?"

"These are smaller circuits, Gayle. While they have some decent fighters with great potential, they may have only fought a handful of amateur fights and a couple pro-level fights. I'm part of the biggest cage fighting organization in the world. I really have an unfair advantage."

"Oh, I'm pretty sure there will be at least one guy there who'll be more than willing to fight Mac 'The Snake' Hannon and gladly take the ass-beating just for the bragging rights."

A soft laugh. "Looking at it that way, you're probably right."

"You won't get into trouble with your contract or anything?"

He shook his head. "As long as they're not advertising me and I don't accept money or wear sponsor gear, I'm good."

"So I finally get to see you in action, huh? And this will be my first actual fight, too. Hot."

"I'll show you hot afterward."

She grinned. "Oh. I'm counting on it."

Mac plated the food, handed one to her, and she sat down at the table. As her gaze bounced between the beautifully golden chicken breast and the crispy potato patty, she couldn't decide where to start. Her stomach grumbled in protest. She finally dug in to the potatoes and her taste buds shot to their feet, cheering. Jesus, the man could cook.

"How is it?" Mac asked.

She paused in chewing and sent him an incredulous look. "Really? You seriously have to ask?"

Chuckling, he cut into his chicken and took a bite. They ate without speaking, because there was no talking when consuming Mac's meals. She savored every delish morsel of the amazing talent he no longer shared with the public. It really was a damn shame.

As she enjoyed the food, she watched him eat—watched his lips part, then close around the fork, his jaw work as he chewed. He made even the simple act of eating hot as hell.

So much so, when she felt the belt of her robe loosen, instead of tightening it, she left it alone, shifting occasionally to encourage more slacking. Slowly the robe began to gape, widening until it hung off one shoulder and displayed the top of her breast. If the way Mac kept pausing during chews was any indication, he'd noticed. She pretended to be oblivious.

As much as she loved it when Mac took his time with her, right now she throbbed for a mauling. She hoped with this tease, she'd either be up against a wall or bent over a table as soon as they finished dinner. The moment he placed his fork on his plate, she stood and leaned over, letting the front gap as she gathered the plates. He stilled, his gaze latching onto her.

Fighting a smirk of triumph, she straightened. As she turned, the weak knot barely keeping the robe closed gave way completely, and the fabric fell open. With her back to him, he couldn't see, but he knew she was now exposed. The ultimate tease. She couldn't have planned that better if she'd tried. And, one…two…three…

His chair scraped against the hardwood.

Pursing her lips in satisfaction, she continued to the sink, listening to his steps advancing behind her.

When it came to sex, she and Mac were totally eye-to-eye.

Knowing she was seconds from having him attack her, she quickly placed the dishes in the sink. They had not even stopped rattling before his arms were around her, his hands roaming over her bare stomach as he buried his lips into the side of her neck, nipping along the sensitive skin. Cupping both breasts in his large, capable hands, he kneaded the mounds, then tweaked both nipples. Pleasure rushed straight down to pulse at her clit. She gasped, leaning her head back against his chest. God, she *loved* when he did that.

As he ground his cock against her ass, making her rub against him, making her throb harder for him, he slid his palms over her belly until they rested on her hips, and he started walking them backward. When they'd cleared the counter, he turned and started moving forward. The entire time his lips trailed across her neck and shoulder, sucking on the skin. Closing her eyes, she reached behind her and threaded her hand in his hair, holding his face closer to her. Pressing her backside to the hard ridge poking her from behind. She throbbed for him. Needed him.

The kitchen table met the top of her thighs. He pushed her down with a hand in the middle of her back and she went without protest, laying her cheek on the cool wood. He shoved the robe up off her backside and she widened her stance, anticipating his invasion, waiting for him to fill her in one quick thrust.

There wouldn't be foreplay, touching, or caressing. This was going to be hard and fast. And she enjoyed that as much as she did gentle and slow. Prone as she was, and with him behind her, she was at his mercy. He controlled everything, from the pace of how he took her, to how deep he went and how hard. Knowing that only increased her lust for him.

There was a rip of foil, then she felt him probing for her, the hard, wonderful head that would lead to the long, solid length of him inside her. She held her breath, waiting. Would he do it quick? Or agonizingly slow?

He took the slow option. One excruciating inch at a time. Wanting to have all of him buried inside her, she whimpered and pushed back, trying to shove him in, but a sharp smack on the ass stopped her. *Inflamed her.*

"*My* way, Gayle." He slipped a little farther inside and a groan erupted from him. Her clit pulsed in response. "I want to feel every inch of you welcoming every inch of me."

When he finally had his pelvis pressed against the back of her thighs, cock embedded to the hilt, he ground against her. "Fuck me, woman, you feel so good."

He withdrew and thrust forward. A slow, methodical pace that continuously filled her to the brim, then left her empty, filled her, left her empty.

She moaned his name, helpless to do anything to make him speed up. She tried to lift up onto her elbows and met the resistance of his palm between her shoulder blades. He gently pushed her down and held her there, keeping the pressure of his hand on her back as he kept the torturous pace he'd set. "What do you want, Gayle?"

"F-faster."

"Slow not working for you?" He thrust harder, making her gasp.

"N-no." Again he withdrew slowly, then thrust forward hard. The impact on her clit made her groan as pleasure erupted through her.

"Really? You sure about that?" He did it again, and she cried out as pressure built between her legs. God, if he'd just go at it she'd come, but this slow build was keeping her right at the brink, building fuller and fuller inside her so she felt ready to explode…but she wasn't going over the edge. Again, he withdrew and thrust hard.

"Mac!" she groaned. "Please."

"Oh, you're going to get it, baby, but you have to pay for that little tease over dinner. Don't think I didn't know what you were doing."

She'd done this to herself. If she'd just left well enough alone, she'd be getting the taking she wanted, but instead Mac was teasing her as mercilessly as she'd teased him. There was no clit play, no end to the slow-withdrawal-and-hard-thrust pace he set. Just the increasing, almost uncomfortable, detonation building inside her.

Hell, if that was the way he was going to be—

She wedged her hand between her body and the table, intent on relieving herself, since he was being so mean. All she got in was one awesome groan-inducing rub before strong fingers snatched her hand away and held it fast on the table beside her head.

"You want me to fuck you, don't you?" he asked.

"Yes!"

"I will, but you have to come first."

That's what she was trying to do. *Jerk!*

"Think about what you want, Gayle. You want me going hard, like this," he thrust forward again. A smack filled the air as their skin met. "But faster, right?"

Almost painfully aroused, all she could do was curl her hands into fists and nod.

"Faster like this?"

He gave her a few seconds of hard and fast, and just as the sensation of pending release gave her hope, he slowed again. In frustration, she yelled, "Damn it, Mac!" She thumped her fist on the table. His responding chuckle was grounds for a good smacking.

"I'll give you what you want. All you have to do is come."

It wasn't going to happen. He had her so aroused, wound so tight, so ready for release, all she could do was whimper her need for it. And with the way he continued his slow onslaught, he had no intention of reaching around to give her the stimulation she needed to push her over the edge. She needed to touch herself, she needed *him* to touch her.

"Imagine it, Gayle. I just gave you a taste of it. Think about it. Think about how that felt."

And she did, the sensation of him pushing deep inside her, fast and hard, the pull on the sensitive skin of her inner walls, the feel of him circling her clit. And everything inside her clenched.

He groaned and ground out, "That's fucking it, baby, keep imagining it just that way. Tighten around me more."

His words, the images he'd made her paint in her head, had her entire body shaking from the need for release. She pictured him with his hands on her hips. The bite of his fingers into her skin as he relentlessly bucked into her. Heard the sounds of their flesh smacking from the power of each thrust, their pleasure melding. The tip over the edge was slow, but she felt herself go. The orgasm started softly and built in force with each thrust until she cried out from the intensity as it tightened every muscle in her body.

Mac growled behind her with a guttural, "Yes."

The energy shot out of her, taking every bone in her body with it, and he let loose behind her, giving her everything she'd begged for. All she could do was groan over and over, "Oh, God. Oh, God. "

Every sensation was heightened, every touch, every thrust, *everything*, and she found herself wound just as tight as she'd been only seconds before, whimpering for release again. This time, he circled her throbbing clit with his glorious fingers. She immediately fell into another orgasm. His low moan signaled his release as his thrust slowed. He braced both hands on either side of her body and rested his forehead on her lower back, his breathing choppy.

For a minute they both stayed still, then he eased up and helped her rise. Her legs shook as he lifted her to sit on the table. She flinched as her oversensitive center met the hard wood.

A supremely masculine expression crossed Mac's face. "A little tender?"

"Tender? Really? My vajajay is screaming, 'Let's do that again.'"

Mac threw his head back and laughed, then he moved between her parted thighs and kissed her. Long and slow. His tongue swept across hers as his palm cradled the side of her face. She wrapped her arms around his neck as he shifted closer.

She couldn't get enough of him.

Was worried she never would.

And where would that leave her?

She broke the kiss and pressed her forehead against the middle of his chest, trying to collect herself.

His body tensed against hers, letting her know he'd picked

up on her change. "Hey, you okay?"

Inhaling, she looked up and saw the concern in his eyes.

"I didn't hurt you, did I?"

Not yet, he hadn't, but one day he could. Badly.

She attempted a smile. "Just wore me out completely."

"We've had a really long week. Why don't we call it a night?"

"That sounds like a good idea."

After he helped her clean up, she expected him to tell her good-bye and go back to Lance's. Instead he laced his fingers with hers and led her upstairs.

And she didn't have the strength to send him home.

CHAPTER TWELVE

After being with CMC, Mac had forgotten the crazy setup of the smaller circuits. The event he, Gayle, and Lance were headed to was being held outside at a popular bar and grill in Wichita. A portion of the parking lot had been sectioned off and about a hundred folding chairs surrounded a cage. Already the area was packed with people. A bunch of them were standing since all the seats had long since been filled.

To keep a low profile, Mac had worn a baseball cap. If they let him fight, it wouldn't be long before everyone realized who he was, and he'd rather spend time with Gayle than be swarmed by well-meaning but persistent fans.

As they followed Lance into the bar, Mac wrapped his arm around her bare shoulders and brought her close to his side. She didn't hesitate to melt into him. He loved that about her. She just gave over everything freely, without thought, without question. Pride at having her on his arm swelled through him, especially as he noted some appreciative once-overs from other men as they walked by. In a black corset-type halter top and short jean skirt, she looked like walking dynamite. He couldn't blame the men for noticing her.

They could look all they wanted. Gayle was his.

This morning, he'd enjoyed waking up beside her, had enjoyed even more sneaking downstairs and cooking her breakfast while she slept. Afterward, she'd spent the morning watching him and Lance train, and then he'd spent the rest of the stormy afternoon with her, kissing his way down her body without one thought to the crashing thunder and flashing lightning.

And he'd come to realize that what Lance had told him from day one was right.

Gayle *was* good for him.

Not only for letting go of the past, but also thinking of a future…with her.

The idea terrified him, but when they'd gotten home the day before yesterday and he'd gone to Lance's and she'd returned to her place, he'd missed her. Like crazy. It hadn't taken much for him to find his way over to her place with a bag full of groceries from his friend's fridge.

He hadn't left her side since.

Though there was fear lurking in such closeness, having her beside him felt right. Made him believe that as long as he had her he could do anything—possibly even including moving back to Kansas.

Of course, then he'd think about the storm chasing and how close she'd come to being hurt, and his gut twisted. Even though she took every precaution, it was still too damn dangerous.

Yet she did so much good with her job.

He was so fucking torn on how he felt about it.

He looked down at her. No reason to mull over it now. They still had a few weeks together before any big decisions needed to be made. Best see how things played out before he got wrapped up in all the other stuff.

Just enjoy being with her and how she made him feel.

"Man, with you incognito like this I feel all special," she whispered.

Chuckling, he hugged her tighter. Lance pushed aside a black tarp that hung at the back of the bar and held it aside as Mac and Gayle ducked underneath. Behind it were a registration table and the group of fighters with the coaches waiting for the event to start. Lance sauntered up to the coordinator.

Mac waited until his friend pointed over at him, then removed his cap.

"Holy shit," the coordinator muttered.

"I was hoping I could get in on the action tonight."

The man grimaced. "The cards are full. I don't have anyone available to fight you."

Damn. He figured that was the way it would go, but he was disappointed, nonetheless. The ego wanted to show off his manliness in front of Gayle. Though he got to do that during training, it wasn't the same as the raw testosterone of a real fight. Yeah, he was all man in bed, but after the emotional crap she'd witnessed him struggle with, he wanted her to see him as a man in life, too.

"I'll fight his sorry ass." A deep, gravelly voice boomed from behind him.

Mac twisted around and exhaled in a burst of surprise. "Fuck me. Are you serious?" He released Gayle to pound the back of the powerhouse of a man he hadn't seen in years. "Man, what are you doing here?"

"I own a training facility in Wichita. A few of my guys are on the card tonight."

"That's great, man." He couldn't believe Ragin was here. They'd trained together back in the day, when Mac was treating MMA as more of a hobby than a career. Ragin had never gone pro, had stuck with the coaching route. The six-foot tall, light-haired man was still rock solid. "I see getting older hasn't softened you any."

"Nah. I'm stronger at forty-one than I was in my twenties."

"Have you gotten in the cage with a kid?"

"I'm about to, ain't I? Think your young ass can keep up with my old one?" He nodded at the coordinator. "What do you say, Trent? Surprise everyone with a special last minute fight? I think the fans will dig it."

Mac grinned. He dug it, too. He just hoped he wouldn't pound the guy too far into the dirt.

Lance helped Mac tape his hands and put on his gloves. His friend sported a nice shiner under his left eye from his fight a bit earlier, but other than one good clock from his opponent, his friend had dominated the other man—a more skilled and *younger* fighter.

"You didn't need me to come out here," Mac said. "Submissions you've been struggling with during training, you executed flawlessly. What have you been doing? Faking it while we trained?"

Lance stilled guiltily for a second, then he shoved the last glove on Mac's hand. "No. I didn't need you here," he finally admitted.

"Then why ask me?"

"Because I missed you and I was worried about you." His friend straightened and met Mac's gaze. "I couldn't figure out any other way to get you to come here willingly. The fight seemed like the perfect excuse."

Mac was silent for a long moment. "Thank you."

"Wow." Lance shook his head. "Gayle really has done wonders for you."

"Gayle has done a lot, but it's not been all her. It's being back in Kansas and having you all up in my grill. Nobody else does that kind of shit to me, Lance, just you. If you hadn't decided to be a lying, sneaky bastard, I'd still be in my apartment in Atlanta haunted by the past." He pulled his friend forward and beat a fist against his shoulder blade in a bro hug. "I love ya, man."

"Yeah. Yeah. Feeling's mutual," Lance muttered as he returned a couple of thumps to Mac's back.

They broke apart, and Mac studied his friend. "I don't guess your money situation…" He let his sentence trail off, hating himself for even bringing it up, but he hoped the reason his friend had been so adamant on not accepting any financial help was because he didn't really need it.

Lance gave a weary smile, but there wasn't any resentment at him for bringing up the topic. "I wish I'd been faking that, too, buddy, but no, I still owe a shitload of money. And I'm still banking on getting into CMC to help." He cleared his throat. "But enough of this heart-to-heart shit. Go out there and kick Ragin's ass."

Mac nodded as he popped in his mouth guard. After going out the back entrance, he followed a roped-off area that led to the cage. A guy in jeans stood in the middle with a microphone. As Mac started passing people, the whispers started. Multiple, "Holy shit. Did you see who that was?" and, "Fucking-A! It's Mac 'The Snake' Hannon!" made him smile. His tattoos made him easily recognizable to any fan of CMC.

He jogged up the stairs and through the cage's door. He scanned the area for Gayle and found her sitting in the front row—something he'd made sure would happen as soon as

Trent agreed to let him and Ragin fight. What he didn't expect to see was some motherfucker sitting next to her hitting on her hardcore. She was not encouraging the attention. If anything, she was discouraging him, but the asshole wouldn't take the hint. As he laid a hand on her knee, which she smacked away, Mac started for the exit. Lance held up his hand to stop him. His best friend walked over to the man, squeezed his shoulder roughly, and said something in the fucker's ear. He beat a hasty retreat and Lance took the empty seat. The tension eased out of Mac.

"We have a special treat for you guys and gals tonight! Mac 'The Snake' Hannon is in the house." The place went nuts. "He's agreed to fight the well-respected and fucking awesome, Ragin Coolier." Wild applause and screaming roared around them as the announcer turned to them. "You guys know the rules, go fight." He left the cage.

Not used to the casual introduction, Mac shook his head. Ragin raised his arm and Mac tapped his glove to the other fighter's, showing his respect. Then the fight was on.

Until that very second, he hadn't realized how much of a disadvantage he was really at. Usually he spent weeks to months preparing for a fight, which included studying his opponent. He had no idea what Ragin's strengths or weaknesses were, what he could use to his advantage, or what could be used against him. This was a blind fight...and it energized the hell out of him.

He threw the first jab, catching Ragin on the cheek. The hit seemed to light a fire under the old man, as well, and he returned the favor. The next two minutes were an all-out brawl. There weren't any clenches against the cage, no knees, no kicks. The fight stayed in the middle of the canvas and consisted of two men punching the ever-loving shit out of each other. Blows were given with so much strength the impact cracked loudly, making the crowd cringe and yell, "*Ohhh!*" A few shots were missed, others dodged. By the end of the first round, Mac was covered in sweat and was blinking blood out of his right eye. Ragin didn't look any better, with a gash opened up across the bridge of his nose.

One thing was for fucking sure, his old buddy still had one hell of a punch. Lance came up in the cage, while a couple of guys from another team helped stop the blood from the cut on his brow and give him water.

"You should hear Gayle squealing. It's fucking hilarious."

"Really?"

"Oh, yeah. Flinching, slapping her hands to her face, muttering 'crazy idiot,' the whole nine yards."

Mac gave a pained laugh. "The woman can walk into the eye of a tornado without blinking, but can't watch the man she's sleeping with take a punch? Who'da thought?"

Lance clapped him on the shoulder and trotted out of the cage to rejoin Gayle.

As the second round commenced, Mac and Ragin circled around each other. Mac threw a couple of soft jabs to feel out the other fighter. Ragin just weaved back and forth. Apparently, he wasn't up for another slugfest. That was just fine with Mac. He dove into the fighter's side, taking him off his feet and crashing him to the canvas on his back. Within seconds, he had Ragin's arm locked in an arm bar. Immediately, he felt four quick taps to his shoulder. The referee waved his arms, signaling the end of the fight, and Mac released him.

Ragin pounded him on the back. "There's a reason you made it into the CMC, Hannon. You're tough as fucking nails. If you ever decide to move up this way, I'd love to have you in my gym."

And there was that moving topic again.

"It's definitely something to consider."

As he walked out, Gayle and Lance came rushing up. She searched his face and kept coming back to rest on his eyebrow. "Are you okay?"

"Trust me, I've been a lot worse."

"I knew MMA was about fighting, but seeing it firsthand — holy shit. Are you *sure* you're okay?"

"I'm fine. Let me get cleaned up and I'll meet you guys in the bar. I could use a beer."

He gave Gayle a quick kiss, then hurried back inside the area behind the tarp. The wife of one of the fighters, who also happened to be an ER nurse, was volunteering. Knowing he needed at least to get the wound taped, he sat down.

She cleaned it and put a butterfly bandage over it. "Looks like you took some good hits out there." She peered at him. "Along the jaw and the nose."

"Ragin packs quite a punch," he said as he stood up. "Thanks."

In fact, he had a slight headache. Nothing a couple of aspirin wouldn't cure, but it had been a long time since he'd had his noggin rung hard enough in the cage to leave a dull throb in it.

After he showered and changed back into his jeans and T-shirt, he stepped into the bar. Rock music was thumping from the speakers. Some of the fighters had stayed to enjoy the rest of the night. The place was jamming. He ordered a beer from the bartender, then scanned the room for Lance and Gayle. Neither of them were to be found. A momentary sense of panic rushed over him, then rational thought took control. Gayle probably had to go to the bathroom and Lance had escorted her there so she didn't get hit on by any more men. That made sense. Something bad happening to her, didn't.

"I saw you kissin' Gayle."

At the intrusive voice, Mac glanced over. The brown-haired motherfucker who'd dared touch Gayle was standing beside him. Sort of. The man reeked of alcohol, and he swayed alarmingly. A glassy sheen of inebriation glazed his eyes.

Goddammit, this was all he needed.

"What the fuck do you want?" he asked with no attempt to cover his hostility. Seemed the old Mac was still in there.

"*Ah*. You did see me hittin' on her." Chuckling, the jackass shrugged. "Can't blame a man for tryin'. So you're her current boy toy. Go, Gayle."

This drunk ass was seriously starting to get on Mac's nerves. He took a long swallow of beer, eyes sweeping the bar for her. And then she was there, stepping out from the hallway where the bathrooms were.

The guy grunted appreciatively. "*Damn*, I miss that fuckin' body."

Taken aback by the audacity of the man, sloshed out of his senses or not, Mac slowly turned his head and glared at him. "Dude. Are you fucking *asking* to get your teeth shoved down your throat?"

"What? I only got a piece of that a couple of times." He smacked Mac on the back like they were buddies. "Enjoy it while it lasts, bro, 'cause she's gonna drop you fast and then you'll be just like me, wishin' for one more round." As Gayle neared them, he muttered, "Hell, why not?"

Next thing Mac knew, Gayle was in the drunk's arms, his mouth all over hers, and Mac saw red. Slamming down his glass, he yanked the fucker around and clocked him one on the jaw. The drunk crumbled on the spot. Mouth dropped open, Gayle stared down, then looked up at Mac with an expression that clearly said, "What the *hell* are you doing?" then stared back down at the guy.

Mac threw up his hands. What the fuck had he done wrong? *He* wasn't the one mauling her, that asshole was.

"Kevin," she said as she stooped beside him. Hot, potent jealousy flared bright at her obvious concern for the dickweed. "Are you okay?"

Mac clenched his teeth.

Kevin rubbed his jaw. "Holy shit. Gayle, did you see that? I just had a CMC fighter punch me. How fucking cool is that?"

She rolled her eyes. "He's fine."

As she stood, she didn't even glance in Mac's direction, just marched her beautiful, furious ass out of the bar. And all Mac could do was follow, wondering where the fuck he'd gone wrong.

The tension in the car was palpable. Gayle shook her foot with all the anger she was feeling as she stared out the window of the back seat. While Mac drove, Lance fiddled with the music stations, most likely because he wanted out of the car.

Gayle did not understand what had crawled up Mac's ass. Yeah, Kevin had kissed her. He was drunk. There had been no reason to punch him, especially when throwing the hardest, fastest punch was how Mac made a living. It was totally unfair and uncalled for. That was probably the first punch Kevin had ever taken. If Mac would've just chilled out for a damn minute, she would've handled the situation on her own.

Mac parked the Jeep behind Lance's house. His friend jumped out and was gone within seconds. She opened her door, intent on doing the same.

"Stay in the car, Gayle."

She stared at the back of his head. Yeah, she found the

dominating thing hot in bed, but now? Not so much.

"Yeah. Screw you, Mac."

She hopped out, slammed the door, sent him an eat-shit expression through the driver's side window, then stormed off across the field.

She'd made it halfway to her house before he came up behind her.

"You are such a pain in the ass!" he yelled.

She turned but continued walking backward. "Why? Because I didn't obey and sit like a good doggie? If you want me to stick around while *you* are being a complete pain in the ass, don't *tell* me what to do, *ask* me, or you're going to get the exact opposite. Do you understand?"

He thrust a hand through his hair and inhaled deeply. "You're right. I apologize. Gayle, I would like to talk about tonight please."

"That's better." She stopped. "What the hell got into you?"

He strode up to her, put his hand on her lower back, pivoted her around again, and led her to the bottom step of her stoop. He linked his fingers between his knees and hung his head. "I got jealous."

"There was no reason to be jealous of Kevin."

"It wasn't actually him. It was something he said to me before you walked up."

"What?"

"He told me to enjoy you now, because you would drop me and move on fast. He called me your current boy toy."

"Did he, now?"

"He also alluded to the fact he'd like a second go at you, right before he grabbed and kissed you, thus, my momentary chest-pounding moment." He was silent for a moment. "You date a lot, it seems."

It was a statement, but she answered, "Yes," anyway.

"Why?"

As long as they were being brutally honest… "Better to be the leaver than the leavee."

She could almost hear his teeth grind. "I'm hoping there's more behind those words than smug bitch."

Gayle exhaled. Was she really going to tell him all the sordid details? Studying his hanging head, she realized, yeah, she was. He already knew about Sam, and about him dying in the tornado with her family, but not the rest. Not the part that still drove her.

"Sam was my first love. We were together for almost eight years. We made it through a lot of hurdles most high school sweethearts can't get past. If he hadn't died, we'd be married now. But he did die. He left me. Not willingly, but that's what happened."

"It must have been tough on you."

Squinting, she looked out across the yard. "It took me a long time to date again, to dig out of the grief and find myself. Two years, in fact. Then I met Brian. We had a whirlwind relationship and I moved in with him four months later. A year after that, he kicked me out. Told me I was a cold woman who was too career-driven to be good wife material for any sane man."

Mac scowled. "Are you fucking kidding me?"

She shrugged. "I *was* working on my doctorate at the time." She pulled at a thread on her jeans. "So I picked up the pieces of my life for a second time. Six months later, I met Mark. We had tons in common. He had a master's in meteorology. He was also a storm chaser. We went on so many chases together. I thought maybe I'd finally met my kindred spirit. I loved Mark. Truly thought about a future for the first time since Sam died. We were together six months when I caught him in bed with a co-worker of his. His explanation? I knew how to have fun. But he needed someone more serious."

Mac swore, but a sarcastic laugh escaped her.

"For the third time in four years, my heart was broken. And I was tired of it. I've spent the last two years being Gayle Matthews. Making no connections, but enjoying a warm body from time to time, then moving on to the next. It works for me."

Mac was silent a long time. "And what about me?"

"What about you?"

"Me. Us. What about *us*?"

"Just a few weeks ago you made it extremely clear to me that this relationship is temporary, and you aren't looking for anything more. I thought we agreed that's what we both want. Has that changed?"

She held her breath. Why she wanted him to say it *had* changed was beyond her. The odds were stacked against them in every possible way, even if they attempted to make a go of...more.

He turned and regarded her seriously. "Honestly, I can't answer that yet. But I can tell you for the first time in four years, *I'm* thinking of a future—with you, Gayle."

She swallowed hard, her head warring with her heart. Her head won.

"How could it ever work between us, Mac? I'm not going to give up storm chasing. How could I ask you to live with my job when I know exactly how you'd feel every time I leave to go after a promising system? On top of that, I won't move away from Kansas. My life's work is here, which means you would have to come back here to live. What about *your* career? You would have to completely uproot yourself. Again."

He made a growling noise in his throat and looked away.

She peered at him for a long moment. "Seriously, can you see yourself accepting any of that? Truly accepting it?"

He turned to regard her. "I can train anywhere, Gayle. As for the rest of it, I've thought about all of that. Trust me, I've been thinking of nothing else lately. And…a part of me thinks I could."

A *part* thinks. Not that he'd actually do it. "So, you're still not sure."

"No, I'm not. But I *am* sure I'm starting to have feelings for you."

The desperation to put distance between them, the need to save herself from further inevitable heartache, had her trying to convince him otherwise. "Maybe you're just confused. Maybe all you're feeling is gratitude. Have you thought about that? I *am* the first woman you've met who's gotten past your defenses. Not tooting my own horn here, but…I didn't just get past them, I've brought them down."

He slowly nodded. "You have."

She turned toward him and took his hand. "You haven't had time to get to know *this* Mac yet—the type of man you'll be, now that you are no longer hiding behind those walls. I'm most likely nothing more than the wrecking ball that freed you."

"Or maybe you were the *only* one who could free me, because you were the only one with the power over me to do it. Maybe it's *you* I need in order to be the man I'll become."

Panic clawed at her chest. "What are you saying?"

"Something selfish. That I want the chance to figure all of this out without worrying you'll get scared and run. I want to be confident you're completely in this with me."

"So *you* can leave when you decide I'm no longer what you want."

Frustration crossed his face. "No. Damn it. My life has been turned upside down in the span of a month. I'm allowed to be confused. I didn't even want to come here—Kansas was the last place I ever wanted to be. Now? I'm actually thinking about moving back, and it scares the shit out of me."

"Mac—"

He held up a hand. "Four weeks ago, I hadn't so much as *looked* at another woman, and now I can't get you off my mind. I want to be with you every damn second. The idea of not seeing you hurts"—he thumped his fist right above his heart—"here. Over two weeks ago, I learned the woman who was getting under my skin faced down my worst nightmares for a damn living, and I wanted nothing to do with that shit."

He jabbed his fingers through his hair. She remained silent, her heart pounding.

He turned to her, looking almost awestruck. "And yet, here I am. I've been pelted by hail, almost swallowed alive by tornado-force winds, and helped rescue people from EF-5 destruction…when before the mere *thought* of those things made the past consume me. That day…back at the tornado, when that little girl tugged on my shirt… Gayle, she was the spitting image of Ally, and I was seeing the child I'd lost. I knew trying to find her mother was going to be one of the hardest things I'd ever done, but I felt like I'd been given a second chance for a reason."

"Oh, Mac."

"I might not be the most religious man, but I truly believe Ally reached out to me that day. Showed me a way to get past the guilt her death had burdened me with and move on."

The look in his eyes—the vanishing sadness, and the dawning seed of hope—nearly melted her heart.

"*None* of this has been easy, Gayle. It's been confusing as hell. The *only* thing I am certain about is I really do want to be with you, but I'm going to be upfront—the storm chasing is a huge problem."

"Are you asking me—"

"Never," he interrupted. "It's *my* issue. The chase we went on helped me with the past…but it also worried me about the future. What you do *is* dangerous. I keep remembering you screaming and covering you head when the windshield broke. Remembering how close we came to that tornado twisting right over us. I can't forget those things. And I'm not sure it's something I can live with. But, I'm trying my damndest to find a way to make that happen, okay?"

She heard the truth in his words. And was aware of one thing. If she agreed to his terms, she wouldn't be the only one putting her heart on the line. They both would be.

And somehow, that made all the pain they'd inevitably face at the end of all this just a little bit easier to bear.

She took a deep breath. "Okay," she agreed. "So, how do we do that?"

He swallowed heavily. Which made her suddenly nervous.

"I have an idea," he said. "Something I feel we both need to do, before either of us can be certain about the future."

She was almost afraid to ask. "Yeah?"

"I think it's time we both go back home," he said. "To face our pasts. So we both know we're ready to move forward."

She jerked up. "W-what?"

"I've spent years running from the past. You haven't been running as much as you've been trying to make up for it, to make it right. But we both need to stop for a minute and take a step back…and confront what we've been most afraid of."

"I'm not sure I understand."

"I know I'm not completely healed yet, but with your help

I've taken a huge step in the right direction. And you've been doing great with your life, pulling meaning out of tragedy. But you just admitted you have relationship issues."

She frowned. "I'm fine with my issues."

"Well, I'm not. I need to go back and face my issues. In my hometown. And I think you do, too."

She looked away and thought about that for several long minutes. Then she slowly nodded. "Back home. You may be right."

"After that, I'm just waiting for the next big system to hit and I'm going to stay behind."

CHAPTER THIRTEEN

Strong fingers entwined with Gayle's and squeezed as she stared at the two-story farmhouse she'd grown up in. She hadn't been here in so long...

Damn Mac for making her come back.

So many bittersweet emotions clogged her throat. The one that hit the hardest was that someone else lived here now. For eighteen years, she'd woken up and gone to sleep in this house. Even after she'd left for college, every holiday, every break, was spent under that roof. Until they'd all died and she'd been left utterly alone.

But now a new family was making sweet memories here. That was good, right?

"Come on." Mac tugged her hand as he took a step forward.

She remained rooted at the end of the driveway. "I-I don't think I can."

Already, the changes done to the outside felt wrong. All wrong. What would the inside be like? She'd probably lose it completely.

"Gayle, this is what we came for."

Tears burned her eyes. Oh, how the tables had turned. She'd spent weeks encouraging and helping Mac to let go of his past, and now he was encouraging *her*.

"The house used to be a soft, buttery yellow," she whispered. "Every few years, my dad would make me and Zoe—my sister—help him paint it. It was such a pain in the butt, and we hated every second of it."

Gray vinyl siding had now replaced the original wood, and she would've given anything to be painting side-by-side with her dad and sister again.

At least the owners took care of the place. From the immaculate lawn and the freshly weeded beds, she could tell they'd put their heart and soul into making the house a home.

Acknowledging that didn't make it hurt any less.

"Gayle. I'm not leaving you, baby. I'll be here every step of the way."

As she looked at Mac, his steadfastness and confidence flowed into her. Holding his gaze, she nodded, and he squeezed her hand again.

Together they walked up the driveway. The closer they got to the house, the more her resolve slipped. But instead of having to face it alone, she took what strength she needed from the man by her side, without guilt, without feeling weak…without hesitation. Confident he was giving support to her freely, just as she had in his moment of need.

A true couple, always there for each other when one of them couldn't face something alone.

New emotions flooded her chest, expanding it. She loved him. Probably had from the moment she'd soaked him with her water gun that very first time. Damn, but she loved Mac Hannon. Not just the Mac he had become, but the wounded man he once was, as well.

She rested her head on his bicep, a soft smile curving her lips as he kissed the top of her head.

I'm not leaving you, baby.

Only time would tell if those words were true, but in this moment, he was here and he wasn't leaving. And it was more than she'd had in a very long time.

Mac shouldn't have pressed her. As he and Gayle neared Emerald Springs, he understood a bit more of what she'd been going through earlier this morning as she'd stared at her childhood home.

He didn't *want* to see how Emerald Springs had changed, or remember why it had.

Even though she'd been resistant at first, the visit had ended up being healing for Gayle—or so she'd told him afterward. After the new homeowner had allowed them in, Gayle had cautiously stepped over the threshold. A soft, stuttered laugh had rushed out of her as she'd gazed around, filled with speechless happiness, and it had reached right into his chest and squeezed his heart.

According to Gayle, the décor had changed a lot. But the important details were still there—the staircase she and her sister used to clamber down each morning when their mom called them to breakfast, the window nook Gayle and her father used to curl up in to read a book together, the dining room where they'd eaten dinner as a family every night. The renovations hadn't changed all that, and Gayle had seemed so much lighter when they left.

He just had to keep telling himself that.

As they passed the WELCOME TO EMERALD SPRINGS sign,

Mac shifted uncomfortably in the passenger seat.

"How you doing over there?" Gayle asked.

"Nervous as fuck," he admitted. Whose idea had this been, anyway?

Oh, yeah. His.

She sent him an understanding smile. The most comforting thing was, she *did* understand. He reached over and took one of her hands off the steering wheel and entwined their fingers, linking them physically, just as they were emotionally.

"Where to first?"

His own healing journey would consist of two stops—the demolished neighborhood where he'd shared a home with Ally, and where the restaurant was that he'd been working in when the tornado had struck. According to Lance, the owners had rebuilt the restaurant, as had most of the other businesses. As for the neighborhood, he was sure what he was going to see.

"Let's get the neighborhood done first."

Nodding, she squeezed his fingers. As he gave her instructions, he started to notice the changes in the landscape where the tornado had torn through the town four years ago. The park that had been surrounded with lush, mature trees had been bulldozed. Young trees now dotted the area, and reconstructed shelters, bathrooms, and a playground stood proud amidst them. It wasn't the same, but it wasn't necessarily different, either. Not in spirit. He could still see himself out there playing Frisbee or grilling burgers.

Gayle was right. Even though the surroundings had changed, nothing could erase the memories he'd made there— the good memories.

A sense of peace washed over him.

As she turned into the neighborhood, he stared in stunned amazement. When he'd left, some of the owners had started to rebuild, some were still struggling with the decision to stay or go. Four years later, the community thrived with freshly built homes, pristine sidewalks, and bright flowering shrubs and trees. Had he not lived here, seen the destruction himself, he would never have believed every one of these homes had once been leveled.

The community had picked up the pieces of their lives and started over.

He knew it was high time he did so, himself.

"Take a right," he said.

Gayle remained silent as she took the turn. He appreciated that. He needed to just absorb all of this now. Talking would come later.

They approached the small piece of land where his home had once stood, and he whispered, "Slow down."

Nothing about it was the same. Nothing. Whoever had bought the lot of land had built a single-story ranch, replacing the two-story Cape Cod. An aboveground pool sparkled in the side yard where three kids ranging in age from about six to twelve splashed around. A mom and dad sat on the steps leading to a small porch, laughing. Someone had made the piece of land he associated with grief and death into something beautiful—they'd made it a home. Emotions almost got the best of him. Clearing his throat, he blinked.

"Do you want to get out?" Gayle asked softly.

"No. I've seen all I need to see."

"You want me to do *what*?" Mac blinked at Gayle. There was no way he'd heard her correctly. After they left the neighborhood, they'd come straight to the restaurant.

Being that it was late afternoon, they'd decided to go ahead and eat while they were here. Except for some upgrades, this place hadn't changed. Still had the deep cherry wood floors and accents throughout. The black padded booths and the open kitchen. Bill and Paulette had said they loved the restaurant the way it was and when they rebuilt, they'd had every intention of bringing it back to look the same.

"You heard me." She shoved a forkful of rolled spaghetti in her mouth.

"I can't do that."

"You don't have a choice. I believe I won a bet that allows me to collect the reward at any time for anything. This is what I want."

"I'd thought it would be more of a…sexual collection," he whispered as he leaned across the table toward her.

"That's your bad. I talked to Bill and Paulette while you went to the bathroom and they are so stoked." She sent him a smug smile. "Grab your chef hat, baby, and get your hot ass in the kitchen."

"I haven't been in an industrial kitchen in four years."

"So? You haven't been back to Kansas in four years, either. Seen a tornado, slept with a woman, or returned to your hometown. You've done all that now." Seriousness crossed her face. "Mac, of all you lost, this is the only thing left to reclaim. Go take back your talent."

Inhaling, he held her gaze for a moment, then nodded and slid out of the booth.

Her muttered, "So hot," pulled a smile out of him as he strode toward the kitchen. Though it slipped a little as the stainless steel appliances came into view. Okay, more than a little. He'd been trapped under one of those, pinned helplessly as a car's bumper inched closer and closer, intent on crushing him—in that very kitchen.

Working his shoulders, he pushed open the door, his gaze immediately landing on the area under the sink. Prickles of panic made his hands go numb and he could feel the tornado-force winds, hear its roar, as if it were happening at that exact moment.

"Mac, so glad you decided to cook for us!" Paulette's excited voice jerked him out of the horrific memory.

Forcing a strained smile, he glanced over at the older woman. In her early fifties, she had blond hair secured back in a bun and the typical white dress shirt and black slacks uniform of an establishment like this. She and Bill had been married over twenty years now, and had owned this restaurant for most of it. She ran the place, while Bill was the businessman. Neither one of them had any culinary skills, but they did have superior taste in hiring chefs.

"Are you sure your head chef doesn't mind?" Mac asked. The kitchen was the head chef's domain. There was a sense of possessiveness that went along with it, if the chef really valued his restaurant. Mac used to be anal as hell about his.

"Not at all. Michael is very excited to meet you. He used to eat at your restaurant."

Well, there went that out.

He followed Paulette to the back, where a man, maybe in his early thirties, with black hair, was waiting with a chef's jacket.

The man offered his hand as soon as Mac stopped in front of him. "I'm Michael Ross. It's an honor to meet you, Chef. I used to eat at your restaurant all the time. The food you create is inspiring."

Ross's use of the formal address took him aback for a second. Damn, it was weird to be recognized for his culinary skills instead of his fighting skills. He couldn't remember the last time a stranger had approached him without referring to him as "The Snake." It was quite refreshing.

He took Michael's hand and shook it. "From the Coda Di Rospo I just tasted, Chef, I'd say you're the one who is inspiring."

Pride illuminated the man's face as his chest puffed out. Man, he used to feel the same way anytime a customer had wanted to compliment the chef. He'd loved those moments. Still had them occasionally—like when he watched Gayle eat his food.

The other chef lifted the white jacket. "For you."

Overwhelmed by conflicting emotions from hesitation, to need, to excitement, he took it and slipped it on. As he stood in front of a mirror, he fastened the pearl buttons, then tugged on the hem. The reflection staring back was like coming home. Chef Mac Hannon.

And he grinned.

For three hours, he lost himself in the chaos of an in-the-weeds kitchen, making dishes he hadn't in so long, calling out orders, expediting and beautifying plates. Not once did the horror that had happened in that very room cross his mind. He was in the moment and no longer in the past. After he finished the final ticket of the night, he realized how much time had passed—and he'd left Gayle by herself. Excusing himself, he hurried out of the kitchen.

She sat back in a booth, playing around on her phone. She looked up, her brows shot up her forehead as she said, "Damn," appreciatively. "Baby, we need to do a little roleplaying." She motioned up and down with a finger. "You wear that, and I'll be the disgruntled customer, and you're willing to do whatever the customer wants to make her happy. *Mmm-hmm.* That'll be *fun.* That jacket is *rrawr.*" She made a feline motion with her fingers.

Grinning like a fucking fool, he strode over to her. "Get up." When she did, he tugged her to his chest and kissed her gently. He gazed down at her. "You are the most amazing woman I have *ever* met."

And he meant it. Ally had been wonderful, would always be remembered. But Gayle, with her unwavering patience, her support, and unflappable personality...no one topped Gayle. No one.

M ac smothered a chuckle at Gayle's impatient huffing from the passenger seat of her car. For the first ten minutes of the forty-five minute drive, she'd been excited about the surprise he had planned for her, but for the last twenty or so, some very unlike-Gayle complaining had started. He was learning all kinds of interesting things about the woman, now that he was staying at her place twenty-four-seven. For instance, he'd learned she was all about spur-of-the-moment fun, but riding along in pitch darkness irritated the piss out of her.

"Can I take this damn blindfold off yet?" she asked as she lifted her hand to the black satin sleeping mask he'd bought especially for tonight's events.

"Touch it and you can forget your surprise," he warned.

"You are *so* mean," she said with a pout.

He allowed himself a small chuckle before his humor faded and fear of losing what he had with Gayle clobbered him again. For the most part, he kept a lid on the unwanted feeling and enjoyed being with her. The other night, though, after she'd gone on a chase that took her away overnight, his nightmares had returned full force.

Except Ally was no longer the star player in them. Gayle was. It seemed he'd put the guilt he'd carried, for not being there the day his wife died, to rest. But it had only been replaced with his gut-wrenching fear a tornado would rip another woman from his arms—a woman who actively pursued them. The nightmares were vivid, stemming from the tornado that sideswiped them while they lay unprotected in the ditch. But this tornado didn't miss them; it yanked Gayle from him every time, and tossed her around like a ragdoll before it hurled her to the ground. It was her hazel eyes staring lifelessly up at him, not Ally's blue ones.

He'd begun to dread the next big system. Thankfully, all remained quiet. He wasn't ready for the powerless feeling of putting his faith back into trust and hope. Because once Gayle left, he would be powerless to stop anything that happened to her, and that made him feel defenseless, vulnerable. He hated that feeling.

Shaking out of his ugly thoughts, he forced himself back to the present and how she made him feel when he was with her, which was happy. Content.

One of his favorite parts of the day was curling up on the couch watching TV before they went to bed. He'd forgotten how nice it felt just to have someone sitting beside him. Someone to share the shock or laughter when something unexpected happened in the show they were watching.

Four nights ago, the idea for tonight had planted in his mind from one of their nightly couch cuddling sessions, and he just couldn't pass it up. She'd been more than diligent in making him step outside his comfort zone since they'd met, and it was time to return the favor. And do something extra special for her.

He parked her car in front of a line of overgrown shrubs and cut the engine. She immediately went for the blindfold.

"Don't," he warned.

She growled at him, and he had to clamp his teeth together to keep from laughing. Man, he couldn't wait to see her reaction. He grabbed his duffle bag from the back seat, then climbed out of the car and hurried around to the passenger side. She had already unbuckled her seatbelt. As soon as he opened the door, she thrust her hand out and said, "Get me out of here."

Taking her fingers, he helped her out of the car, pausing a second to admire the tan legs her denim shorts showed off and the purple halter top which dipped enticingly between her breasts. Hopefully, she'd still let him touch them after this.

He guided her across the uneven pavement until they stood in front of a run-down porch with peeling gray paint. Now, where did he want to be? Definitely somewhere he could see her reaction. He stepped off to the side so he could witness every emotion but not obstruct her view.

"Okay, you can take it off now."

"Oh, I can't wait, handsome." A grin curved her lips as she clapped her hands and ripped off the mask.

Mac stilled, anticipation making him almost giddy.

She blinked a couple of times, then focused on what was before her and blinked some more. The grin twisted into a confused scowl. "What the hell is this?"

Time to have some fun. He tugged a piece of paper out of his back jeans pocket and offered it to her. She eyed it suspiciously, then unfolded it. "Graymore Manor." She studied the page a second longer and her head snapped up. The expression on her face screamed, "You bastard!"

"*Hell*. No." She took two steps back. "What the fuck, Mac?

You brought me to a *haunted house*?" She spun around and started for the car. "Screw this. I'm going home."

"I. Dare. You," he sing-songed after her.

She whipped around and shook a finger at him. "*Uh-uh*. That's *Gayle's* bag of dares, not Mac's bag of dares. Don't be trying to coin in on my trademark, handsome, or you're asking for a hurting."

"So, what? You can issue *me* all kinds of challenges, but you're too chicken to accept one?"

"Damn straight, I'm chicken." She whirled around and circled her finger over her head. "Take me home."

Damn the woman. She didn't even hesitate when she *refused* to do something. The fact she flat out refused shocked him. He'd expected a slight hesitation, but not an outright balk. He'd learned about Gayle's absolute loathing for poltergeist movies after she'd unenthusiastically watched one with him the other night. There hadn't been a moment she hadn't had her hands covering her face as she peeked between her fingers, screaming like the events were actually happening to her.

But after the movie ended, he'd become even more tickled. Every creak and pop, even him clearing his throat, had made her jump. Just seeing the woman who never backed down from anything so jumpy, well, it was an opportunity he couldn't pass up.

"You give me ten minutes in here, and I'll streak through the field behind your house. Naked."

She paused, then slowly turned around. Cocking her head to the side, she narrowed her eyes on him with interest. "Make it five. And you streak in broad daylight. You will frolic through the field, skipping and dancing with your arms in the air, singing, *Oh, What a Beautiful Morning*."

Jesus Christ. Where did she come up with this stuff, and so

quickly? "You drive a hard bargain, woman."

"That's my offer. Take it or leave it."

Five minutes was more than enough. "Get that fine ass in the house and let the countdown begin."

Another scowl twisted her face as her gaze darted to the rundown shack, and she didn't move a muscle.

"Holy shit." He laughed. "You thought I'd back down."

Making a frustrated *grrrr* noise, she stalked past him. "You're spending too much time with me. It was a lot more fun when *you* were the one hemming and hawing."

The little show of attitude filled his chest with warmth. God, he loved being around this woman. She just made life better, filled it with laughter and happiness. Even if she was pissed off to the gills right now.

As she stomped up the porch steps, he followed her. She froze at the door and he reached around her to grasp the knob, which he'd unlocked earlier after getting permission and the key from the owners, and opened it. A loud, creepy *crrrreeeak* greeted them.

Her eyes widened and she jumped back. Putting his hand to her lower back, he kept her from backing any farther away, which earned him the same eat-shit expression she'd given him the other night. "If you don't make it the entire five minutes, our deal is off."

Her lips pinched as her gaze skimmed over him. "I see you have a duffle bag." She held out her hand. "I assume that means you came prepared. I want a flashlight."

He'd come prepared all right, and thinking about the bargaining about to happen was turning him the hell on. "That's going to cost you. No singing *Oh, What a Beautiful Morning* for me."

The glare she sent him would've knocked him out cold if

they'd been battling it out in the cage.

"Fine," she said between clenched teeth.

He lowered the bag and dug into it. To have the upper hand for a change was fucking awesome. Other than the watered-down training session he'd put her through, she had steered every activity they had done together. Every one. Yeah, there was a tiny bit of guilt about the creepy-shit factor, but this was Gayle. She chased fucking tornadoes. He didn't have much to work with.

He found his stopwatch, then handed her a flashlight. She immediately turned it on. Leaving the bag sitting by the door, he motioned her inside. "Ladies first."

"How very gallant of you."

He knew better than to laugh, but goddamn it, she was making it hard not to. The utter hostility in her voice was amusing as hell. As soon as she stepped over the threshold, he said, "And your five minutes starts...*now*."

She jumped back outside and faced him. "How can I trust you will tell me when the five minutes are up?"

He dangled the stopwatch in front of her.

"I don't trust you. Give it to me."

Fine by him. "And the price for that is no frolicking for me."

She sucked her teeth as a challenging spark flared in her eyes. "Oh, handsome, you have no idea what a can of worms you've opened."

Actually, he did, and he couldn't wait to find out the revenge she was dreaming up in that creative mind of hers. "That's my price."

Her hand shot out. Even her fingers motioning for him to hand the stopwatch over screamed with attitude. Softly laughing, he placed the watch in her palm. She fiddled with it for a moment then shoved it in his face. Yep. Set for five minutes. As she stepped over the threshold again, she clicked the button on the watch.

And the five minute countdown began.

She shuffled slowly inside, flipping the beam of light everywhere and nowhere. Mustiness from being closed up for years made the air heavy and dank. Cobwebs hung from the ceiling in long strings. Dust coated the floor. Lance had been the one to tell him about the house when Mac was trying to figure out how to pull this off. His friend had been right. The place was eerily perfect.

Seeing she had barely taken ten steps, he said, "You're going to have to pick up the pace."

"You want me to speed up? Then be prepared to frolic your handsome naked ass off," she retorted.

Even in a faux haunted house, she never missed a beat.

"Done."

She moved a little faster into the large, empty living room. A staircase leading upstairs was off to their left. Shadows made spooky images dance across the ceiling and floor. She started humming. Distraction. Mac followed behind her silently, letting her get wrapped up in the surroundings…and forgetting he was there.

A loud *thump*, like someone pounding a fist against the wall, came from upstairs. Without even a squeak, Gayle did a one-eighty and bumped straight into his chest. He gazed down at her. "Going somewhere?"

"You will *so* pay for this." She spun back around and crept forward.

"Does this mean no frolicking for me again?" he asked after she'd taken no more than five steps.

A mumble that sounded very much like, "I'll show you frolicking, you jerk," came from her, but her strides increased.

Seconds later, a low moan echoed throughout the house. Every muscle in Gayle's body stiffened, then she shot behind him and pressed against his back.

"Holy shit, did you hear that?"

He about lost his composure, but he cleared his throat. "Just the house settling. Now, get back in front of me."

"Hell, no."

"Well then you know—"

"I'll take back the fucking frolicking. I'm *not* going first." The flashlight clattered to the floor, then his T-shirt stretched taut against his chest as she grabbed two fistfuls of it.

Creaking footsteps sounded above them, moving closer and closer to the staircase. She climbed up his back, wrapped her legs around his waist, locked her arms around his throat and pressed her face against his neck, whispering, "Shit. Shit. Shit."

"Jesus." He coughed as her grip dug into his windpipe. "Let up, for God's sake."

Thankfully, she loosened her grip. He knew she'd be scared, but her choking him unconscious hadn't occurred to him.

With her piggyback on him, he squatted for the flashlight, wishing he'd thought to video tape this. He might never see Gayle this ruffled again.

As he straightened, a movement from the stairs grabbed his attention. At the tiny white figure slowly making it way downstairs, he stiffened.

"Why'd you stiffen? Oh God! Why'd you stiffen?" The words warmed his skin as her arms tightened around him until he gagged.

"Gayle," he rasped. "Can't breathe."

"I don't care. You're an ass!" she said, but her death lock loosened.

Seconds later, he lost a few decibels of hearing from her earsplitting scream and he smacked his palm to his ear, groaning. "Fuck!"

"That's it. I'm out." The weight of her body left his back and when he turned around, she was gone.

Scrubbing his palm against his aching ear, he walked over to the tiny ghost, hoisted her up into his arms and tapped her on the tip of her white painted nose. "Good job, kid."

Skylar grinned. "Man. Gayle can scream. Did you hear her?"

Her childish cackle brought a smile to his face. "Oh, I heard her all right. Where's your dad?"

"Right here, "Lance said as he jogged down the steps. "I had to get Skylar's DS before I came down. Man, I didn't know Gayle was capable of screaming like that."

Mac hadn't, either. Chuckling, he motioned for them to follow him. "Come out. Let's find her and let her in on the fun."

Finding her wasn't hard. As they stepped outside onto the porch, she was already in the car. Lance waved at her. Gayle's eyes rounded in disbelief, then she flung the door open. "Are you friggin' kidding me?"

Grinning, Mac walked over to her just as the stopwatch in her hand started chirping. He tsked. "You didn't make it the five required minutes. It seems our deal is off."

She gaped at him, then she looked past him to Lance and Skylar on the porch. Her eyes narrowed. "This isn't Graymore Manor, is it?"

"Nope. Rick made the flyer and printed it off for me. That man has some serious talent with art."

"*Rick* was in on this."

She shook her head, then stared at him for a moment longer. The shock slowly faded to amusement. A small laugh came from her, then another, until she was laughing so hard she doubled over. "Oh, my God." She gasped, pressing her hand into her side. "You people could give *Scare Tactics* a run for their money. That was awesome."

"And you." She stepped over to him and wrapped her arms around his neck, gazing up at him with her eyes full of happiness and awe. "Baby, you just took Gayle's bag of dares to a whole new level. You just wait for what I pull out for you to do next."

She tugged his head down and pressed her lips against his. Her warning was something to look forward to. Hell, he had a lot to look forward to. Finding out more of Gayle's Achilles' heels and using them to do crazy things like this were one of them. Yeah, he could definitely see himself spending a lifetime concocting his next dare for her.

And a lifetime anticipating hers. He hoped nothing changed that.

Chapter Fourteen

How was she going to tell him?

Gayle leaned against the doorframe of her workroom and studied Mac as he sat on the couch watching a fight. Things between them had been going so well. After the ghost prank three days ago, she had been racking her brain for a dare that would top it. So far, nothing had come to mind.

Now it was possible that even if she thought of something, she'd never get to issue him the challenge.

The storm had arrived. Both literally and figuratively.

The two fronts that were about to collide would bring another massive outbreak of severe weather. She wouldn't lie to him, though she was ashamed to admit she was real tempted.

This was the last hurtle.

The real test—another huge, dangerous system. The last one they'd experienced together had turned deadly. And this time he wouldn't be with her. Could he take it—the fear for her safety? Or would he turn tail and run back to Atlanta?

The reality that she could still lose him—really lose him— hit her like a ton of bricks.

Because she'd gone and done the one thing she'd sworn to protect herself from—she'd fallen in love. With a man who was as wrong for her as it got. Even while he was so damn right.

Love alone wouldn't save them, wouldn't keep them together. She was terrified it wouldn't be strong enough. Not against a killer storm and the fears it brought to the surface.

At the thought, her stomach knotted.

The fight on TV ended, and Mac clicked off the set. Concern furrowed his brows when he saw her expression. "What's up?"

"Rick and I are leaving in the morning," she said, stepping into the living room.

"Okay."

No hesitation, just quick acceptance. She wavered about telling him the rest. But shook off the idea of lying. No. The only way to know if they were going to work was complete honesty.

"Mac. It's a big system. I'll be gone for a few days."

The blankness in his eyes slowly diminished as her words sank in, replaced by anxious understanding. He swallowed, then averted his gaze. "Like the one we went on before?"

"Yeah."

Nodding, he sucked on his teeth, then inhaled deeply. "Well." He scrubbed his hand over his mouth. "We knew this was coming."

Not really the reassurance she was looking for. "Yeah, we did."

Tension crept between them. Mac vigorously shook his head, then grabbed her hand. Next thing she knew, he was tugging her up to her room. As they reached the edge of her bed, he spun her in front of him, cupped her face between his hands, and attacked her mouth with his.

That's when she realized he was just as terrified of the outcome as she was.

Throwing her arms around his neck, she parted her lips and welcomed his tongue. Frantic hands fumbled with clothes and tossed them across the room. Naked, they fell on the bed, legs tangled. As he rolled her beneath him and settled between her thighs, their gazes locked. While he brushed back her hair, she cupped his jaw. No words were needed. Everything needing to be said was being done so by the fear saturating this moment.

As he entered her and began to thrust, they never lost eye contact. Taking a moment to just feel the other. Because the feelings were becoming too much. They stayed together, connected. Both knowing that tomorrow their connection could be forever broken.

Afterward, Mac tucked his body against her side, his arm wrapped tightly around her waist. He kissed the top of her head, and muttered, "Everything will be okay."

As she squeezed closer to him, she could only hope that was true.

Feeling like a hundred pound barbell had formed in his stomach, Mac watched Gayle pack the SUV. Yesterday when she'd told him about the huge system she was going after, he'd felt like he'd been hit with a blinding right hook. The daze still hadn't cleared from his head.

Gayle was about to put herself in harm's way.

All the good she did while racing after those storms didn't matter one fucking bit to him. The only thing that mattered to him was *her* safety. He couldn't help the resentment that she was about to put her life on the line again when she didn't need to. Understanding there was nothing he could do to stop her only increased the bitterness and frustration.

The thing was, those were *his* issues to get over, because he'd never try to stop her.

Storm chasing was what Gayle was. *Who* she was. If he couldn't accept that side of her, he didn't deserve her. So, as much as he wanted to yank out the suitcase she'd shoved into the SUV and toss it on the lawn, he forced himself to pick up a toiletry bag and help her.

She brushed her hands on her jeans and started toward him. "We're ready to hit the road."

A lump of panic threatened to choke him, but he swallowed it back. Would he always feel like this when she left, or was it because this was the first time? Would it become something he got used to?

He hated how he felt right now. Hated it. "Be careful."

She stopped in front of him, shoving her hands in the back pockets of her jean shorts. "Always."

He wrapped his arms around her waist, linking his fingers at her lower back as she looped hers around his neck.

"I'll be careful, Mac," she said with more fierceness. "I promise."

Pulling her close, he hugged her tight, not wanting to let go. At one time, in his naïveté, he'd once believed himself invincible. That he and his wife would have a family, grow old together, and have a plethora of grandkids to spoil. The universe had given him one hell of a reality check.

Everything could change in an instant. He'd learned that with a woman who *hadn't* taken risks with her life. How was he supposed to let Gayle go, knowing the immense risks she took? That she was willingly putting her future—their future—in such danger?

He squeezed her hard, feeling torn. She wasn't a daredevil. She might go after these monsters, but she did it to save people, just like the brave men and women in law enforcement and the military. He had to be strong for her, just as their loved ones were.

He loosened his grip, and she lifted her head, leaning back. "Are you going to be okay?"

As always, she was worried for him.

He brushed back her hair. "I'm going to worry. No reason to pretend I won't, but I'll keep myself busy. So, don't give me another thought. You just stay focused on what you're out there to do."

Please.

The idea that her concern for him could distract her into making a dumb and deadly decision shot another stomach-twisting jolt of anxiety through him.

She tugged his head down and kissed him hard on the mouth. "When I get back, I'm going to turn all that focus on you, so you'll know how focused I can be," she whispered against his lips.

Despite his fears, a smile pulled at his mouth. "Then you better focus real hard, woman."

Laughing softly, she pulled out of his embrace and climbed into the car. She rolled the window down. "I'll call you."

"I won't call you." Surprised hurt flashed through her eyes, so he quickly added, "Wouldn't want to interrupt you during a crucial moment."

The tension left her muscles and the carefree Gayle returned. Her eyes slowly ran over the length of his body. "One of my many talents is multi-tasking, handsome. I'll be sure to make that clear in a few days."

Rick put the SUV in reverse, and right before they zoomed

off to go after their storm she gave Mac one of her filled-with-suggestion winks. Then they were gone.

He stared at the empty driveway, dread weighing heavy on his shoulders. *This was it.* Either they were going to get through this ordeal, or it would end them. The final square-off with his inner demons was at hand.

Gayle settled back against the seat and rubbed her forehead. Tension crept back into her as she let out a tired breath. Mac had let her leave without laying on a guilt trip. Why did that fill her with both happiness and trepidation?

As she'd packed up the car, she'd been aware of his anxiety. Knew he'd wanted to beg her to stay. But he hadn't. He'd kept his fears to himself, and she had to give him credit for that. He really did want this relationship to work between them. And in just a few short days, they'd both know if a future for them was possible.

The outcome terrified the hell out of her. She didn't want to lose him. At this point, the odds of him leaving her were just as great as the odds of him staying. If this whole situation had been a storm she was tracking, she would have backed off for sure because of the extreme unpredictability.

Safety first. Protect herself, always. She hadn't followed those rules with Mac. Now she was in danger of one hell of a hurting.

"What are you thinking?" Rick asked, breaking the heavy silence.

"That I might have just kissed Mac for the last time."

Rick sighed, shaking his head. "You've seriously got to let go of the past, Gayle. Mac's not Mark or Brian."

"No, he's not. He lost his wife and unborn child to the very thing I chase for a living. That's a pretty big hurdle to jump."

"Not really. You lost your family to the same thing."

"I didn't experience the horror myself, though. I didn't find my house destroyed. Didn't have to frantically look for Sam and my family, praying they were okay. I didn't find them *dead*. I don't have memories like those branded in my mind, Rick. Mac does." She tapped the pencil against her knee. "A big part of me feels I'm being selfish to keep doing this."

Rick shot her a what-crazy-talk-is-this look. "What in the hell makes you say that? You wouldn't consider giving up your career for him, would you?"

"No. Even though I know how hard this is on him, I'm not willing to stop—not even for him. That's selfish, isn't it? If I really loved him, wouldn't I be willing to give it up?"

"You act like this is some kind of drug addiction, Gayle. It's not. Your work does a lot of good for a lot of people. Even Mac sees that, or he would've demanded you stop."

"He's going to want kids one day."

"So? You do, too."

"Yeah, I do. But I'd always thought I'd end up with someone with an understanding of meteorology. Maybe not another chaser, but someone like me with a love of weather, who wouldn't balk at what I do. After everything Mac has been through, how can I ask him to stay home while his wife and the mother of his children goes off looking for the very thing that killed his last family?"

"Gayle—" There was a warning in Rick's voice. "You're *looking* for reasons to run."

"I'm trying to think ahead."

Because there was no way this was going to end well.

"Listen, I've been there with you through all of this.

Trust me, I do get the skittish act. But I'm telling you, Mac is different. It's time to take a leap of faith. He's not going to ditch you because of your job."

She wanted so badly to believe Rick. But it was so hard. Knowing the next few days would make or break her relationship with Mac. And decide whether she would be happy for the rest of her life…or was destined for a life filled with storms and loneliness.

//H ow's Gayle?" Lance asked as he hopped from foot to foot. The mouth guard and protective blue headgear around his face muffled his voice.

Mac lowered his arms and removed his guard. His friend did the same. He and Lance had been sparring for the better part of an hour. It was time for a break, anyway.

"Good. They've seen a few touchdowns and she's gotten some decent data. They are down toward the border of Oklahoma and Texas today. Hopefully, they'll be headed back up this way in a day or so."

Gayle had been gone for three days. Surprisingly, each day had gotten a little easier for Mac. He missed her like crazy, but the fear had abated more with each passing minute. And with the abatement, his nightmares had stopped *before* she was even finished with this chase. A very, very promising sign for his and Gayle's future.

She called or texted him constantly. Sent him pictures over the phone of the storms she was chasing, and kept him informed almost every hour she was out there. The fact he wasn't completely cut off from her made it easier not to worry.

"How are *you*?" Lance asked.

Sighing, Mac tugged off his headgear and tossed it on a bench. "What am I supposed to say? That I like her chasing tornadoes? I don't, probably never will, but if I'm going to be with her, I have to accept it. Hell, the way she loves weather, it'll be my luck she will one day become an extreme weather reporter and branch out to more than just tornadoes. At least right now this worrying will only be a few weeks out of the year."

"Do you think you'll be able to handle it?"

"After she left, I was really nutted up over it, but she's been out there with some huge storms this time and it's not been as mind-fucking as I built up in my head. I'm feeling pretty damn positive."

"So, does this mean you're going to become my neighbor?" Lance asked with a sly grin. "I've liked this arrangement we've had since you got back."

Mac chuckled. "Things are certainly looking that way."

Lance thumped him on the back. "That would be so fucking awesome. I've missed you, man. What would you do about training?"

"Let's not get ahead of ourselves. One thing at a time. Gayle and I need to have a long talk when she gets back. Hammer out our relationship, now that this obstacle is out of the way."

When he finally told Gayle Matthews he loved her, it would only be when he was certain his demons wouldn't surge forward and ruin what they had together. When he was completely confident he was the man she deserved. Not before.

They walked back into the house, and Lance flipped on the TV. Breaking news immediately caught Mac's attention, and he froze at the grainy video clip of a monster tornado churning a path of epic destruction through a city in Oklahoma. His throat closed as dots formed before his eyes. His knees threatening to buckle, he reached around for something to hold on to. He finally found the back of a chair. He latched onto it, squeezing until his knuckles turned white.

"I'm sure she's fine, Mac."

"She fucking speeds ahead of these damn things to warn the people in its path. What if she doesn't get out? We barely did the last time."

Had she called while he'd been sparring with Lance? Had he fucking missed her call? He frantically searched for his phone.

Lance must have picked up on what he was looking for, because he reached over onto a side table and handed it to him. The phone trembled in Mac's hand. No missed call. No text. Nothing.

Oh, God. What if he'd already lost her? What if the last time they spoke had been the last time they would ever talk to each other?

Just as he was about to press the number to autodial her, his phone rang and her name appeared on the screen. "Oh, thank God," he breathed. "Where are you?" he demanded as soon as he answered.

"Mac?"

It was difficult to hear her from all the static filling the line—that, or howling wind. Something was also pounding in the background. Goddamn hail. She *was* near that deathtrap.

"Mac? Can you hear me?"

"Gayle?"

"Listen, you must know about the tornado by now. We're not near that one. About fifty miles away." There was a loud *pop* and a muttered, "Shit. Just wanted to let you know I'm—

Rick! Watch out!"

Screeching tires sounded. Scrunching metal, screams, and muffled groans of pain.

"Gayle?" No response. "Gayle!" he yelled, his heart pounding hard.

What had he just heard? Had a tornado just taken out the SUV?

Terror quaked his body as his gaze snapped to Lance, who was standing ramrod straight, paler than usual.

"Gayle, please, baby, say something. Anything."

But all he heard was the long, strident blare of the car horn.

A lmost seven hours later, Mac rushed into the hospital in Fort Smith, Arkansas. Seven of the longest fucking hours of his life. He couldn't catch a flight because the storm system had caused delays everywhere. Driving had been the only option.

The only information he'd gotten was what someone on the scene had told him after he'd stayed on the fucking cell phone yelling her name for what had felt like an eternity. An unfamiliar voice had finally answered him—a chaser from another team. They'd been driving behind Gayle and Rick when they'd wrecked. They were on their way to a chase target and got caught in a severe storm.

According to the guy, the wind had been intense and knocked a tree down in the road. Rick had swerved to miss it and lost control, careening down an embankment. The people behind them said the SUV had flipped about four times before landing hard on its hood. Both Rick and Gayle had been knocked unconscious. Because of the storm, it had taken a while for emergency crews to get to the accident. Once they did, the Jaws of Life were needed to rip open the car.

Rick, by then, had been awake. He hadn't sustained many injuries—just a few lacerations and a broken arm. Gayle was another matter. All they could tell him was she still hadn't regained consciousness when the ambulance had finally left.

After that, the doctors had taken over and fucking HIPAA kept him from finding out anything. And Rick wasn't answering Gayle's fucking phone.

When he and Lance finally got to the hospital, Mac sprinted up to the front desk. "Gayle Matthews."

The woman typed on the computer. "She's in room 350."

She'd been admitted. He rubbed his forehead. "Fuck."

Lance rubbed his shoulder, but Mac knocked him off. He really wasn't in the mood for any comfort right now. He raced to the elevators and punched the button. What the hell was going to be waiting for him up there? She wasn't in ICU. That was good. It had to be.

The elevator took its damn time reaching the third floor. The second the doors parted, he sprinted for room 350. As he passed the waiting area, Mac noticed Rick sitting there. Fury had him charging the man. "Why the fuck didn't you answer Gayle's phone? I've being going insane with worry the entire goddamn drive down here!"

Rick held up his good arm to stop him. "Her phone must still be in the SUV. I didn't think to grab it. I just got in the ambulance with her. I didn't realize until I got here that I had no way to get in touch with you. I'm really sorry."

Mac inhaled a breath, trying to calm his fury. "How is she?"

"She looks worse than she is. She regained consciousness

on the way to the hospital. She hit her head pretty hard, but the doctors don't see any sign of a concussion. They're keeping her for observation because of how long she was out, and giving her IV fluids for dehydration. She's resting right now."

"I'm going to go see her."

Mac left the two men in the waiting room and found Room 350. He walked in and froze, horrified at the bruises and lacerations all over her beautiful face. An IV was taped below her collarbone, and a large bandage was wrapped around one arm.

The lifeless hazel eyes that had haunted his dreams for the last couple of weeks formed in his mind. He blinked, shaking his head. Instead of Gayle's usual bright smiling face, he saw the battered and bruised woman lying so still in a hospital bed—because she chased destruction, because she took her safety out of his hands. He couldn't trust, couldn't hope, that she would come out of her chases unscathed. Not with Mother Nature. It was unpredictable. He was going to lose her, eventually. He knew it.

Lifeless hazel eyes flashed before him again. Panic became crushing, stole his ability to breathe. He stumbled backward.

He couldn't do this.

He loved this woman so fucking much, but he couldn't do this again. He would not lose another woman he loved to a tornado.

She'd survived the terror they'd gone through together, she'd survived this one, too…but how many chances did a person get to escape death?

This crash wouldn't stop her. She'd be right back out there the moment she was able to. Leaving him to worry, terrified of seeing her like this again, about losing her forever. He just couldn't.

He slowly backed out of the room, then spun and sprinted down the hall. As he passed the waiting area, Lance yelled after him, but he kept going—his only goal was to get the fuck away.

Once he had himself back in the truck, Lance slammed into the driver's seat right after him. "What the hell are you doing?"

He shook his head. "I won't go down this road again, Lance."

"Give it a few days, Mac. If you leave right now, you're going to regret this."

"What I regret is coming back to Kansas. This place has never brought me anything but grief. Gayle knew I might not be able to hack it, we both knew this was possible. She won't be surprised."

Lance stared at him for a moment, then sighed. "All right. But this is on you, Mac. Not Gayle. That woman is perfect for you. And you're letting fear of something you have no control over—that *no one* has any control over—ruin the future for you. Like I said, that is all on you."

He breathed deep, the pain in his heart agonizing. There was only one thing he could do to keep it from being completely crushed. He had to allow it to tap out—surrender as he would in the cage when the only choice he had was between gracefully accepting defeat and leaving a broken man. He stared morosely out the window.

This opponent was bigger than him. Gayle deserved more than a man who'd only try to change her. Because now he didn't think he could ever let her go out there again. He'd use guilt to make her stay, so he wouldn't have nightmares of seeing her like this again, over and over.

And she'd grow to hate him for it.

Either way, their relationship was doomed to fail. Why put either of them through the agony? Better to leave now and accept defeat.

Gayle stared out the window of her hospital room. So far, she had been able to pretend she was asleep so she wouldn't have to face Rick, but it had now been three hours since she'd opened her eyes just in time to see Mac flee the room. She could no longer pretend.

He'd left. Just as she'd known he would. She cursed the sting attacking the back of her eyes. She would *not* cry.

"Gayle?"

Damn it, this was exactly why she'd pretended to be asleep. She barely had control over her emotions. No way did she want to talk about this. Or anything.

But none of this was Rick's fault. So she blinked, plastered on a fake smile, and turned to him.

"Hey," he said.

God, puppy-dog eyes. Really? She was feeling bad enough as it was, she didn't need everyone else feeling bad for her, too. "Don't look at me like that. I told you he would leave, and he did. Big shocker."

"So you know?"

"Opened my eyes in time to see the man jackrabbit out of here like the coward he is." Bitterness crept into her words, giving them a biting edge. She pressed her lips together. At least she hadn't called out to him and begged him to stay. She'd saved herself a sliver of dignity.

"He was really freaked the hell out, Gayle. When he passed the waiting room, there was no color whatsoever in his face. When Lance called after him, he didn't even slow down."

And she'd known that. Given him the benefit of the doubt, and allowed him a freak-out session. He *was* entitled to one, after going through the hell he had.

"But he hasn't come back, has he?" she said evenly. "It's been three hours. He hasn't called, sent a flower, card, or even a text. I'm in the *hospital*, Rick. I've made concessions for this man from day one. I've been there for him—put up with him—through *everything*. The one time I need him, he runs away. I'm better off without the jerk."

That's right, girl. Stay angry. Keep angry. Then you won't feel the pain.

But she was lying to herself. Mac *had* been there when she'd needed him. The night in the shower after the EF-5, and later, when they'd visited her hometown. He'd been her rock. She hadn't had a rock since Sam died. Okay, so she had been there for Mac more. But his wounds were fresher.

And there she went—making concessions for him again.

Disgusted with herself, she rolled her eyes.

"How you feeling otherwise?" Rick asked, looking at her bandages.

Thankful he'd dropped the topic of Mac, she said, "Sore as hell."

"Seen the doctor?"

"Few hours ago. She said they'd release me in the morning."

But Gayle had no interest in returning home to face Mac. How much longer would he be in town? At this point, she wanted him to leave immediately.

So she could pick up the pieces. *Again.*

God, that road was so familiar. Fool that she was, she'd hesitantly started to believe all the heartbreaking roads she'd traveled until now had been in preparation for Mac—her final road, her final destination. *Wrong.* He'd been just another man aiming to come into her life and tear it all to hell.

She was so over men. Permanently. This time for real.

There, that felt better.

"The SUV is totaled. We'll have to rent a car to get back home," Rick said.

She shrugged. They could stay right here, for all she cared. "Were you able to salvage any equipment?"

"I haven't really had a chance to look."

"Probably should get on that," she said.

"You'll be okay if I leave for a while?"

She knew why he was hedging, not wanting to leave her alone because of Mac's abandonment, and that made her stomach cramp. "I'm a big girl. I can take care of myself."

She always had.

Still, he hesitated.

"Rick. Go."

"All right. I'll be by later."

Once he was gone, she leaned back against the pillows and returned her gaze to the window. She tried to concentrate on the side of the other building, counting windows, bricks, people coming and going, but her mind kept wandering back to those last seconds before everything had gone black—the desperation of phoning Mac so he would know she was safe, not wanting him to worry for one minute that she'd been involved in the large tornado. Knowing he'd be going nuts if he didn't hear from her. Then the tree falling. Their car flipping. The pain. And the vague awareness that Mac was hearing every single second of it.

And, as the darkness had claimed her, she remembered wishing she had told him she loved him, just once. So he'd know. In case she didn't wake up…

Now that she was, she was so glad she hadn't.

God, that was messed up, but the damn truth.

A light tap sounded on her door and she turned to find Lance standing there. For a second, her heart stopped. The disappointment that pierced her was physically painful when he walked in…alone.

"How you doin'?" he asked.

"Banged up. But I'll live."

There was a long silence, then Lance hung his head. "He's gone, Gayle."

She'd known that, but she still wasn't prepared for the punch to the heart or how it knocked the air out of her lungs. She forced a shaky laugh. "What did he do? Have you drive him to Little Rock so he could jump on the first plane to get away from me?"

"Gayle, it wasn't you. You know that, right?"

Wow. He really had.

"Wasn't it?" she muttered.

Lance pulled a chair beside her hospital bed. "I'm not going to defend him. Honestly, I wanted to knock his teeth out the entire drive to the airport. But, Gayle, I was with him when he got your phone call. I was with him the entire drive down here. And I've been with him the last three hours. As much as I believe he is making a huge mistake, in the span of seven hours I watched that man go from terrified, thinking you were in that huge tornado, to relief knowing you were safe, to petrified and insane with worry wondering if you were dead or alive after the crash, to running out of a hospital with all the ghosts from his past tearing at his heels. I just think he needs some time. He'll come to his senses."

She was already shaking her head. "I can't, Lance. Don't think I'm cold, okay? I have my ghosts, too. Mac knows that. He knew what leaving would do to me. I'll never trust he won't run out on me again. I can't spend my whole life worrying he will. I can't. Even if he comes to his senses, we're over."

CHAPTER FIFTEEN

Mac pummeled the bag over and over again with only one goal: drain every ounce of energy from his body and mind.

For over a week, he'd punished his flesh with ridiculous hours of grueling training in an attempt to exhaust himself… just so he could get some fucking sleep instead of lying awake obsessively thinking about Gayle. His efforts had all been in vain. No matter how physically fatigued he was, memories of the woman pursued him every second of the day. The questions bludgeoning him were even worse. What was she doing? What was she thinking? Where was she? Did she hate him?

Of course she fucking hated him. He'd *left* her in the goddamn hospital.

Disgust had him driving his fist into the bag, sending it spinning high into the air.

What fucking loser did that?

That the loser was *him* made him sick. Lance had told him he'd regret his decision to leave. At the time, he'd been unwilling to listen. He'd allowed his fears to control him, had allowed them to control him all the way to fucking Atlanta. It wasn't until that night, as he lay in his bed staring at the ceiling, that he'd realized Gayle had been awake the whole time, had witnessed his entire fucked-up decision, and it'd truly hit him what he'd done.

He'd left her, out cold, in the hospital—like he hadn't given a rat's ass about her.

Which was the furthest thing from the truth. He loved the damned woman, even if he wished he didn't. But because of his actions, Gayle would always think of him as the man who'd left her when she'd needed him most. God, he fucking *hated* that. Had even thought about calling her to apologize, but it felt selfish to give himself peace when he couldn't be with her.

He deserved having her think badly of him.

One day, after the hurt and betrayal passed, Gayle would look back on their time and realize she'd dodged a bullet by not getting shackled to a man with the obvious baggage he carried.

She'd meet a man who wouldn't freak out when he thought of her going out there and putting herself in danger, who wouldn't let his fear motivate him to *leave* the woman he loved in the damn hospital. *Fuck.*

Sweat dripping into his eyes, he went ape-shit on the punching bag, yelling between clenched teeth from the searing agony scorching the muscles in his arms—and in his heart.

"Man, you need to chill out," Tommy "Lightning" Sparks said from behind him. "You're going at it like you're fucking losing your mind."

Mac grabbed onto either side of the bag and leaned his forehead against the vinyl. "Go the fuck away."

His friend muttered beneath his breath. Motherfucker was going to say something. Mac hoped he did. A fight was exactly what he needed.

"Dude, I don't know what's crawled up your ass since you've been back, but you've got to get the fuck over it."

Spinning around, he pressed his nose into Tommy's face, whose brows shot up in surprise as his head jerked back. Satisfaction egged Mac on. "How about you tell me to get the fuck over it again? Let's see what happens."

The other fighter's momentary surprise fled as his temper came roaring forward. He puffed up, chest butting Mac back as a nasty curl drew up one corner of his upper lip. "Is that it? You itching for fight, big boy? Bring it. You've been biting people's heads off for days. It's time for someone to bite back."

If there was anyone in this gym Mac could provoke into a fight, it was Tommy. And he could use an all-out brawl right now.

"Really? Think you have the fucking balls to take me?" Knowing how much the other man hated it, Mac drove his fingertips into Tommy's shoulder and pushed him backward.

A muscle jumped in Tommy's cheek. "Touch me again, and I don't care how much I like you, I'm going to knock you the fuck out."

Mac deliberately poked him again...and waited.

Tommy worked his neck back and forth, then he charged. Mac landed hard on his back. Unleashing all the anger and disgust he had at himself, he had Tommy under him and in a full mount in seconds.

"What the fuck has gotten into you!" Tommy ground out between his teeth as he twisted his body, trying to knock Mac off his straddled position.

Mac landed a punch on the other fighter's chin and his head swung sharply to the left. Tommy turned his head back. Rage contorted his face. "Fuck you, motherfucker!"

A bare-knuckled blow caught him on the sweet spot. His vision fleetingly tunneled as brilliant white dots exploded before his eyes. As he refocused, the taste of blood flooded his mouth. *Goddammit.* Snarling, he drew his arm back, ready to deliver another fist to his friend's face. Arms grabbed him around the torso and hauled him to his feet. Mac whipped around and came damn close to decking his other friend, Dante, but the expression on the man's face froze him in place—disgusted horror.

"What the *fuck*, Mac?" Dante asked, who'd apparently just walked into the gym, since he was still in jeans and a T-shirt. He gave a sideways glance at Mac, then sidestepped him and offered a hand to Tommy, who took it, rubbing his jaw. "You okay, buddy?"

"Yeah." The fighter glared at Mac. "That was *not* cool, dude."

The first threads of mortification shot through Mac. What the hell had gotten into him? Even Lance hadn't provoked Mac into actually taking a swing at him, even with all the shit he'd said while he was in Kansas. He'd come damn close, but had never followed through. Tommy hadn't even *done* anything.

He had picked this fight because he was desperate not to think about Gayle.

"Fuck, Tommy." He fisted a handful of hair at the front of his head in self-loathing. "I'm sorry."

"Yeah, well, you get to explain to Julie about the cheap shot you just took. You think *I'm* bad, she'd going to have your ass, man."

Yeah, Tommy's fiancée would have his ass, and he deserved it.

Dante studied him. "Dude, you've been stalking around here like a jacked-up tiger since you got back. It's time to talk. This shit cannot be going on in here."

"I know." As the adrenaline fled, a dull ache lingered in Mac's temples. He rubbed his forehead. A bare-knuckled punch would do that. Thank God, he'd had on open-palmed gloves when he'd hit Tommy.

"Come on, you two," Dante said. "Mike's across town in a meeting. Let's all go to his office."

As soon as Tommy closed the door behind them and they'd sat down, Mac started talking. Told them everything. Losing Ally, the baby. Why he stopped cooking, why he'd moved to Atlanta, why he'd started fighting, why he'd gone back to Kansas. Meeting Gayle. What she did, how she'd gotten hurt, and finally about him leaving her.

Dante stared at him, aghast. "You left her in the *hospital*?"

"Don't think for a second I'm proud of that moment. I'm not." He blinked against the pulse behind his eyes.

Tommy shook his head. "You do understand you don't have any control over stuff like this, right?"

"Yeah, I know that. That's the thing. I *worry* about the stuff I can't control. Big-time. But *she* chases tornadoes willingly. She puts herself at risk every time she does it, even knowing she has zero control over anything, ever. How am I supposed to be okay with that?"

Dante shifted on the edge of the desk. "Caitlyn had a huge issue with me being a fighter, but she realized she loved me more than what I did for a living. We just found out we're pregnant. I can't imagine my life without her and the family we're going to have. She feels the same way, and now she feels foolish over how she balked at my career. Maybe one day you can change your feelings about what Gayle does."

"You're comparing a kitten to a damn lion, Dante. There have only been two documented deaths in regulated MMA. What Gayle does can be seriously life-ending. Tornadoes take way too many lives each year. I know this. I've *experienced* this."

Dante exhaled harshly. "I'm just saying, one day you may wish you had taken *any* time with her, rather than none at all. Everyone takes a chance when we fall in love. Caitlyn is my whole life, just as Julie is Tommy's. Neither one of us has lived through the tragedy you have, thank God. I can't even begin to fathom how something like that would change me when Caitlyn is in every thought I have of the future."

"I can't. I just can't."

Dante leaned forward. "Here's the thing, Mac, you didn't think you would have a second chance at love, and you still found it. Would you rather be alone knowing the woman you love is out there, one day learning she died and realizing you'll never, ever, be able to be with her, or would you rather take what you are given, which could possibly be forty years or more, and just enjoy being with her as long as you can?"

Mac stared ahead. He got Dante's meaning. He really did. The rational side of his brain saw completely what he was saying. The irrational side however, didn't. "But I *have* lived through losing a woman I loved. Had to learn how to wake up every day to the empty spot beside me. Her laughter gone. Live with the emptiness she left behind. I didn't recover *until* I met Gayle. If she were ever taken from me, I would *never* recover. Not this time. So, I feel like it's better to save us both a lot of heartache. Besides, she would grow to hate me. After her getting hurt like she did, I would never feel safe with her out there chasing. It would be a constant source of friction between us."

Tommy and Dante exchanged glances. "It's your life, man. We can't make you do anything. Just know that life sucks, going at it alone. *Especially* when you have a woman out there who loves you."

Who said she loved him?

And even if she had, he'd surely killed that love by walking out.

He was done with this conversation. Slapping his hands on his knees, he stood. "I don't want to talk about this anymore. Don't we need to train?"

"You going to stop being such a dickhead?" Tommy growled. "If you don't want to go after your woman, that's your deal, but the rest of us ain't putting up with your bullshit. You need to get any aggression out, you do it inside the ropes. Don't pick fights with your friends."

"I hear you." He worked his neck.

"Since you're so berserked out, how about a sparring match with Maurice?"

Yeah, that sounded good. Maybe then he could go home and sleep. His damn annoying headache was probably more from lack of sleep and stress than Tommy's actual punch. Not saying the guy didn't have power behind his fist, but as a heavyweight, Mac had taken some herculean blows much stronger than Tommy's.

Ten minutes later, he was circling Maurice in the boxing ring. The other fighter had his fists up, a calculating look letting Mac know he was searching for the best move, too. Maurice made a movement, and Mac went immediately for a straight jab. Maurice dodged and came around with a powerful left hook, landing it square on Mac's jaw. His head whipped hard to the side.

And blackness engulfed him before he hit the canvas.

The strong gusts of wind continuously pushed against Gayle as she peered through the camera lens and took another photo of the breathtaking mothership supercell hovering above a golden field of wheat. The storm that came out of that one was going to be a humdinger.

She dropped the camera, letting it hang around her neck, and sighed. Unless something popped up between now and Monday, three days from now, this would most likely be her last chase of the season. The thought was depressing, but the TV news station she worked for was ready for her to claim the helm as chief meteorologist. With tornado season winding down, she really had no excuse not to.

Because "I need the distraction chasing gives me" wasn't a practical reason—though it was the truth.

After the doctor had released her from the hospital, she'd spent one week at home recovering from the muscle soreness that had mocked all muscle soreness, and it had been hell. Being trapped in her house had done nothing but allow the damned man to consume her thoughts. As soon as she could move without wincing, she'd apologized to Lance for leaving him in a bind with Skylar, but she had to get away for a while. He hadn't even blinked, just told her to do what she needed to do.

Over the last four weeks, she'd checked in with him. The last update hadn't gone well. Lance had lost the fight he'd been training so hard for. He tried to sound like his usually energetic, positive self, but she'd heard the disappointment and worry behind his false cheer.

She understood that struggle. At least she didn't need to pretend to be happy. She'd just thrown herself into every possible storm she could—even the ones she knew would be a bust. If she got nothing more than a few pictures or video, she didn't care. She was distracted.

She missed Rick, could've really used the familiarity of their good-natured banter, but with his broken arm, driving was impossible. Another team had selflessly lent her one of their crew. Nick was a good kid in his early twenties, eager, with a passion for meteorology. His continuous barrage of questions had been a distraction in itself.

Not that she hadn't thought of Mac anyway. At night she had, and she resented it, especially as the weeks passed, and he'd never made any attempt to contact her. She'd come close to calling him a few times, to make sure her accident hadn't caused him to regress, but ended up not having the strength to dial. One of her biggest fears was that he *was* fine. The fear made her a loathsome person, but it was hard to forget he'd left her in the hospital and hadn't looked back.

The motivation seemed obvious to her. Her prediction that night on her porch steps had come true. She was Mac's wrecking ball. When he'd returned to Atlanta and the horror of her accident had worn off, he must have realized the feelings he'd had for her were simply gratitude. That was why he hadn't reached out to her. Simple.

The possibility—probability—had driven her insane, had made bitterness churn in her gut, had made her wish she'd never met Mac...which made her feel even more of a horrible person. No matter how their relationship had ended, the man *had* needed her to come into his life and change it. After five weeks of soul-searching she was confident that, given the choice, she would help Mac heal all over again—but just do a much better job of protecting her heart.

Being heartbroken sucked.

She was pulled from her depressing thoughts as a wall cloud descended from the mothership. *Time to roll.*

She hurried back and jumped into the SUV, slammed the door, and immediately grabbed the map to study it. "Let's go down a few a miles and get a little closer."

Nick pulled back onto the road. Gayle peered out the passenger window at the mountain of dark clouds. "Those striations are beautiful."

"Almost as beautiful as you."

At the familiar deep voice rumbling from the driver's seat—a voice *so* not the young kid she'd been listening to for weeks—every cell in her body froze. Lightly shaking her head, she blinked. Was she freaking *hallucinating* now? Only one way to tell. Turn and look. But for the life of her, she was too terrified to do so. Because if Mac wasn't sitting there next to her, she would have to give Nick directions to the nearest psychiatric hospital. She was finally losing her mind.

"I personally like that the mothership has a rain-free base so it doesn't seem anchored to the ground and appears to be hovering in the air."

Wide-eyed, she stared at the supercell. Yes, the person speaking had Mac's voice, but the words coming out of his mouth didn't sound like Mac at all. Rain-free base? Anchored to the ground? That was chaser talk.

She took a calming breath and twisted to peer over at him. Her mind was having a hell of a time computing things. This wasn't possible. It went against all logic. Mac had left her in the hospital because she had been in a wreck while storm chasing. This Mac was sitting behind the wheel in an active chase—driving the damn chase vehicle down the road, calm as could be. That made no sense.

Sending her a quick glance, he arched a questioning brow. "Baby? Are you okay?"

"Wh-" Shock had sucked the moisture from her mouth.

She licked her lips and tried again. "Where's Nick?"

"Where's Nick…" The Mac look-alike sucked his teeth. "You asking for another man was not the homecoming I was hoping for, but what the fuck, I'll play along. I just paid him a crazy amount of money to return my rental car for me. He has no loyalty, Gayle. He snatched the money and took off."

Eyes locked on Mac, she leaned back against the seat. "Why are you even here? You left me."

A pained grimace contorted his face. "I did, and I regret that."

"Without one word, you left. It's been weeks." And the festering hurt was still there in spades. And the fury. Seeing him made it all bubble to the surface again.

"I've been recovering," he said.

She crossed her arms, filled with anger. "From what? Terminal stupidity?"

A deep chuckle filled the SUV. "As a matter of fact, yes." He tapped a finger to his temple. "Sometimes it really does take a good punch to the head to knock some sense into a guy." He grasped the steering wheel again. "Am I supposed to turn or keep going, or what?"

"How about you drop me off and then keep going… straight back to Atlanta."

"Nope." He sent her a lazy smile. "I'm good right here."

Her mouth dropped open. He hadn't even blinked at her retort. His laid-back reaction only goaded her anger more. "Really? You're good…*right here*? Holy shit. Where's the Lollipop Guild to welcome us, because we sure as hell ain't in Kansas anymore."

His soft laugh made her want to smack him. Hard. Why was he so damn relaxed and unresponsive to her hostility? Grinding her teeth, she folded her arms tight across her chest and stared out the windshield. Did the ass really think he could just show up and all would be forgiven? Not damn likely. He left her. In. The. Hospital.

After a quick glance at the weather monitoring screen, Mac took a right turn onto a side road. Gayle struggled to hide her surprise. She would've instructed Nick to take that same route to follow the clouds.

Come to think of it, how had he known proper terminology? He'd deliberately dropped those words to make her curious and, damn it, the ploy had worked. She snapped her head around. "How did you know that cloud has a rain-free base?"

"I've been studying. A person can learn a lot if they open their mind instead of letting fear close it."

She dragged her gaze up and down him. He sure looked like the man she'd fallen in love with—correction: *thought* she'd fallen in love with—but something was definitely off. "Man, what a shocking discovery. I mean, who knew ed-u-*ca*tion made you smarter?"

Her snippy tone only earned another chuckle from him.

If the man didn't stop laughing, she was going to kill him. She fisted her hands in preparation.

"I know, right? Those books and videos showed me a lot." He paused for a long moment. "But it was life happening that taught me the most important lesson. And made me a much smarter man. I've learned something invaluable with you, Gayle. Something losing my family didn't ever teach me. In fact, their deaths made me live in fear of it."

She shot a sideways glance at him. Questions pushed at the back of her teeth, but she wasn't ready to let go of the anger.

"Want to know what it was?" he asked, then paused for a heartbeat. "Life happens. And some things I simply have no control over. None. All I can do is accept that, and live every moment I'm given to the fullest."

The raw sincerity in his voice grabbed her undivided attention, and she narrowed her eyes to study him. Something *was* different. It wasn't just the complete freeness about him, either, which was disconcerting to say the least. Even when he'd been trying like hell to make things work between them, there had always been an underlying tension, a constant he-would-bolt-at-any-second vibe when it came to the future of their relationship.

Holy shit. *That was it.* The tension and the vibe were gone. He felt...at peace.

The man sitting next to her was not the one she'd left standing in her driveway, uncertain if he could handle her profession or not. This man was the one who'd gone to Zumba, who'd run with her in the mud, who'd found a little girl's mother, held Gayle while she'd cried. The man who'd helped her face her past and cooked with such joy after he'd faced his own.

And now he was driving her chase vehicle, the very thing that had come between them, with that same damn determination and steadfastness.

That other man in the driveway, *he* would leave her. He *did* leave her.

Somehow, she knew this new man wouldn't. Knew it to the depth of her soul.

She swallowed, terrified of allowing him back in, in any form. But she was unable to ignore what he was trying to show her.

"Th-that's quite an epiphany," She cleared her throat against the nerves suddenly taking her body hostage. "What made you decide to let go and accept all that?"

He smiled wryly. "When life decided it was my turn to look death in the face again. I've done it before, trapped under that refrigerator, but any lessons learned were erased when everything I loved was taken from me. That time, I had no reason to live. This time I did." He shot a quick glance at her. "You."

I've been recovering. Looked death in the face. This time.

The real meaning of those words suddenly hit her square in the chest. "What happened to you, Mac?"

He sent her a sideways smile. "I'm fine now. Doctors released me yesterday. It's the only reason I didn't come sooner, and I sure as fuck wasn't doing this over the phone."

"*Mac.* What happened?" A rising dread was making it difficult to breath. She wanted to claw at her throat to loosen the grip this unbidden panic had around it.

"P-pull over."

She had to get out of this damn car.

As soon as he stopped, she jumped out and ran into the adjoining field. The robust winds whipped her hair and she wrapped her arms around her waist, inhaling the air greedily. It smelled of hay and wet earth with a hint of ozone. Familiar smells that usually comforted. But not now. What was freaking her out so badly?

Mac came to stand beside her.

"I had a brain contusion. Seemed I'd been walking around with a very mild concussion ever since I fought Ragin. Then I got clocked twice at the gym, and the second punch did me in. I was out before I hit the floor. Didn't regain consciousness for hours."

Gayle hugged herself tighter. And she had been completely unaware of it. This entire time, she'd thought he was moving on with his life, but in reality he'd been recovering from a *brain injury*. He could have *died* and she wouldn't have known the truth until it was too late.

The realization twisted her gut so sharply the pain nearly brought her to her knees.

"After they released me from the hospital, I spent a week and a half lying in bed. I couldn't read, watch TV, or anything. All I could do was think." He looked down at his feet. "About how much I love you, how much I miss you, how much I regret running out of that hospital…and how the hell I was going to win you back. The second week I could do small periods of activity, so I started watching YouTube videos about chasing, learning everything I could about what you do. See, I was planning my own chase. But my goal isn't to catch a tornado. My goal is to catch you."

Tears welled in her eyes, making his frame swim in front of her. Mac had faced death, and returned to her ready to accept everything she came with.

That she had come so close to losing him, without knowing it, was giving her a wake-up call. She'd forgotten life could step in and change her world in an instant, regardless of how happy or sad, protective or carefree she lived day to day. Even if Mac had stayed with her after the crash, his silent brain injury could have taken him from her at any minute.

As much as she wanted to believe her live-in-the-moment philosophy shielded her from the pain of loss, the truth was, she'd been no different than Mac. She'd tried to control life, but all she'd really done was keep herself detached from other people for fear of losing them.

And how fucked up was that?

She closed her eyes and drew in a lungful of fragrant air.

Could she take a leap of faith? *Truly* live in the moment, as she'd believed she had been all along…this time with Mac by her side?

Did she dare?

"What happens next season, Mac?" she asked him. "Or in the future, if we get married and have kids? What if I get hurt again? I won't give up chasing. I can't, Mac. I owe it to my family to make sure their deaths weren't in vain. That others don't die the same way. If it's not my own research that makes the breakthrough, then maybe it's something I do, something I record, that will be the missing piece for another scientist's work. I need to know I will, in some way, further our understanding of tornadoes. It's what gives me hope for the future."

He let out a long sigh. "When we met, I scoffed at the idea of hope." He lifted his shirt and ran a finger over TRUST inked on his side. "Scoffed at that, too. Thought they were useless emotions meant only to crush a person's spirits when they inevitably failed." Dropping his shirt, he cupped her cheeks in his hands. "You gave them back to me. I have hope for a future now." His grip on her tightened. "With *you*. I have hope for children, grandchildren. *You* are the one by my side when I see those things."

A tear escaped and slid down her cheek. "And trust?"

"I trust you. I trust you with my life and my heart."

She let out a soft sob, and Mac gathered her to his chest. Wrapping her arms around his waist, she clung to him.

"I *love* you, Gayle Matthews," he whispered. "With everything in me."

Her heart swelled. He'd said the words. All three of them. Hope. Trust. Love. And she believed him. Believed the changes in him that she could see written so plainly in his earnest eyes.

She drew strength from his certainty, from him, and lifted her head to look up at him. "Even though I always knew you might leave me in the end, when you walked out on me at the hospital I was devastated."

A pained grimace contorted his face, and he started to say something.

She stepped out of his embrace and held up her hand. "Let me finish. You never made light of your baggage. You've always been honest with me. Now it's time for me to be honest. I've come to realize I've spent the last three years doing the same thing you've done for the last four."

His throat worked on a swallow. "Gayle, I—"

She shook her head, cutting off his words. "I'm carefree, fun, live-in-the-moment Gayle Matthews. She embraces life, right?" She paused, allowing the truth to seep deep within her before saying it. "But I *don't*. Not really. When you truly embrace life, you embrace it all, including the possibility for pain. You gamble your heart because the joy is worth it. But I took my heart off the table years ago, terrified of being hurt."

Mac reached for her, but she waved him off. As she studied him, awe expanded her chest. "After everything you've been through, here you are, gambling on a future of uncertainty with me. Not knowing what tomorrow will bring. Fully knowing what you have to lose, because you've lost so much before." She inhaled a shaky breath. "That's the real risk of winning love, isn't it? Loving someone, even knowing one day you could lose them."

He swallowed and gave a jerky nod. "Yeah. But I know now it's so worth the risk."

She smiled. "I do, too. And I'm so ready to win, so ready to give my heart to you."

A curse burst out of him as he scrubbed his palm over his face. "Thank God. You scared the crap out of me."

"Mac Hannon, I love you so much. I'm all in. You have me. All of me—my hope, my trust, and my love."

He pulled her to him and gazed down at her. "Gayle, you brought me back from the dead. You've made me live again, enjoy life again. I will never be able to show you how much I love you." Caressing her jawline, he kissed her gently. "But I will spend every damn day trying."

Smiling at last, she looped her arms around his neck and tugged his head down. As he made good on his vow, her heart swelled to bursting. Here in Mac's arms, facing the uncertainty of the future together—*that* was truly living in the moment. That was what love was about. Whatever they faced, they would do it together.

As they pulled apart, a funnel lowered from the wall of clouds in a distant field. Mac wrapped an arm around her shoulder, and she leaned into his side as they watched it descend and make touchdown. No tension crept into his body as the twister grew in size, whirling across the horizon. He simply kissed the top of her head and said, "Dorothy was right."

She tilted her head back. "What do you mean?"

He gently kissed her lips one more time, then whispered, "There's no place like home."

ACKNOWLEDGMENTS

Writing Winning Love was the biggest challenge I've faced, so far, as a writer. I worked on this book, off and on, for over a year, which included two tornado seasons. The EF-5 tornado in Moore struck when I was just starting the writing process. Then El Reno, where three well-respected research chasers lost their lives when that tornado took them by surprise. Most recently, the tornado outbreak at the end of April that caused extensive damage across multiple states and over thirty-five deaths.

Each instance has given me pause. I found it difficult to write. I worried over every word and I doubted. What kept me going was reminding myself there are people like me who don't truly understand the devastation these storms cause. We see it. We watch it. We pray for those affected, but there's not a true understanding. I hope that the feelings of those who have lived through the experience, crawled out of debris, who have lost loved ones to the fury of Mother Nature, or lost everything they own, comes across in this book. My heart goes out to these people, and my ultimate goal was to respect the tragedy they've experienced.

With that said, I've wanted to write a storm chaser character for a very long time. From the many years I've spent watching storm chaser-related documentaries, YouTube videos, and reading blog posts, I became aware of how the media sensationalizes what storm chasers do and how most chasers resent it. Are there thrill-seeker chasers? Of course. But the vast majority of these men and women are not cowboys, yahoos, or any other name that has come to be associated with storm chasers.

People do not realize the amount of science that goes into chasing. Days of planning, watching, waiting...calculating. I had the most exciting interview with Gerard Jebaily. Gerard works as a meteorologist in South Carolina...and he also chases. It was an amazing interview with some great stories I won't forget. I thank him immensely for taking the time to speak with me and answering my questions.

Now to take a few moments to thank those who helped and supported me during the writing of this book.

To Liz Pelletier—thank you for being super excited over the proposal. Though I spent most of the time while writing Winning Love repeating, "What the hell have I done?" and doubting my ability to accurately portray tornado destruction and storm chasing, I challenged myself as a writer and, in the end, I am very proud of this book. Winning Love, in my opinion, is one the best books I've written to date.

To Nina—thank you for being one of the best editors a girl could ask for. As always, your editing and suggestions helped me take the book that step further. We're a kickass team.

To the art department–I was only halfway finished with the book when I received the cover. The TRUST tattoo was a surprise for me. But it unleashed a torrent of ideas for Mac that added a level to him that I wouldn't have achieved if you guys hadn't put it there. Thank you.

To my fans—I love each and every one of you. Thank you for loving my writing, for anticipating the releases, and just being awesome. Without you my dreams wouldn't be coming true.

To my CPs, Angie, Christina, Christyne and Tina—I've said it before and I'll say it again, and I'll say it with every future book—I wouldn't know what to do without you girls.

To my parents, sister and friends—thank you for being supportive. I know I'm an ogre when I'm under deadline, you guys just wave it away, knowing that's not typically me. I wouldn't know what do without that understanding and support.

A special thank you to Chad—I always acknowledge those who inspire me to be better. I once sent you a cryptic text saying, "Thank you for making me a better writer." I wouldn't elaborate on how. Mostly because I was waiting to write my acknowledgment to do so. I told you before there is always some truth behind a book. An insight into a writer's mind, their thoughts, insecurities, desires, and their past. Unfortunately, sometimes we haven't experienced something or it's been a very long time since we have and we're disconnected from what we are trying to convey. We have to make it up as we go and keep our fingers crossed that we're doing a good job of it. I've been doing this for years in a couple of areas. You coming into my life gave me the ability to filter more reality into my writing. I'll never forget that. Thank you.

As always, I will complete my acknowledgments by thanking my kids. They are last not because they are a side thought, but because they are the most important. My final thoughts will always be sharing the love I have for my children and how damn lucky I am to be blessed with two amazing kids. I love you.

For more page-turning books from Entangled, try these...

A DUKE'S WICKED KISS

by Kathleen Bittner Roth

The Duke of Ravenswood, secret head of the British Foreign Service, has no time for relationships. Miss Suri Thurston knows the pain of abandonment. When Suri appears in Delhi, the Duke's resolve is tested as he finds his heart forever bound to her by the one haunting kiss they shared once upon a time. With Suri's vengeful Indian family looking for her death, and insurgents intent on mutiny tearing their world apart, can their love rise above the scandal of the marriage they both desperately want?

QUEEN OF SWORDS

by Katee Robert

Ophelia Leoni grits her teeth and boards the starship that comes to seal her fate - to marry the Prince of Hansarda. When she's introduced to the ship's commander, it's none other than the gorgeous stranger she just spent a wild, drunken night with. Boone O'Keirna can't be in the same room with Ophelia without wanting to throw her out an airlock—or into his bed. Her marrying his sadistic half-brother is not an option. But while the fates may never lie, the truth is sometimes hidden between them...

HONOR RECLAIMED

by Tonya Burrows

An interview with a runaway Afghani child bride leads photojournalist Phoebe Leighton to an arms deal involving a powerful bomb. Forming an unlikely alliance with a team of military and government delinquents called HORNET, she meets Seth, a former Marine sniper with PTSD, who ignites passions within her she thought long dead. Racing against the clock, Seth, Phoebe, and the rest of HORNET struggle to stop the bomb before it reaches its final destination: The United States.

DEATH DEFYING

by Nina Croft

After five hundred years, Callum Meridian, founding member of the Collective, is bored out of his mind. Until he realizes he's physically changing—into what, he isn't sure. Callum is determined to discover the truth, but his own people will stop at nothing to prevent it from coming out. He turns to Captain Tannis of the starship El Cazador. Sparks fly as they work together to make it out alive, but can Callum really trust the one woman hell bent on using him? Defying death has never been more dangerous...or more sexy.

EAST OF ECSTASY

by Laura Kaye

Devlin Eston, black-souled son of the evil Anemoi Eurus, is the only one who can thwart his father's plan to overthrow the Supreme God of Wind and Storms. But first, Dev must master the unstable powers he's been given. Distrusted and shunned by his own divine family, the last thing he expects is to find kindness and passion in the arms of a mortal. But Devlin's love puts Annalise in the path of a catastrophic storm, and in the final Armageddon showdown between the Anemoi and Eurus, sacrifices will be made, hearts broken, and lives changed forever...or lost.

A SHOT OF RED

by Tracy March

When biotech company heiress Mia Moncure learns her ex-boyfriend, the company's PR Director, has died in a suspicious accident in Switzerland, Mia suspects murder. Determined to reveal a killer, she turns to sexy Gio Lorenzo, Communications Director for her mother, a high-ranking senator—and the recent one-night stand Mia has been desperate to escape. While negotiating their rocky relationship, they race to uncover a deadly scheme that could ruin her family's reputation. But millions of people are being vaccinated, and there's more than her family's legacy at stake.

TANGLED HEARTS

by Heather McCollum

Highland warrior Ewan Brody always wanted a sweet, uncomplicated woman by his side, but he can't fight his attraction to the beautiful enchantress who's stumbled into his life. He quickly learns, though, that Pandora Wyatt is not only a witch, but also a pirate and possibly a traitor's daughter—and though she's tricked him into playing her husband at King Henry's court, he's falling hard. As they discover dark secrets leading to the real traitor of the Tudor court, Ewan and Pandora must uncover the truth before they lose more than just their hearts.

SUNROPER

by Natalie J. Damschroder

Marley Canton joins Gage Samargo in tracking down the goddess who went rogue decades ago. Insane with too much power from the sun, she's selling that energy to Gage's younger brother and his friends. But Marley's ability to nullify power in those who aren't supposed to have it means that every time she nullifies someone, she takes on some of the goddess's insanity. Gage falls for Marley's sharp wit and intense desire to right wrongs. Once he discovers she's turning into her enemy, is it too late to back away?

TOUCH OF THE ANGEL

by Rosalie Lario

Night after night, Amara and her fellow succubi are forced to extract special abilities from the strongest Otherworlders for their psychotic master's growing collection. When Ronin Meyers, the gorgeous angel-demon hybrid she believed to be dead captures her, Amara is both stunned and elated. But the happily-ever-after Amara's dreamed about will have to wait. Before she and Ronin can find salvation, they must bring down the madman hell-bent on destroying everything—and everyone—they love. And Ronin and Amara are at the top of his list.